Growing Season

Growing Season

a novel

✻✻✻

by Melanie Lageschulte

Growing Season: a novel
© 2017
by Melanie Lageschulte
Fremont Creek Press

All rights reserved.

ISBN:
978-0-9988638-1-8 (paperback)
978-0-9988638-7-0 (hardback)
978-0-9988638-0-1 (Kindle ebook)

Cover photo: tacojim/iStock.com
Back cover: Author photo © by Bob Nandell
Cover design by Melanie Lageschulte

Web: fremontcreekpress.com

✳ 1 ✳

The bright morning sun burned through Melinda's eyelids, the air already too hot for early May. She forgot to pull the curtains last night, stumbling home later than she should have after downing too many drinks with her co-workers at the advertising agency.

Oh no, not my co-workers, she thought, clenching her eyelids and silently willing her bedroom to stop its slow spin. *My former co-workers.* Because yesterday, along with sixteen of her friends and colleagues, Melinda Foster suddenly found herself out of a job.

"Great," she mumbled, her tongue thick and her throat dry. "Not only am I unemployed, but I'm hung over, too."

She struggled to sit up, but the twisting drop in her stomach brought her head back to the pillow. "I'm too old for this." She rubbed her pounding forehead and gritty eyes. "All of it. And what if I'm too old to start over?"

The only answer was the hum of the box fan in the window, breaking the early-Saturday silence of her Uptown neighborhood in Minneapolis. She tried to breathe deep, to fight off the despair that seemed to be spreading through her body, pushing her down into the bed.

"I'm only thirty-nine," she announced to no one, pounding her fist on the sheets. "It's not too late. I'll find a way. But I just need ten more minutes. No, maybe twenty."

Bracing herself for the spin, she rolled over and tried to fall back asleep, to block out the fear and shock that had dogged her since yesterday afternoon.

We have to cut expenses to better meet revenue expectations, they'd said, as Melinda tried to stop her hands from shaking in a nearly empty conference room at WP&S, one of the Twin Cities' largest advertising firms. Clients had been pulling back on their print campaigns and television spots. In her copywriting department, projects had started to disappear from the white board in the meeting room. Then came whispers last week that one of their largest accounts was about to bail.

We appreciate all your work and wish you well, they'd said, as one of the three mournful-looking guys from human resources handed her a farewell packet and muttered something about her "fourteen years of service" and "insurance extensions" and "severance package." She managed to pick up the manila envelope and wander out to the elevators and was standing there, dazed, not sure which button to push, when she saw Patricia from accounting with her hands over her face, hiding behind the towering fake plant in the corner of the atrium. And Bobby, the newest hire in IT, starting to cry as his supervisor gently took his arm and tried to steer him into the room Melinda had just left.

We'll need you to not go back out on the floor, they'd also said, as if Melinda could have collected her thoughts long enough to make a scathing speech about the company or steal some paper clips on her way out. Someone pushed her purse into her arms and solemnly asked for her security badge. She'd stood there, her feet unable to move and her heart racing, for a good ten minutes and then found her way outside to the bus stop to catch a too-early ride home.

At least I never have to go back, she thought now as she stared at the bedroom ceiling, wondering if the small water stain on the plaster would suddenly start to expand, spreading like the tight feeling in her chest.

But she did. Today. At eleven. To clean out her desk.

Melinda rolled over again and forced herself upright, set her bare feet on the worn hardwood floor. Her two-bedroom flat on Pickard Street, with its multi-paned windows, oak built-ins and little butler's pantry, still held that air of genteel elegance that made her fall in love with it six years ago.

Suddenly affordable after her latest promotion at the agency, the third-floor walkup was unassuming yet filled with vintage charm. Moving into this reviving, hip block had made her feel like she was moving up in the world, too, that life was full of possibilities.

She looked around the bedroom. It was fairly clean, but she must have missed that cobweb in the corner by the window. And that near-tumbling stack of books needed to be sorted. She had so many, they never seemed to fit into the built-in bookcases in the dining room. Dirty laundry, stale and forgotten, waited in the basket at the foot of the bed.

Suddenly, Melinda saw her apartment, and herself, in a new, dimmer light. Would she still be here in ten or fifteen years, shuffling around in a ratty robe among piles of books and laundry, the dust drifting on the built-in buffet, struggling to keep the lights on as she toiled away at some low-paying receptionist job?

No, she decided, that wouldn't happen. Because if she didn't find something good, and soon, she wouldn't be able to afford the rent much longer.

Vintage, pre-war charm would have to be exchanged for some dull, suburban, beige-walled rental complex where the cheap window blinds were always broken and the trash was always overflowing out of the Dumpster.

"I'm sorry." She sighed and looked around at her home. "I don't know if I'll be able to stay here."

Thirsty and in need of an aspirin, she wandered into the kitchen and wrenched open the tiny wood-framed window over the sink, letting in the warm breeze.

The cold, sweet water helped, but there would need to be coffee. Lots of coffee. Before, Melinda would have simply changed out of her sleep shirt into some yoga pants and a tee and walked down to the corner coffee shop, which was as charming as it was expensive.

"There'll be no more of that." She set her jaw as she wistfully recalled the concoctions created by the baristas down the street. There was an aging canister of coffee grounds in one of the top cabinets, behind the cereal, and a thrift-store coffee maker under the sink that she only used when her parents drove up from Iowa to visit. She crouched on the blue-and-green rag rug, the white-painted cabinet door giving a surprised squeak as she jerked it open and peered into the shadows. She reached around the dish soap and assorted household cleaners, feeling for the back. There was some sort of pile on the floor of the cabinet, wedged behind the box of trash bags. Small things. Melinda grasped them and pulled out her hand.

Two pouches of cat treats, mostly gone. And a little blue collar, the brass tag etched with "Oreo." And then, for the first time since yesterday, the tears came.

She had been trying not to think about him, the shy black-and-white kitten she'd found wandering behind the building right after she'd moved in. Oreo had quickly become her best friend, winning her over with his joyful outlook and knack for tricks and games.

And then, so quickly, too soon, he was gone. She came home from work one night two months ago to find her precious boy having a seizure on the kitchen floor.

We're so sorry for your loss, they'd said at the emergency veterinary clinic as Melinda, her hands shaking, removed Oreo's collar. *But there was nothing we could do.*

That first day after Oreo had slipped away from this life, the apartment had been a too-quiet shell of grief. Melinda called in to work and spent the afternoon curled up on the couch, staring out the paned windows as yet another round of snow blanketed the city.

The second morning, she was trying to eat her cereal when suddenly there was the unmistakable feeling of a cat brushing against her leg under the table. The third night she'd gotten up to go to the bathroom and saw Oreo at the end of the hall, sitting next to his dishes in the kitchen. Half asleep, she'd just looked at him, and he at her. He was shadowy somehow, but it was her Oreo. She glanced his way again, but he was gone.

The fourth day, she woke up heavy-hearted yet with a sense of peace. She found the courage to box up Oreo's toys and dishes and take them, with the bag of kibble she'd just opened the week before, to the animal shelter across town.

Now, leaning back against the refrigerator, she held the nylon-knit collar up in her hand as the tears slid down her face. The brass tag danced back and forth, a small sunbeam catching its edge. Two losses in two months. She closed her eyes with a shaky breath.

"I have to get up," she said, quiet, dejected. "I have to find a way to face this day."

She didn't just need to get up off the floor. She had to *move*. Forward, up and out, in more ways than one.

"I have to get up," she said again, this time in a calm, determined voice. She put a hand back under the sink and dragged the coffeemaker forward, its cord fishtailing around the boxes and bottles. Cradling it in one arm, she reached up to the countertop for balance and stretched to her feet. The coffeemaker wasn't so dirty after all, she realized, as she scrubbed it with hot, soapy water, wiped down the controls and plugged it in. The coffee grounds passed the sniff test and soon, a comforting smell wafted around the kitchen.

Melinda gently placed the crumpled pouches of cat treats in the garbage can, then studied Oreo's collar, remembering. She couldn't toss it out, but what to do with it? She carefully tucked the collar into the inside pocket of her purse.

Gulping a mug of coffee and nibbling a piece of toast made her feel more alert. Wrapped in her favorite robe following a steaming shower, she stood in front of her stacked and packed closet. All these clothes. When would she ever get to wear most of them again? There were no high-end designer labels among the rows and piles, but still an impressive collection she had gathered as her career and net worth soared. Even so, the weekends and evenings were always spent in jeans and sweats. And at least for now, her weekdays would be, too.

"What does one wear to the death of one's career, anyway?" Resisting the urge to make a statement by showing up in all black, she wrestled a pair of jeans out of a stack and reached for a blue long-sleeved tee. At least it was warm enough she wouldn't need a jacket for the two-block walk to the transit stop.

Yesterday came flooding back again, but this time she was determined not to dwell on it. Cassie and Susan had already texted this morning with plans for the three friends to go out for lunch. Melinda and Susan met during college, at the University of Minnesota, and the women had worked together at various times throughout their careers. Susan was now a junior executive at Collins and Cartwright, another agency in town. Cassie had stepped off her career track a decade ago to raise her family, a move made easier by the fact that her husband, Jim, came from an old-money Minneapolis family and was a successful attorney.

Melinda had the dubious honor of being the first of the three friends to ever be laid off. And that, she decided, was probably a significant feat given the instability in the media and marketing world these days.

Cassie would pick up Susan and drive downtown to shepherd Melinda and her box of work stuff home. And then what? A string of empty days stretched ahead of her and she had no idea how to fill them.

But first, she had to get dressed. The mirror above the bathroom sink wasn't very encouraging. The fine lines on her face, the ones that started to appear over the last few years, were more pronounced than ever. Her green eyes were tired and puffy, her skin blotchy. Pulling her wavy brown hair back into a low ponytail, she settled for a swipe of moisturizer and a little mascara. She didn't have the energy to try too hard, to put on some sort of show for her former colleagues.

And it was just as well. The tears nearly returned as Melinda realized she wasn't likely to see most of these people again, a loss that seemed nearly as painful as her fears about the future.

She reached for her keys and her purse, a saddle-brown tote that now seemed far too expensive and luxurious. How much had she paid for it last year? Couldn't remember, didn't want to. She pressed her lips together at the sight of Oreo's collar in the bottom of her bag. Under that stab of pain in her heart, she felt an ounce of strength. Oreo was gone, but his collar would remind her that just as she got through that loss, she could make it through this one. She briefly considered snapping his collar around the strap of her purse, like a good-luck charm, but decided against it. Cassie and Susan would think she'd lost her marbles.

Well, maybe I have. But she was going to try to keep up an appearance of sanity.

The hallway was wonderfully empty, her sneakers nearly silent on the beige runner that protected the original hardwood floors. There was nobody in the stairwell, either. She really didn't want to see anyone this morning, not even Charlie, the elderly widower whose apartment was right below hers. Charlie always was ready with an encouraging word and a cup of tea, when he wasn't riding his bike around Lake Calhoun with people half his age. He'd been a kind neighbor all these years, living in his rent-controlled apartment long before this street became fashionable again.

Even so, she wasn't ready to tell him what happened, how she was out of a job and might not be upstairs much longer. "No, I'm staying," she muttered as she stepped across the marble-floored lobby to the oak front door, "this is my home."

The air was warm but still had that spring freshness to it, that feeling that anything was possible. Melinda could almost imagine she was back home in Iowa, walking down the quiet street in front of her parent's home in Swanton. The aromas drifting from the crowded coffee shop on the corner beckoned, but she was determined to stay on schedule. She'd just have to look up some recipes online and create her own custom brews. Surely it couldn't be that hard.

No one else was at the transit stop and the bus, when it finally rolled up to the corner, only held a handful of riders. She swiped her pass and took a seat by a window, a rare treat. Most weekday mornings she had to stand all the way into downtown, gripping an overhead strap as she balanced her tote and coffee, braced against the packed bus of commuters.

The skyline loomed ahead through the windshield, the sun glinting off the angled peaks of the skyscrapers. Melinda found she was holding her breath as they reached the city's core and her heart jumped when the digital screen beeped and "Sixth Avenue" appeared. Her stop was next. Her arm felt weak as she reached up and pulled the cord.

"Have a good morning," the driver said with his usual cheerfulness as she exited the bus, disoriented and uneasy. For years she'd stepped off at this corner, secure and confident in her fashionable blouses and not-too-high heels, the sleek tote under her arm, elbowing her way through the crowds to WP&S. Now she paused on the sidewalk, not ready for what was coming next. She glanced down at her sneakers and felt like a scared little kid on the first day of school.

More like the last day. She fished in her tote for her phone, checking the time. Ten to eleven; would she have to wait? Why couldn't this nightmare just end, and fast? When she dropped the phone back inside, she found herself desperately rubbing Oreo's tag for good luck.

More alarm bells began to clang in her head as she approached the steel and glass office building where WP&S took up the top eight floors of the twenty-story structure. A small, quiet crowd was gathering in the courtyard in front. Melinda counted eight of her former co-workers, all in jeans and tees, scuffing their shoes on the concrete tiles. She couldn't help but smile as she saw Linda, from the CEO's administration office, rocking her pink-and-cream Chanel jacket as if this was any other day.

"Going out in style," Linda said as she draped an arm

around Melinda. The silver streaks in Linda's glossy black hair were elegant, even today. But Melinda saw the telltale signs of tears around the older woman's kind brown eyes. Linda lowered her designer sunglasses and tried to offer an encouraging smile.

"Going to make them wish they'd never tossed *me* out in the street. We're locked out, by the way, like a bunch of criminals. Nobody's key fobs work."

The men, by contrast, looked like they'd been up all night. None of them had shaved and a few carried the sharp odor of stale beer. Melinda was surprised to see Tom from retail accounts with a cigarette in his hand.

"I didn't know you smoked, Tom," one of the other men said, then shyly bummed a cigarette.

"I do now," Tom retorted. "I quit ten years ago but, what the hell, might as well start up again." There were murmurs of understanding from the others huddled by the door.

"Did you guys read that packet?" said a woman with a ball cap pulled low over her face. Melinda realized it was Monica from graphics. "I couldn't sleep and finally got up about three and started going over it. Then I couldn't stop going over it. I've only been here four years, so only four weeks of severance. Anyone know how to sign up for unemployment?"

"Oh, darling," Linda squeezed her hand. "We'll figure it out, all of us, together. I can't look at that horrible envelope. I stuffed mine in the kitchen junk drawer last night and told my husband we'll have our attorney pick it up Monday." No one said anything, but Melinda knew what many of the others were thinking: Linda's husband was an account manager at one of the Twin Cities' largest brokerage firms. Leisurely days of reading by the pool were in her future.

"I think someone's coming." Monica peered through the glass panes of the atrium, her lips trembling as she pulled her cap's brim lower.

"Well, let's get this over with," Tom angrily stubbed his cigarette out in the sand bowl topping the ornate trash can. Melinda instinctively reached in her purse for her badge, then remembered it was gone. Tom was digging in his jeans pocket, too, then pulled his hand out, empty. He looked at her, then looked away.

How strange this all felt. A lump formed in her throat as she gazed up the side of the commercial tower, up toward the fifteenth floor, her second home for more than a decade. All morning she'd comforted herself with the idea that this final stop at the office would be therapeutic.

This was her chance to gather everything accumulated over her fourteen years at WP&S, including photos of her parents and siblings, her friends, and Oreo. She kept an old-school pica ruler in her desk for good luck, and there was an extra umbrella and a page-a-day cat calendar, too. The smallest things mattered now, and she needed to pack them up, take them with her. Even getting her bottle of hand sanitizer back seemed righteous in some way.

But now, she just wanted to go home and go back to bed. Everything felt wrong, from being downtown on a Saturday morning to the thin traffic and the few people strolling by on the usually congested sidewalks.

And then Patrick from human resources came through the lobby, a grim, forced smile on his face. With a *pop* and a *thunk*, one of the glass doors opened as Patrick took a few more hesitant steps forward.

"Everyone, thanks for coming in today." His tone was brisk and overly upbeat for the occasion. "Your managers will meet you at the elevator lobby on your floor. We'll all go up together. We'll keep this as easy as possible, and quick. I'm sure you all have other things to do."

"Sit at home and drink the weekend away?" Monica whispered acidly to Melinda as they walked through the atrium single file, like a group of chaperoned kids on a field trip. "Thanks to him and his, I don't have anything to do come Monday."

Melinda couldn't think about Monday; it made her palms sweat and her heart race. Monday was two days away. She just had to get through the next hour.

* 2 *

Another human resources officer met them at the elevator doors and they were divided into two groups. When her car lurched to a stop on fifteen, Melinda took a deep breath and stepped into the all-too-familiar hallway, followed by a studio photographer and a woman whom Melinda couldn't quite place. Jason, one of the team leads for the floor, tried to smile and hug all of them at once. It was awkward and terrible.

"I'm sorry the other supervisors couldn't make it today," Jason said as he guided them to their desks, as if they'd already forgotten where they were. Despite his casual tone, Melinda could tell he was annoyed the other managers hadn't even shown up.

With no one there to complain the sun was too bright on their computer screens, all the blinds were still open from last night's visit by the cleaning service.

Melinda felt like she was in some sort of strange, disorienting dream, the late-morning sunbeams flooding the open workspace with near-blinding light. She swallowed hard as she followed Jason to her desk, then stopped short. Where were her things?

In the middle of the barren desktop was an unmarked cardboard box. Her monitor was shoved to the side, pockets of dust scattered around the otherwise-blank surface. She glared at Jason, whose cheeks started to flush.

"We're trying to move the process along as quickly as possible," he stammered. Melinda felt her anger rise.

"You went through my things?" Her voice, high and shrill, echoed around the deserted office. Someone on the other end of the floor started to cry. She was about to. "You packed up my desk for me, like I'm a little kid?"

"It's not ... it's not like that, Melinda," Jason wavered. "We just want everyone to move on and ..."

"You went through my stuff." She pointed at the desk, then at Jason, her voice lower and tight. "My stuff. My personal belongings. I've had this same desk for over ten years, you know."

Jason just stood there, looking miserable. Melinda could hardly bring herself to lift the flap and peer into the box. Her photos and other personal items looked small and sad as they huddled in the bottom. *This is all that's left*, she thought. *Shouldn't there be more?*

She began to mentally catalog the contents of her files. All her account folders, her writing drafts, notes on the projects she was working on. Her hands shaking with anger, she jerked open the metal drawers on the desk and the file cabinet. They were all empty.

The hollow clangs they made when they slammed closed echoed her grief and frustration.

She turned, trying to keep her voice calm. "Where's the rest of it? Tell me where they are. All the files. All of it."

"The supervisors are moving quickly to relocate accounts with employees remaining with the company," Jason recited in a tone that told her he'd practiced his talking points at home last night.

Her mouth fell open. "Who ... "

"That's confidential information. And all those projects are legally owned by WP&S, which you ... well ... I'm so sorry, Melinda." Jason appeared genuinely upset, but that only made her angrier. None of those projects were finished. She needed to sort them, make notes for the next writer. Didn't anybody care about that? Apparently not.

Jason came around the desk and began to fidget with the flaps on the box, glanced around and lowered his voice. "I saw some items from past projects I thought you might want to keep, to show the scope of your work here, to help you land something else. They're in the manila folders down in the bottom, under your photos."

Melinda closed her eyes. She didn't have the heart to look in there again. What about the copy for that new grocery store campaign, or the project for the woman starting a consulting business from home? And she'd just sketched out some ideas for that one major corporate client ... the one that she then remembered had dropped her firm.

This firm, she reminded herself, staring at the void on her once-cluttered desk. *I don't work here anymore.*

"I'm so sorry," Jason said again, holding one hand with the other as if he didn't know what to do. Melinda had never liked Jason much, but she could see this was hard for him. Even so, she hoped he wasn't about to go in for another hug. He'd just spent the morning sorting through her possessions and carting her files off to goodness knows where.

"Well, I have to help Kim get her box," he gestured toward the other woman and started in her direction, as if he couldn't get away fast enough. "Please go stand by the left entrance and wait for us there."

Kim. Suddenly, Melinda remembered. Kim had given this firm more than two decades as a top-notch proofreader, even staying late and coming in on weekends when some of the copywriters were slow to make deadline. She never complained, never sought attention for her work. Kim was now slumped in her chair, resting her head on her empty desk. She didn't look up when Jason put a cautious hand on her shoulder.

Melinda picked up her box, felt sick about how light it was in her arms. She considered going to the right-side entrance, just to see what Jason would do. Would security guards suddenly appear? She could imagine the box being wrestled away, her photos flying across the room.

At least, that would free up her hands and give her a much-needed opportunity to slap somebody ...

"But that would just delay my escape," she whispered, obediently going to stand by the left elevator. "And I have to get out of here."

She placed her box on the slick tile floor and waited. The parcel seemed smaller and sadder than it had on her desk. *Everything is in there*, she thought. *Everything that's left.*

The tears were coming again. She knew Cassie and Susan were on their way, but she had to do something. Not just stand there, waiting for this to end. She reached in her tote, fumbled around for her phone, and texted Cassie. "Come get me. I'm done," she typed.

The photographer joined Melinda with his box. They just nodded at each other, then watched as Jason, carrying Kim's tote, gently steered her to the elevators. Kim trailed behind, tears streaming down her face. Melinda tried to offer her a smile, but what could she say? What could anyone say?

Her heart sank with the elevator as they drifted down to the lobby, where Jason and the other floor managers tried to say their goodbyes, offering tentative handshakes and hugs to the shell-shocked former employees. Melinda zigzagged around the huddle and, hugging her box to her chest, put her head down and started for the doors.

"I'll find you on Facebook," Monica gave her arm a squeeze as she passed, her box tucked to her side. Melinda could only nod. Her head was spinning. She was trying to look outside, look ahead.

Then she spotted a cherry-red Escalade double-parked in the loading zone. The horn honked and the lights blinked. Cassie and Susan were there, they saw her coming, saw her trying to make those last trembling steps across the atrium. Melinda's tears switched from anger to relief as she gave the glass door a hearty push with her shoulder and stepped out into the sunshine.

Susan jumped out of the backseat and ran to the entrance, her pushed-up sunglasses caught in her strawberry-blonde bob. She reached for the box in Melinda's shaky hands. "That's it? That's all you got?"

"Yeah." Melinda was starting to feel dizzy, disoriented. "Please get me out of here. I have to get out of here."

"Don't look back. Just get in the car," Susan put her arm around her friend. "We're going to Amadori's for lunch. Just think about what you want for lunch. There'll be wine."

Cassie propped the passenger-side door open and reached out, taking Melinda's purse and guiding her into the cool shade of the vehicle.

"Get in, dear. What do they say? When one door closes ..."

"Those windows don't always open right away," Susan added, settling in the back with Melinda's box next to her on the gray leather seat. "But they'll appear, give it time. Right now, you need some food and some rest. I'd say you need to laugh, but that might be asking too much today."

"Thanks for coming, girls." Melinda leaned back against the seat and closed her eyes, a welcome blast from the air conditioning vent hitting her face.

Cassie, as usual, was overdressed for the occasion. Decked out in a green-and-white dotted dress and high heels, she flipped her shades down over her brown eyes, honked her horn at another driver and whipped the Escalade into the street. "Screw that place," she muttered. "It's their loss."

Melinda felt herself drifting away from the curb. She was numb and scared. And suddenly tired, so tired. She had considered driving herself downtown, picking up her stuff on her own. But Cassie and Susan had insisted otherwise, saying it might be too tough emotionally for her to handle alone. And they had been right.

Cassie let out a whoop when she found a prime parking spot at Amadori's, the ladies' favorite old-school Italian restaurant. "It's a Saturday," she grinned as she maneuvered into the space. "On a weekday, we'd be walking blocks to get over here."

Amadori's was dim and cozy, with dark red walls and ivory tablecloths. Even for a weekend lunch, the restaurant was nearly packed. Melinda began to relax as she settled into the overstuffed booth. She was hungrier than she realized. That piece of toast hadn't given her much energy, and the emotional strain of going to WP&S had chased away the last of her hangover.

The gold bracelets on Cassie's already-tan wrist jangled as she picked up the wine list. "I'm not going to ask what you're going to do next," she reached across and patted Melinda's hand. "Let's not talk about it today, OK?"

"Didn't we agree not to bring that up?" Susan rolled her eyes as she checked her phone. "And you just did!"

Cassie laughed, then grew serious. "Melinda, you need to take care of yourself. Jim and I have an extra bedroom if you ever need a place to stay, we'll help in any way we can. You just let us know what you need."

Cassie and Jim Blake actually had more than one extra bedroom. Their renovated 1920s brick mansion in a small-but-elite neighborhood in Minneapolis boasted a tiled pool, guest house, fireplaces in every sitting room and a manicured lawn that would make Jay Gatsby jealous. Despite Cassie's lavish lifestyle, Melinda always suspected her friend was a bit embarrassed by the Blake family's wealth and status.

"She does have an apartment," Susan tilted her head at Cassie. "And a fabulous one at that. Which is really good, because our place is a little tight." Susan's husband, Ray Vinter, was a software engineer for a large manufacturing company. They and their two small sons lived in Edina.

"Besides, you won't be needing a place to crash." Susan flipped over the wine list Cassie passed across the table. "You're skilled, you're bright, smart, talented, all of it. You'll find something, and fast. Don't worry. My firm might even be hiring in a few weeks, even in this economy."

"You're right," Melinda tapped her menu. "I'll start looking Monday. Isn't that what the kids do? Switch jobs every year or two? I'm overdue for a change, then."

"You get some money, right?" Cassie narrowed her eyes. "Severance? Unemployment? Insurance?"

"I have the packet at home, but haven't looked at it yet."
Melinda rubbed her face, trying to block out the mental image
of the heavy manila envelope that had glared at her all
morning from the top of the bookcase. Maybe tomorrow she
could read its contents. Just not today. She shook her head
when Susan offered her the wine list. She'd had enough last
night. But there would be lasagna, and dessert, and as many
slices of garlic bread as she wanted.

"Whatever they're giving you, it will surely last you for
some time," Susan said as she scanned the list of specials.
"And you do have time, Melinda. Take a break for a few
weeks, clear your head. It's the perfect chance to go home to
see your family, and not just for a weekend. It's been a few
months, right?"

Her hometown of Swanton was in northern Iowa, only a
three-hour drive from Minneapolis but a world away from her
life in the city. Even though it was home to just under ten
thousand people, Swanton retained its title as the hub for
Hartland County because it was the most-populated town for
miles in any direction. Her mom, Diane, had given up her
elementary-school teaching job just last year, and her dad,
Roger, was retired from the local phone company. Melinda
was close to her parents, especially since her siblings lived far
away. Amanda and her family lived outside of Milwaukee.
Mark had moved to Austin, Texas to study engineering and
never found his way back to the Midwest.

Going home for even a few days always relaxed Melinda
and cleared her head, which was just what she needed now. "I
was thinking about that this morning, but ... I still need to call
my parents and tell them what happened."

"You haven't done that yet?" Cassie raised her eyebrows
as the waiter brought their salads. "I would think you would
have called them right away. You're all so close."

"I know, I know," Melinda sighed. "Yesterday was such a
blur, so surreal. I'll do it first thing when I get home."

Home. How long could she keep her apartment if she
couldn't find a well-paying job, and fast? There would be

some unemployment benefits, and she had started to save more aggressively after her last promotion at WP&S. But when she tried to look ahead two months, three months, she couldn't see her way forward. She shuddered as she remembered the flash of insight from that morning, that vision of herself as old and broke, shuffling around in a stale, cluttered apartment.

"What am I going to do?" She put her head in her hands, her voice small, scared.

Cassie reached around and hugged Melinda's shoulder. "It's going to be OK. It will. It has to. You'll see."

"No, really, what's going to happen to me?" She tried to sit up straight, wipe at her eyes. Two elderly women at the next table stared as they sipped their soups of the day.

"I'm nearly forty. I've been at the same company for almost fifteen years and so happy there that I never once considered looking for another job. How am I going to compete with those Millennial kids? And I can't sit home all day, staring out the window."

Cassie gave the eavesdropping ladies a warning look and lowered her voice. "Listen, you're good on your own, better than anyone else I know. Believe me, I wish I was half as self-sufficient as you are." Susan raised an eyebrow, as Cassie had just confirmed what she and Melinda had always suspected.

"Three years ago, when you and Craig broke off your engagement? I would have died on the spot." Cassie reached across the table and grasped Melinda's hand. "But you just held your head up and kept going. Thankfully the two of you hadn't bought that house, the really cute one with the wrought-iron fence and ... well, never mind about that ..."

Melinda winced. She and Craig, a sports reporter for one of the Twin Cities' television stations, had dated for two years before he slipped the engagement ring on her finger while they sat on a park bench beside Lake Calhoun.

Despite the romantic, sunset-lit gesture, she had known deep down that it wouldn't work, that he wasn't the one. It took six weeks of breathless congratulations from well-meaning friends and an offer on a house before she'd gathered the courage to put an end to it.

Susan handed her a tissue and tried to get the discussion back on track. "The point is, you always find a way to move forward, and you will again. Like when Oreo passed away. You cried, of course, and it hurt. But you carried on."

Melinda thought of Oreo's collar tucked down in her purse. Her friends were right, she'd faced hard times before. But still ...

"Even if I can manage somehow to deal with this ..." She felt the tears stinging behind her eyes again. Would she ever get her emotions in check? "What about when the severance runs out? What if I get sick, or I can't pay the rent? I'm just one bad day away from ..."

"From what? Extinction?" Cassie gave a smirk and all but shoved the bread plate in Melinda's face. Amadori's garlic bread was one of her few vices and Cassie knew it. "You certainly won't starve here. Eat up."

Melinda knew she was being melodramatic. The coming weeks and months would be only as difficult as she let them be. Her attitude, her outlook, would determine how well she weathered this challenge. "OK, OK, but I'll probably feel like a dinosaur when I start looking for another job." Then she became quiet. "Eviction, though. Eviction could happen."

"Then you'll just find another place," Susan patted her hand. "You won't be homeless or go hungry, we'll see to that."

"You girls are the best friends I could ask for," she managed a smile for Susan and Cassie.

"You're right, I need to give it time. Maybe I'll just hang out for a few days, try to clear my head. But then, I need to figure out what I'm going to do."

⁎ 3 ⁎

"Do you know what you are going to do?"

Melinda glanced up from the foam cup of coffee she was absentmindedly stirring with one of those tiny plastic straws. It was hospital brew, cheap and hot and bitter. She'd added four little pots of creamer, trying to make it drinkable, but it was a work in progress. She reached in her tote for the packets of sugar swiped from the cafeteria.

Aunt Miriam plopped down in the beige plastic chair next to Melinda, a wad of tissues in her hand, her brown eyes tired. "It's been, what, a month now? Any prospects?"

She had been camped out on her couch, surfing talk shows and house-flipping programs, when her mom called to tell her about Uncle Frank's heart attack. That was yesterday. Today they were at the hospital in Mason City, waiting for Frank to come out of surgery. He was going to survive, the doctor said last night, but needed a triple bypass and, after that, lots of rest.

"Well, I'm looking around," Melinda began her standard answer to the question that had been asked more times than she could count in the past month. That included challenging herself with it at least once a day.

"The market's not good. Most of the larger advertising firms in the city aren't hiring. I might get lucky at a smaller company, but most of them have been snapped up by the larger firms. I've got a few more severance checks coming, and then I can apply for unemployment, I guess."

She sounded defeated and bitter, and she hated herself for it. She was healthy, she wasn't starving, the rent was paid. But some days it had been hard to get up in the morning. Where had the time gone?

Melinda wasn't sure, but knew she'd passed too much of it sprawled on her couch, remote in hand.

There were more important things to talk about now. "How is Uncle Frank, what have you heard?"

"The physician's assistant came out about an hour ago to say the bypass is going well." Miriam folded her hands in a quick praying motion and glanced up at the cream tiles on the waiting room's ceiling. "I'm thankful for that. He'll pull through, thank God. But I don't think he'll be back at the store anytime soon."

Miriam rubbed her close-cropped brown curls and adjusted her glasses. Melinda knew her aunt was about to vent her frustration, and she was ready to listen.

"I've been telling him he needs to slow down," Miriam clenched the tissue still in her hand. "The hardware store doesn't need to be his whole life, we can hire more help. But he loves it so much. I do, too, but I don't know how we can keep it going, if he can't work for even a while. Truth be told, I don't want to retire, either. We've only run the store for more than thirty-five years."

Frank and Miriam, who was Diane's younger sister, had owned the hardware store in Prosper, a little community northeast of Swanton, since just after they married. The store had been in Melinda's family ever since her Shrader great-great-grandparents opened it in 1894. The small town had less than two hundred residents, but Prosper Hardware was its heart. The community's lone gas station had closed more than twenty years ago, and it had been decades since a grocery store operated in the little town. Prosper Hardware remained the only retail business for ten to fifteen miles, depending on which direction you traveled.

Miriam and Frank had no children, and Melinda always suspected she was their favorite niece. She hadn't hesitated to pack a bag yesterday and hurry home to offer whatever support she could. Aunt Miriam was normally quick with a joke and a smile; nothing fazed her and no one intimidated her, especially after years of waiting on every resident within miles of Prosper.

But now, she was quiet and drained. It hurt Melinda to see her aunt like this.

"I know you love the city," Miriam said now, leaning in as if she was sharing a secret, "and you probably can't imagine living out here again. But if you wanted to help me out for a while, I would really appreciate it."

Melinda didn't know what to say. She took a slow sip of her now-lukewarm coffee to buy some time. Miriam assumed the silence was a sign her niece was considering her offer, and doubled down. "I'd pay you, of course, as decent a salary as I could manage, and it would be full time."

It was obvious Aunt Miriam had given this idea some serious thought. Before Melinda could begin to let her down easy, she started ticking off the details of her plan.

"You can't drive back and forth from Minneapolis, but what about staying with your parents? It would give you more time to spend with them. It's just for a while, until Frank gets his strength back and we can decide what to do. We have a full-time employee already, it's not like you'd have to take on that much. I need to focus on the books, ordering supplies and payroll and such. What do you say?"

What Melinda wanted to say was, as much as she loved her parents, she couldn't imagine living with them again. How would she live out of a suitcase, even for a few weeks, when she'd been living on her own for so many years? And what about her life in Minneapolis?

"I know it's a lot to ask," Miriam patted Melinda's arm. There was now a pleading tone to her voice.

"I'll take all the time you can give me. A few weeks, a few months. Whatever you can spare. It would give me more time to care for Frank. And it'll help him recover, too, to know that the store is in good hands."

Melinda started to laugh. "Well, I don't know anything about running a hardware store, so I'm not sure I qualify for the 'good hands' part. But I'll think about it, Aunt Miriam. It would be a big change."

What she didn't say, what she couldn't put into words, was how this idea had suddenly raised her spirits. She didn't want to admit it to her aunt, but the last month had been filled with empty days, tears and frustration. Helping at the store would give her a chance to drop out of her regular life, which wasn't so great right now. It was the easy way out, a temporary escape, but maybe she was willing to consider it.

"Honey, I think you're due for a big change." Miriam's mood brightened. "Sounds like you've had plenty of change recently, but not the good kind. Maybe a little break would be just the thing, give you something else to focus on. I hear that you can apply for jobs online, everyone does that nowadays. You could continue to look while you're here. It'd be like a summer job, like when you were in college."

Miriam's eyes sparkled now. She'd saved her best talking point for last. "I could set you up with health insurance. Does that help? I bet it does."

"Wow," Melinda tipped her head, considering. "You're making a sweet offer now." The premiums on her former employer's insurance plan were going to skyrocket in just a few weeks. And she had already decided that, no matter what else happened, she would never go without health insurance. That was just tempting fate.

"Well, I could pay up my rent a month or two in advance, I guess," she shrugged, "if I decided to do it."

"I won't work you seven days a week. The store isn't even open on Sundays. You'd have days off, I'm guessing Sundays and Mondays. You could go back and forth on weekends."

Melinda was relieved to see her mom coming down the hall with a stack of cafeteria sandwiches in her arms. They couldn't be worse than the coffee, and she was starving.

Even in the harsh glare of the florescent lights reflecting off her glasses, Diane Foster still didn't look all of her sixty-seven years. She styled her steel-gray hair in a layered pixie cut, and decades on her feet as an elementary-school teacher had kept her fit. Melinda couldn't believe it when her mom took up running after retirement, but it was doing her good. She had the energy of a person half her age.

The one thing that dated her mom, that made Melinda cringe even now, was that retired-teacher habit of wearing tops embellished with designs reflecting the seasons. Pumpkins in the fall, kittens with mittens in the winter, that sort of thing. Today's pink top was embroidered with hummingbirds on the right shoulder.

"Ham and cheese is all they've got right now." Diane handed a waxed-paper bundle to Miriam, then one to Melinda. "Is it working, Miriam?"

"What?" Melinda was about to take a bite, then stopped. "Mom, are you behind this plan?"

"Well, not really. It was her idea. But your father and I would love for you to come stay with us for a while. And working at the store will give you something to do, so you won't be underfoot all the time. We like doing what we please, when we please. We're getting used to this retirement idea."

"I'm not," Miriam snapped. Diane took the chair on the other side of her sister and wrapped an understanding arm around Miriam's shoulder.

Diane and Miriam had always been close. It's no wonder they'd cooked up this plan together.

"I know it's a lot to ask," Diane said to her daughter. "And I know you'll head back to the city eventually. But will you at least consider it? Maybe you'd even have some ideas about marketing for the store, like using that social media stuff."

Miriam started to laugh. "I don't know how much a marketing plan would help the store," she said, then took a hearty bite out of her sandwich.

"People know what's in it, things haven't changed much over the years. And the same customers have been coming in for decades. But Melinda, I know how talented you are. I'm open to any and all suggestions."

It was clear her mom and aunt weren't going to drop their idea. "Well, since you two have it all planned out, I'll give it some thought, at least."

"In the meantime," Aunt Miriam began to fish around in the black leather purse at her feet, "can you stop by the store on your way home, I mean, to your parents' house? I need to get this extra set of keys to Bill, our full-timer. He's going to lock up tonight. I was so frazzled when I ran by there this morning that I forgot to hand them over."

"You went to the store today, Miriam?" Diane gave her sister a concerned look. "Let Bill worry about the store. You have to take care of yourself, too, along with Frank."

Neither of them said, *"that's why we need you, Melinda,"* but she saw how tired her aunt looked. The relief that Uncle Frank was going to make it through this health crisis didn't change the fact that Miriam had some long weeks and months ahead of her as she helped her husband recover.

"I'll stay as long as I can this afternoon and come back tonight if you want me to," Diane told Miriam. "Melinda, we'll eat about seven. That should give you plenty of time to stop by the store."

"The doctors say Frank will be out of surgery soon." Miriam hugged Melinda as she got up to leave. "I'll let you know how he is. If all goes well, I could go home tonight."

Melinda threaded her way through the antiseptic corridors of the hospital and stepped out into the blindingly bright afternoon sunshine.

Working in downtown Minneapolis for so many years, she had forgotten how strong the sun could be without all those towering buildings to filter the light. The bubble of silence inside her gray hatchback was comforting after the sudden stress of the past two days. She cranked on the air conditioning, leaned back and closed her eyes.

It had been weeks since she'd been in the middle of this much activity, and she was surprised by how strange it felt.

Her days had dissolved into a slow routine of watching television, reading, walking and cleaning, punctuated with occasional dinners out with friends and a weekly scroll through the online job boards.

The woman who had been so busy, who had so much work to do and so many commitments to fill her days and nights, where had she gone?

The chaos of the last twenty-four hours had shown her how lonely she was, how much she missed the hustle of her former life. The projects she'd planned to take on during her sabbatical, like a scrapbook for her sister's kids, a deep clean of her place, some creative writing, had yet to be started.

She was bored. Bored, and lonely. The longer she was out of a job, the less connected she felt to her old self. With nothing new to replace them, she drifted through the days and weeks, waiting for something to happen.

And now, it had. She opened her eyes and realized she was still clutching the keys to Prosper Hardware. She dug down into her tote, reaching for a safe place to stash the nothing-special ring and its two keys.

Oreo's brass tag winked at her from the bottom of the inside pocket. Seeing it made her heart ache for a moment. Then she realized that, for the first time in a long time, she was free to do whatever she wanted. Wherever she wanted.

"It is a sign?" She raised an eyebrow at Oreo's collar. "We'll have to see about that."

She made her way out of Mason City and merged onto the interstate, heading east. She'd changed her car radio's presets yesterday, a task she completed each time she crossed the Iowa-Minnesota state line on her trips to and from Swanton. She cranked up her favorite country station as the fields and pastures began to fly by. Pop and alternative rock were her favorites, but the tunes of Willie, Merle and Dolly always seemed a better fit for rolling through the open spaces of northern Iowa.

It was about a forty-minute drive to Prosper, punctuated by a handful of towns once she turned south onto a two-lane state highway. It was always interesting to check for any changes in the communities along the route, but it was the fields and family farms that she loved the most. No matter what was happening in the Twin Cities, no matter how crazy her life was, she could always breathe easy out here.

It was early June, and the young corn and bean plants were just starting to poke up out of the fertile soil, each stalk just one miniscule stitch in a rolling green blanket that stretched to the horizon, the fields interrupted only by the small streams meandering through this part of the state and its grid of gravel roads. Melinda was always amazed at how many shades of green were visible out here, from the pale tones in the tender leaves on the trees to the deep hues of the grasses in the freshly mown yards. Red-winged blackbirds sang atop road signs as they kept an eye on their nearby nests, which were tucked into the wild-growing bushes along the ditches.

Melinda played a little game as she passed each farm, seeking out anything new, such as a garage being built or a re-shingled house roof. Fall was her favorite time of the year to make this drive, but early summer was a close second. New calves appeared in some of the barn lots, and baby goats and lambs frolicked near their mothers in the front pastures.

Once Melinda passed the place with the white barn and the red house, whose color scheme was the opposite of most of the farms along the state highway, she started watching for the turnoff to Prosper. She smiled when the green sign with the white letters appeared on the side of the road. It told her the little community was still incorporated, a point of pride for places this small. That meant a mayor and city council, a library, and a little tax money to keep up the streets. There'd been rumbles a few years ago that Prosper might officially disband, but its few business owners rallied with residents to keep the town on the map.

She turned east at an intersection with a county blacktop, the tower of Prosper's co-op punctuating the horizon about a mile away. Platted in the 1890s along the railroad line, the community's founders had big dreams that didn't quite pan out. The irony of the town's name wasn't lost on any of its residents, however. Melinda laughed as she passed the wooden welcome sign, which offered a quaint, colorful painting of Main Street and the town's motto: "Welcome to Prosper, the great little town that didn't."

There was the inevitable bump-thump as the county highway crossed the railroad tracks just before Prosper Feed Co., where the co-op's name was still prominently displayed in bold, black letters on the cream stucco of its tallest tower. Prosper's first commercial structure, a wood-frame train depot that once doubled as a feed store and creamery, was still huddled next to the tracks, its white paint peeling and its windows dark. The current co-op office sat closer to the county highway, square and smug in its cloak of tan metal siding. Several trucks were parked out front, and one man was coming out the front door with a bag of animal feed slung over his shoulder.

The blacktop next crossed First Street, made a little diagonal jag to the southeast, and began its three-block run as Prosper's Main Street. The opposite end of the business district was marked by the sea-green water tower just past Fourth Street. Beyond that, the county highway bended again, this time turning straight south, and crossed the river.

The first block of Main Street was filled with houses built at the turn of the last century, a few grand Victorians surrounded by bungalows and the occasional four-square house that would have been at home on any area farm. The Methodist Church, a stately brown-brick structure, stood the corner of Main and Second.

"This is where all the action is," Melinda grinned as she rolled into the second block of Main. Prosper Hardware crowned the middle of the block on her right, a two-story, red brick building with limestone-block details above its windows and on its corners. Display windows flanked both sides of its dark-green front door. A matching awning sheltered the first floor from the ever-changing Iowa weather.

The swinging metal sign jutting out between the second-floor windows wasn't original to when Melinda's ancestors opened the store. That one had been repainted and repaired over the decades until it rusted right through.

Uncle Frank thought a more modern sign would be best, but residents made it clear they loved the old one, a sentiment that Aunt Miriam shared. Uncle Frank had grumbled about the expense, but then combed over the books for the extra cash to have a replica made by a Chicago company. Aunt Miriam turned the new sign's arrival into a grand celebration of the store's history. She loved to remind Frank that the extra revenue brought in by the publicity stunt had, in the end, covered the cost of the custom sign.

And that wasn't the only detail on Prosper's Main Street that reflected Aunt Miriam's love for her community. This block was dotted with benches of iron scrollwork and wood slats, encouraging people to stop for a chat and to soak up the little town's welcoming atmosphere.

Hanging baskets of purple and white impatiens, reflecting the colors of the local high school's teams, danced in the early-summer breeze on decorative iron hooks installed on the light poles. Miriam had rallied the business community a few years ago to get both projects completed, and Melinda suspected her aunt had pulled a large chunk of the cost from her own pocket.

Right across from the hardware store stood Prosper City Hall and the next-door library. The library was just one story and City Hall was two, its upstairs housing a community hall once used for plays and social events. Behind those buildings, back across an alley and facing Oak Street, was the metal shed that housed the volunteer fire department's single fire truck and its only ambulance. There hadn't been a Prosper Police Department for several years; instead, a Hartland County Sheriff's deputy cruised through town a few times a day.

A squat, gray stone building between Prosper Hardware and Third Street held the town's post office, its American flag listing in the slight breeze. Melinda was glad to see the post office was still operating. Some tiny communities, even though they were still incorporated, had seen their post offices closed.

As she turned into one of the diagonal parking spaces in front of Prosper Hardware, Melinda peered down Main Street to see how the rest of the town was faring.

The old bank building, a grand, two-story brick structure just past Third Street, kitty-corner from the post office, still appeared empty and unused. She had noticed the former gas station, across from the Methodist Church, also remained vacant. Shades were pulled in the windows of several other properties along Main.

The farm crisis of the 1980s, along with an ongoing exodus to larger towns and cities, had been tough on small communities like Prosper. And there had been further strain when the Prosper school district consolidated with Swanton a decade ago, resulting in the middle- and high-school students being bused fifteen miles to the county seat.

That left only the elementary grades at the renovated, century-old building a block off Main, across Oak Street from the fire department.

Even so, Prosper's residents loved their town and were determined to preserve its identity. The buildings in the third block of Main Street weren't as grand as the second, instead being single-story structures in various states of upkeep, but there were still several vehicles parked there.

Melinda guessed most of those people were inside the Watering Hole, Prosper's only bar and restaurant. But across from the tavern, one of the buildings had additional flower baskets out front and its concrete steps appeared to have been recently painted. A modest sign above the door declared it was an insurance office.

As Melinda got out of the car, not bothering to click the door locks, she thought about how urban residents always bragged up city life, that everything was so convenient and all the neighborhoods had their own shops within walking distance of most people's homes.

"It's no different here," she said, feeling the blast of summer heat radiating off the asphalt-coated street. "Get your mail, pick up some nails, grab a free book and chug a beer, all within about a hundred feet."

Melinda craned her neck and looked to the end of Main, down past the Catholic Church. Although she couldn't make out the sign, she was sure the dark green building with the gleaming white trim was still the home of Prosper Veterinary Services. Her search was rewarded when she spied an adorable black-and-white calf, its red halter tied to a yard stake, munching the emerald-green grass under the front lawn's oak tree.

The shade cast by Prosper Hardware's awning was inviting. She was tempted to flop down on one of the two benches out front, close her eyes for a minute or two. But it had been at least three years since she had last been inside the store, her most-recent visits with Miriam and Frank being at their house on Cherry Street, a few blocks away. Melinda was curious to see if anything had changed at Prosper Hardware, and secretly hoped it hadn't.

✳ 4 ✳

The familiar scent of sawdust and lemon-oil polish drew her into the cool, air-conditioned store, the bells on the inside of the heavy oak door jingling to announce her arrival.

In an instant she was four again, toddling down the main aisle to press her face against the glass window of the wooden showcase, which still held a selection of candy. The oak cabinet stretched down the center third of the store, its weathered top serving as Prosper Hardware's checkout counter. She could still see Grandpa Shrader at the register, smiling as his metal scoop dropped her carefully chosen candies into a rustling paper sack.

Frank and Miriam had modernized the store over the years, filling its four rows with metal shelving and hanging industrial florescent lights from the pressed-tin ceiling. All the candy in the case was now shrink-wrapped, and the ornate cast-iron register had been replaced by a digital version with a credit-card reader. But the plaster walls retained their creamy hue, and the worn oak floors were still buffed until they glowed with a soft sheen. The oak counter was just as it had been decades ago, when Frank and Miriam took over the business from Miriam and Diane's parents.

Melinda wondered if Frank and Miriam really loved the counter that much, or simply couldn't figure out any possible way to haul the twelve-foot-long cabinet out of the building.

Her reverie was broken by the smiling, inquisitive woman behind the counter. Even on this warm day, she wore a corduroy shirt with embroidered kittens romping on the front. She was short and stout, her whitish blond hair tucked behind her ears, her hazel eyes studying Melinda.

"Can I help you?" She leaned her elbows on the counter, and Melinda noticed the gold kitten earrings she was wearing.

"I'm Melinda, Frank and Miriam's niece. Miriam asked me to drop off some extra keys for Bill. She forgot to leave them here this morning and ..."

"Oh, Melinda! It's wonderful to see you again!" The woman hurried to the far end of the counter and came around to offer a proper welcome. Melinda didn't recognize this woman, but sensed a big hug was on the way. And it was.

"How was your trip down from the city? Miriam called an hour ago to say Frank's on the mend, thank goodness." The woman reached for a flannel cloth resting on the counter and began rubbing the glossy oak surface, as if she couldn't stand to be idle. "Knowing him, he'll want to get out of bed tomorrow and be back here stocking shelves. But he needs his rest, poor man. And Miriam was fretting this morning that the front windows haven't been washed in a week with everything that's been going on. You've got to get out the big ladder, you know, and I'm getting a little far along in years for all that. Besides, we've been pretty busy today anyway."

Melinda couldn't place this woman, even with her obvious love of cats. But then, she hadn't visited Prosper Hardware for some time.

"I'm sorry, I don't think I know you." She offered her hand to the woman. "How long have you worked here?"

"Oh, I don't work here, honey. I'm retired from the school, worked in the kitchen for thirty years until that silly merger." She grasped Melinda's palm in a warm squeeze with one hand and continued to dust the counter with the other.

Melinda tried again. "And you're? ... "

"Esther Denner," the woman said with a nod that jangled the golden kittens in her ears. "Frank and Miriam's neighbor.

As soon as I heard Frank had that heart attack, I rushed right over here to help out in the store."

Esther tossed the dust cloth down and started fussing with the top of the counter, which held a small glass bowl for spare change and a red tin bucket of pens with silk flowers taped to their tops.

"Miriam's asked me to keep an eye on things and wait on people when Bill's working in the back. Good thing we had these new digital cash registers at the school, or I'd be lost running this thing." She gestured over the counter, then turned to straighten a cardboard display of garden seeds across the aisle.

"I grew up with Miriam and your mom," she smiled over her shoulder at Melinda. "I was in your mom's grade in school. But it's been so long since I've seen you! I heard about your ... unfortunate situation."

"Err, yes." Melinda grimaced, still not quite sure when she had seen Esther last, if ever. As always, word traveled fast in a small town, and she was sure Esther prided herself on always knowing the latest. She didn't want to give Esther too many details. "It's been tough the past few weeks. But I'm looking, and I'm sure something will turn up."

"Those big-city corporations are just terrible," Esther set her jaw and shook her head. "My daughter Kate lives down in Iowa City, does telecommunications. She lost her job one time, at some big company down there, and it took her a year to find another one. But never mind," Esther waved her hand as if swatting at an annoying insect. "You'll do fine, just fine."

Melinda could only nod. Then she realized she was gripping the counter tightly, bracing herself against it. A year? It took Kate a *year*?

"Well ... I can leave the keys with Bill, if he's here."

"Bill's in the back," Esther called over her shoulder. Melinda took it as a sign to follow.

As they passed a display of kitchen and bath towels, the oak floor creaking slightly under their shoes, Melinda was reminded at the store's range of inventory.

Prosper Hardware stocked everything from a few pots and pans to flashlights and holiday decorations, and that was just on the shelves to one side of the main aisle. It also appeared to carry just about anything anyone would need for day-to-day life in a rural area. In an open space toward the back, where a set of sturdy wooden stairs made a turn and climbed to the second-floor office and storage rooms, there were shelves stacked with tee shirts and jeans, and two circle racks crammed with rugged jackets and work pants.

Melinda knew another aisle was stocked with pet food and supplies and seasonal items. One row was filled with boxed and canned groceries, and the outside aisle still carried all the hardware and home improvement inventory. A battered wooden cubbyhole cabinet on the far wall was filled with dozens of sizes of screws and nails.

Esther leaned her small shoulder into the gray steel door that separated the main store from the cavernous back room. "It sticks," she told Melinda as she cranked the knob and shoved the door, which burst open with an indignant squeak.

"Bill!" A high-pitched mechanical squeal assaulted Melinda's ears. "Bill! Melinda's here! Turn off the saw!"

The screeching noise lowered its pitch and stopped. Bill Larsen slid the cover over the table saw's blade and pushed his safety goggles up to settle them over the bill of a faded purple ball cap.

"I'm cutting that order for George Freitag, that chicken coop he wants to build. He's got quite the Taj Mahal drawn out here." Bill set aside an unfolded sheet of white paper scribbled with measurements and shook Melinda's hand. He was in his middle thirties, she guessed, a stocky guy, wearing a gray tee shirt and jeans. There was a carefully arranged stack of two-by-fours next to the work table.

"I didn't know you still cut wood here," she said, noticing the boards and plywood piled nearly to the ceiling on metal shelves along two of the back room's walls. "I knew Frank and Miriam still kept quite an inventory of hardware supplies, but not all this. It must be really popular with customers."

"Well, yes and no," Bill laughed. "Many people around here have a table saw, do their own cuts. Nearly everybody's got a truck or van to haul home what they need. But this makes it easier for them." Bill leaned in, his gray eyes twinkling. "Some guys wouldn't dare admit they get their cuts done here. It's an ego thing. But we've got a great setup and it saves them time."

He turned back to the plans, then reached for a smaller sheet of plywood and the pencil stuck behind his ear. "It's perfect for guys like George, who's older and now living in town, since he doesn't have his own shop anymore. Still wants to build his own stuff, though, no prefabs for him."

Melinda was surprised to hear people were allowed to keep chickens inside the Prosper city limits, even in a town this small. Bill noticed her expression and grinned.

"Yeah, chickens are legal birds here, in case you're wondering. Been that way for a long time. Not sure if they were ever outlawed, really, but the city did take a stand last year and wrote them into the bylaws, as some younger residents were wanting to have them."

"I'd rather keep mine in the freezer," Esther guffawed, "pick them up at the supermarket over in Swanton, dressed and ready to go. But I do get my eggs here when I run low."

"Here?" Melinda raised her eyebrows. There weren't any chickens strutting around in Prosper Hardware. But then, she hadn't been out back yet, and Frank and Miriam did seem to have a wider array of merchandise than she remembered ...

"Did you see the refrigerated case up front, on the wall by the side window?" Esther pointed in the general direction. "Used to be, there was just a cooler for a few gallons of milk and some pop. But Frank ordered that bigger unit last year. They keep it stocked with more milk than before, a few cartons of orange juice, eggs, and some butter, even. The stuff folks tend to run out of. It's fifteen miles over to Swanton, a long drive for just one or two things."

"And about twenty miles east to Charles City," Bill added as he set up the saw for an angle cut. "North to Mason City, it's even farther. Everyone around here stocks up, of course, but someone's always in need of something probably two, three times a day. Frank and Miriam sell things in the refrigerator case at cost, people say they really appreciate it."

Melinda could see the expanded grocery selection was a savvy move to draw more customers into the store. "Once they're here for a gallon of milk, they realize they need other things, too," she said. "It's a great marketing tool."

The discussion reminded her of the suggestions she had prepared for her small-business client, the one who was always looking for ways to draw more visitors to her pottery shop. She wondered who had that account now, then tried to put it out of her mind.

"Exactly. And it's being a good neighbor," Bill said, tapping the work table with his pencil for emphasis. "Just like this order I'm cutting here. Good service and caring about the customers, that's what keeps this store going. Keeps the town going, too, when you think about it, people looking out for each other."

Esther leaned her shoulder into the steel door. "Speaking of customers, I'd better get back up front. Melinda, it was so good to see you." Esther waved and disappeared as the door gave out another angry squawk.

"I know, I know, it's a hardware store and we've got a door that sticks," Bill rolled his eyes. "We've tried everything. WD-40, wax, you name it. But this building is over a hundred years old. The higher the humidity, the more shoulder action it takes to get that door open." He glanced toward the door to make sure it was closed all the way before he leaned over the table. "So, Miriam says you might help out for a few weeks. Are you really going to do it?"

Did the entire county know about Miriam's plan? It started to seem like she had rallied everyone in and out of Prosper to put the heat on Melinda until she agreed.

"I'm thinking about it, but I don't know." She dropped her eyes from his questioning gaze and picked up the drawing for the chicken coop. Its descriptions and measurements were written in the firm, slanted handwriting of an elderly man. "I think the world of Frank and Miriam, but haven't been back here for more than a week at a time since high school. I don't know if I'd fit in here, really."

Or if I even want to, she added to herself.

Bill put down his measuring tape and leaned against the workbench. "It would be a big adjustment from what you're used to, I'm sure. My wife and I lived in Des Moines for a few years after we got married. We'd met at Iowa State, and both of us said Ames wasn't big enough. We loved Des Moines. Always something to do, great restaurants. But once we started a family, we decided we wanted what we'd given up."

He shook his head, his voice turning thoughtful. "Isn't that the way? You're in one place, but then always think you want to be in the other. Anyway, she was willing to come to my hometown instead of going to hers, and we moved back about five years ago. We've never been sorry."

"I'm glad you like it here so much."

Melinda didn't know what else to say. Coming back for a few weeks to help at Prosper Hardware was one thing; she couldn't imagine moving back to the area for good. But Bill seemed content enough. And proud of his work, too, based on how carefully he was marking cuts for the chicken coop.

"Well, we could use the help if you've got some time to spare. I'd better get this done. George said he'd be by to pick everything up before the store closes."

Bill slid his safety goggles down, then stopped and pushed them back up. He pulled two quarters from his pocket and handed them to Melinda. "Be sure to get a pop before you hit the road. On the house."

"I'll do that." She laughed and took the money. "And I'll pay you back, Bill. Maybe in person." He waved and replaced his goggles, and the saw screeched to life as she headed out the back entrance.

Behind Prosper Hardware was a gravel drive where customers and suppliers could back up to the overhead door. A stretch of grass between the drive and the property line was the home of a towering oak that shaded the back of Prosper Hardware as well as the post office and the lawns across the gravel alley. The rusting pop machine at its base had somehow weathered the elements for more than four decades, the round nests that offered several flavors of refreshment still tucked behind the glass door.

The unit was anchored to the tree with a crisscross of heavy log chains, a precaution that was more about keeping the cooler upright in strong winds than deterring thieves seeking a conversation piece for their man cave. A thick, black cord snaked across the drive to an outside electrical box near the store's overhead door.

"It's still here," she marveled, jingling the quarters in her palm. "But I thought it might be."

Grandpa Shrader had rolled the contraption out of Prosper Hardware's back room the day the town's last grocery store closed, saying folks needed a place to get refreshment any time, day or night. What started out as a joke became one of the quirky things Melinda loved about the town. Community leaders had lobbied for years to get a convenience store built within the city limits, or as least out on the junction with the state highway, but to no success.

Uncle Frank kept the pop machine stocked with plastic bottles, since glass containers weren't available these days. People were on the honor system to drop their coins in the slot, and proceeds were collected once a month and added to the petty-cash box in the safe upstairs.

Bill was right about the price. It was still fifty cents. Melinda mulled her options with the same exuberance she had as a child. Regular cola? What about grape, or cherry? Orange, she decided. She'd just ignore how many calories were in this toothache-sweet stuff compared to the diet soda she normally drank.

Her car was stifling inside. She set her orange soda in the cup holder and powered all the windows open to let out the heat, grateful she'd chosen a short-sleeved tee and a pair of cotton shorts out of her duffle bag that morning. She was about to crank on the air conditioning, then changed her mind. It was hot, but there'd be a strong breeze blowing through the car once she got out on the highway. How long had it been since she'd driven with the windows down?

Guzzling her soda, she passed the co-op and tracked the mile back to the stop sign at the state road. If she turned left, the highway would take her south and then west into Swanton. She sat at the intersection a moment, deferring to a semi and then a truck cruising past, and changed her plans.

The visit to Prosper Hardware and the orange pop had her in a nostalgic mood. With her errand for Miriam complete, she had some time to herself before dinner. The blacktop went straight west from this corner, coming into Swanton "the back way," as everyone around there called it.

"I'm in no hurry," she shrugged, clicking off the left-turn signal and giving the hatchback a little gas. "It's only a bit out of the way. Why not?"

A few miles down the two-lane blacktop, she still hadn't seen any other vehicles. Then she came over a small rise to find a tractor creeping along just ahead of her, its safety lights flashing as it towed a hay wagon. She slowed and fell in behind, taking a moment to admire the Queen Anne's Lace nodding a greeting from the roadside ditches. Striped yellow gophers darted out of the grass onto the gravel shoulder of the blacktop, possibly surprised to see two vehicles making their way down this road at the same time. Stacked, billowing clouds lazily chased each other across the vibrant blue sky.

Melinda took a deep breath. She felt her mind clear, then turn to Miriam's proposal. What if she did come back, just for a few months? Her calendar was blank and she was free to do as she pleased. She could spend the summer out here if she wanted to. Maybe it wouldn't be so bad to move in with her parents for such a short time. Maybe ...

There was something on the side of the road. "For rent" was painted in bright red letters on a scrap of whitewashed plywood, the sign pounded into the ground at the upcoming crossroads. A roughly drawn arrow pointed south.

Crawling along behind the tractor, she had time to peer down the gravel road as she passed the intersection. The farm closest to the highway was at least a half mile away, its treeline just a green, leafy clump on the horizon.

"Must be aways down the road." She glanced in her rearview mirror, searched the other side of the sign for clues, but found only a repeat of what she'd seen before.

She hoped the tractor would turn into the next farm yard, then thought it might choose a field driveway up ahead. When it didn't, she settled back in her seat. There were places on this road where she could pass if the way was clear, but years of driving in congested city traffic made her a little nervous to pull out, even on a quiet blacktop like this one.

Melinda had never lived in the country, but these rolling fields and gravel roads still held a special place in her heart. She had many happy memories of visiting the farm her dad grew up on just west of Swanton. Grandma and Grandpa Foster always had dairy cows, a few chickens, and several cats and a dog. She and her siblings couldn't wait to run off to the back meadow or down to the creek. When they came into the house, Grandma Foster always had freshly baked cookies cooling on the kitchen counter.

Despite her trip down memory lane, Melinda's mind kept going back to the sign. "Who rents out a house around here, in the middle of nowhere?" she asked the radio, which was blasting classic George Strait.

She tried to imagine what it might be like, this mysterious house down a rambling gravel road. Rent surely had to be cheap around here. What if ...

"Wait a minute!" She slapped her palm on the steering wheel, pulling herself out of her reverie. "If I'm so curious about this place, does that mean I'm coming back? Even so, I'd be crazy to live out here alone. I'd never spent more than a few nights at Grandma and Grandpa Foster's. Besides, I've got rent to pay in Minneapolis. Just forget about it."

The tractor slowed to a near stop, its right signals flashing in advance of the next crossroads. As the driver turned off the highway, he looked in Melinda's direction and quickly lifted two fingers off the steering wheel.

It took a second for her to remember what this was all about, then she hastily returned the salute. The "farmer wave" was part of rural life, a quick greeting to friends and strangers alike along the country roads and small-town streets.

"People really are friendly around here," she mused as the tractor chugged away down the gravel road, the hay wagon barely visible in a cloud of dust.

She took another satisfying gulp of her orange soda, nodding along with the music. The way ahead was empty, no more farm machinery to slow her down. She should have stepped up her speed, but instead found herself watching for the next field drive, the next chance to turn back.

"There's plenty of time before Mom gets home from the hospital," she told herself when one appeared. She pulled in, double-checked the vacant road and started back east. "This won't take long, and it's too nice of an afternoon to sit inside at home, anyway."

Soon the sign came into view, and she felt her pulse pick up. She'd never been down this road before, never strayed off this blacktop, even as a teenager.

Her curiosity was just getting the better of her, that's all. She'd see where this road went, what she could find, and then turn around and head for Swanton.

The rattle of the loose gravel startled her as it bounced up under the car. She slowed to fifteen miles an hour and aimed for the rough track pounded by the locals' tires into the center of the road. Too late, she'd forgotten the other rule of gravel-road travel: Roll up the windows.

"Crap!" The tan powder was settling on the charcoal-colored dash of the car, sifting through her hair and onto her scalp. She powered the windows up and started watching for another sign, taking care to drift right with the track each time the road met a rise that temporarily obstructed her view.

She passed the farm she'd glimpsed from the highway, then another, but nothing. She hesitated when she came to an intersection, but there were no markers there, either. "Must be straight ahead, then? How far away is this place?"

If she continued south, the road should eventually meet up with the state highway. But that had to be at least another five or six miles. And sometimes, gravel roads would abruptly end at a "T" intersection or begin to twist and meander. She wished she had GPS in her car.

"I'll go another mile or two, but then I've got to turn back. I have no idea where I'm going."

She spotted a breathtaking bed of peonies, their bowl-sized, vibrant pink blooms waving from the front of yet another immaculate farm yard. The gray house with cream trim was comfortable and square. She leaned forward, hoping. No sign. She rolled through another crossroads and soon, the road started to veer toward the right. A line of trees was visible ahead, a modest metal bridge marked with a yellow "curve" sign.

"Great," she muttered, "this is where I start to get lost."

But the waterway wasn't much more than a gurgling brook, twisting here and there through a lush green pasture. To her relief, the road quickly swung back to the left past the bridge and straightened out, the sparse grove falling away to reveal a sweeping, emerald patchwork of fields ahead.

There was another cluster of trees coming up on the right side, this one much larger, a dense wall of dark green. It had to be a windbreak, sheltering a farmstead from winter's ferocious northwest winds. A small white square at the edge of the driveway morphed into a sign as she came closer. "This has to be it," she said as she danced in her seat. "Finally!"

But suddenly, she felt self-conscious. What was she doing out here, anyway? Was she really going to turn up the drive, knock on a stranger's door and start nosing around?

She slowed the car to a crawl as she neared the edge of the property, noticing the windbreak included an impressive stand of evergreens as well as deciduous trees. A cluster of lilac bushes, still in bloom, marked the northeast corner of the yard. And then, the house came into view.

The scene was so charming that her heart nearly stopped. The two-story's narrow, white wood siding was complimented by soft gray trim. Gray-green shingles clad a steep roof offset by large gables on the second floor, lending the house a cottage-like air. A screened-in front porch stretched across nearly the entire first floor. A towering maple tree in the front yard was surrounded by hostas and a neatly trimmed lawn. Another gracious tree, probably an oak, shaded the small stretch of grass between the south side of the house and the gravel drive.

Melinda couldn't quite bring herself to pull in, but she couldn't wait to see more.

She rolled past the "for rent" sign at the end of the driveway, aiming for a small stand of volunteer bushes at the far corner of the front pasture. They might block her car enough to let her get a better look without being noticed.

The barn was across the drive from the house and otherwise surrounded by pasture. Like the rest of the outbuildings, it was painted a deep red with white trim. She noticed a sturdy building in the southwest corner of the yard that Grandpa Foster would have called a "machine shed." It was smaller than the barn, one story with a steep-pitched roof and a sliding door across its front. To the north of that was another, smaller shed somewhat in disrepair, and then a cozy chicken house with a row of four-paned windows along its south side that looked out on a spacious wire-mesh run. A two-stall garage, painted white, stood under the yard light just west of the house.

There looked to be a substantial garden plot behind the garage. An enclosed porch on the west side of the farm house probably led to the kitchen door. She now could see a bump-out on the south side of the house that hinted at a built-in buffet in what must be the dining room. "So it's as cute inside as outside, then. Oh, this is wonderful."

There was a field drive just past the bushes, and she backed around and turned again to the north, determined to get a better look. She pulled as far over to the edge of the road as she dared, determined to keep her right-side tires out of the steep, grass-filled ditch, powered down the windows, and cut the engine.

Magenta peonies nodded in the bright sun on the south side of the house. More mature trees dotted the yard, stretching their protective arms over the home and outbuildings. The refreshing breeze brushed her face and brought trilling notes of birdsong into the car, then an echo of the quiet rustle of the leaves dancing on the trees. She closed her eyes and took a deep, calming breath.

Maybe she could see herself in that garden, picking fresh cucumbers off the vine. Hanging her laundry on the clothesline to catch a sweet breeze. Or exploring the chicken coop, plucking eggs from the nests for her breakfast ...

Suddenly, she sensed she was being watched. The yard was still silent, but someone was most certainly home. She opened her eyes to find three curious sheep, the cream-colored kind with fuzzy ebony faces and legs, eyeing her over the pasture fence. One of them stomped a hoof and let out an indignant bellow.

Before Melinda could introduce herself or apologize, a sharp, warning bark answered from somewhere behind the barn. Of course, every farm has a farm dog. He hadn't shown himself yet but his yips were getting louder, which told her he was on the run to see who was trespassing on his property. She snatched her phone off the passenger seat and snapped a photo of the sign. This one had a phone number scrawled at the bottom.

"What am I doing? I don't belong out here." She flipped the ignition and buzzed up the windows, then glanced back just in time to see a furious flash of brown and white tearing down the drive. How she hoped the farm's owners hadn't been watching her from the house! But Melinda found she was smiling as she neared the little bridge over the creek.

✳ 5 ✳

Melinda pulled up to the curb in front of her parents' house in Swanton, her mind still on the charming farmhouse and the "for rent" sign. Aunt Miriam's offer was tempting enough on its own, but there was something about that acreage.

She had made the rest of the drive into Swanton in a preoccupied daze, questions and details spinning through her mind. She was excited, yet skeptical. Maybe it was all too good to be true.

"It's just an old house down a gravel road," she reminded herself as she gathered her tote and phone. "A house I know nothing about in the middle of nowhere."

Her father popped the front door open just as she came up the sidewalk. Roger was still in his golf "uniform" of pleated khaki shorts and a pale-blue polo shirt, his close-cropped hair a mix of sandy blond and gray.

"Is Mom back yet? How's Uncle Frank?" Melinda gave her dad a warm hug.

"She just got home. Sounds like he had a good day, all considered." He stepped back into the foyer of the 1950s brick ranch. "He's back in his room at the hospital and his heart rate's steady. Miriam's beat, though. Says she still plans to spend tonight sleeping in the chair in Frank's room, although the docs said she could go home. I heard you had a special errand. How's the store?"

"Same as ever. Not much changes at Prosper Hardware, as you know. Bill was cutting some lumber in the back and Esther Denner was running the register. Says she's Frank and Miriam's neighbor."

Diane was chopping vegetables in the kitchen. "Oh, yes, Esther," she said with a wry grin. "Miriam said Esther jumped as the chance to run over and help out. Now that she's retired from the school cafeteria, she's got a lot of time on her hands." Diane carefully slid the vegetables from the cutting board into a bowl. "We're having burgers and baked fries and salad, if you want to wash up and mix the dressing."

"I'd love my fries the way they should be," Roger said, winking at his wife as he snatched a chunk of cucumber. "You know ... fried. Should I get out the deep skillet?"

"Sorry, dear." Diane elbowed him out of her way as she stepped to the refrigerator. "We're trying to stay healthy, remember? Real fries will have to wait for a treat sometime when we eat out. How about you start the grill, instead?"

"I'll put my purse away and help." Melinda turned down the hallway and into her former room, where her duffel bag was open on the floor, stacked with clothes she'd hurriedly grabbed the day before. Her parents had repainted, of course, but her old bed was still positioned along the long wall and the dresser remained tucked in the corner by the window. The room held good memories, but the thought of staying longer than a week or two made her claustrophobic.

She was used to having her own space, her own routine. She scrolled through her phone and stared at the photo of the sign at end of the farm drive, the lilac bushes so beautiful in the background. One call, and so many questions could be answered. But the mouthwatering aroma of grilling burgers was drifting through the open window. It would have to wait until after dinner.

Roger reached over and patted Melinda's hand as they sat down to eat. "I hear you might come stay for a few weeks, help Miriam at the store until Frank's back on his feet. Sure you're up to the challenge?"

"Really, Dad, how hard could it be? I can't imagine the store's that busy. And I did retail jobs in college, remember?"

"Oh, you'd be surprised." Diane brought the fries and salad to the table, took her seat.

"You're capable, honey, we both know that. But that store carries a little of everything, and customers expect the employees to be experts on all of it. You'd be selling everything from milk to dog food and drill bits."

She passed the plate of burger patties to Melinda and raised an eyebrow at her daughter.

"And it's a delicate balancing act to deal with all the small-town intrigue. Some people want you to keep their confidences, others secretly want you to share them with everyone that comes in the door. If you're looking for a part-time job to tide you over, you'd probably have an easier time at some little boutique up in the city."

"Not that we wouldn't love for you to come back for a visit," Roger quickly added. "We've always got room for you here. But if you come back, promise you'll leave eventually."

"No worries there, Dad. I love you both but I'm used to being on my own. Actually, I discovered something interesting today, on my way over from Prosper." She told her parents about the slow tractor, the sign, the barking dog, the peaceful farmhouse.

Diane's face lit up. "I think that's the old Schermann place. My Grandma and Grandpa Sonberg, your great-grandparents, had their farm not far from there. If you'd gone south to the next crossroads and made a left, and went up the hill, it was on the right side." She chewed on a fry, thinking. "A few of the Schermann boys never married. They were still living on the place you're talking about, last I knew. But they'd be around ninety now. It's likely the farmhouse has already changed hands."

Roger whistled as he smothered his burger patty with mustard. "Your mother continues to amaze me with how she knows everyone in the county. And where people lived fifty years ago. And who's related. I've been around here most of my life, too, except when I was away at college, but I can't keep all these families straight."

"When your parents run Prosper Hardware, you meet everyone eventually," Diane smirked. "And like I said, that store's a hub for gossip. But back to this house. There's really a 'for rent' sign out front?"

"Maybe it's the fields that are for rent, not the house." Roger took a gulp of his iced tea. "That's more likely. Especially if someone bought the Schermann farm but works in town. People make good money these days renting out their fields to neighbors farming full-time."

Melinda found her heart sinking at that thought. She was drawn to the welcoming house, the vast garden, the big maple in the front yard. The driveway sign said "for rent," but what exactly had the sign on the county highway said? She couldn't remember. "House for rent" and "for rent" suddenly had two different meanings.

"Besides," Roger passed Melinda the salad. "Thought you were a city girl these days. And if the house is indeed for rent, they'll likely want a renter for more than a month or so."

He stopped, reading the disappointment on his daughter's face. "You're really drawn to this place, aren't you? I don't want to discourage you, honey, but living in the country is very different from what you're used to."

"I don't know how to explain it." Melinda twirled her fork in her fingers. "I saw the sign and drove on by at first. Then felt I needed to turn back, to see what was down that road. I got so excited when I saw the house, the yard, all of it."

She was rarely at a loss for words, but this time, she wasn't sure how to describe what she was feeling.

"Maybe I'm just tired. The last few months have been hard. I love the city, I love my friends and my life there. But without a job, I'm sleepwalking through my days. I need something to do, somewhere to belong. I didn't realize how much of me was wrapped up in that job until it was gone."

Diane reached around to rub Melinda's shoulder. "You've been pushing very hard with your career, especially the last few years. And things have been tough lately." Then she brightened. "Maybe you just need a break. Maybe that's why that farm affected you so. It is a charming place, for sure."

Roger shook his head. "I doubt Miriam can pay you much to help out at the store," he said gently. "To pay rent at two places, even for a few months, I don't see how you could swing that."

Melinda hesitated to let on about how much of this she already had worked out in her mind. She was jumping ahead too quickly and might end up disappointed.

"Maybe I could sublet my place in Minneapolis," she said casually. "But if I sublet, it can't be for just a month or two. It would have to be at least for the summer. Maybe I can find a student who's going to be out of their dorm until late August. But it's already June. I'd have to move fast, and ..."

"And," Diane raised a finger, "you haven't even seen inside the house yet. Who knows what it's like?"

"I know, it could be in horrible shape. Why are we even talking about this?"

But she a knew the answer. Seeing this charming homestead had lifted her spirits, just as visiting Prosper Hardware had that afternoon. She yearned for something, but wasn't sure yet what it was. She couldn't give up her life in the city. It wasn't just her career. It was her friends, her habits, and her home there. But maybe it was time for a change, if only for a few months.

"First things first," Roger gestured at the cordless phone on the kitchen counter. "How about you find out what the deal is? You're staying a few more days before heading back, anyway. It's worth a call."

A guy named Kevin answered and confirmed the farmhouse was for rent. The next day was Saturday, and he offered to drive down from Mason City to show her around.

"So, it's vacant, then?" She tried not to sound too eager.

"Well ... not yet," was his answer.

That was enough to make Roger insist on riding shotgun the next morning as Melinda retraced the miles back to the farm. She hated to look as if she couldn't handle her own affairs, but had to admit it was a good idea to not go alone. Kevin sounded like he was about her age, and friendly, but she was still meeting a stranger at a remote location.

"Not bad," Roger said as they turned up the drive. "That's some house. Does look like it could use a little TLC, though."

The morning sunshine that gave the yard a warm glow also cast an unfiltered spotlight on the house. Now that she was getting a closer look, Melinda noticed the wood siding was a little tired, the white paint a bit faded. The roof was older that she had expected, but no big patches were visible. And the flowers clustered around the yard were as vibrant now as in yesterday's late-afternoon sun.

She angled her car in next to a pickup parked by the garage. The truck was newer, a tasteful dark blue. It didn't look like something a serial killer would use as a getaway vehicle. She had her seat belt unsnapped in a flash, her hand on the door handle. It had been hard to fall asleep last night, wondering what she might discover today.

"OK, Dad, let me do the talking here. You're just on security detail."

"Should I stay in the car, then?" He crossed his arms and tried to look tough. "Pretend I've got a gun under my jacket?"

"Of course not. Just hover in the background, like the Secret Service. Front or back door?"

"Back door's the kitchen door, the one everybody uses. Let's try there."

The second of the three weathered wood steps wavered slightly under her sneakers. Her heart was pounding. There was only one way to find out what this place was really like. She knocked.

"It's so good to see you."

An old, wavering voice came from somewhere near her elbow. She jumped, relieved the top step was sturdier than the second. "Are you here to buy some eggs?"

A short, slight, elderly man with striking blue eyes was giving her a curious-if-friendly look. His faded brown cap was a little too big for his head. She could see the dull gleam of the buckles on his overall straps under his tan cotton jacket. One hand balanced a galvanized bucket full of delicate brown eggs, and the other reached out for the steadying support of the stair rail.

A medium-sized brown-and-white dog of unknown parentage tagged along behind, then stopped short next to the old man. The dog looked from Melinda to Roger, raised its ears and offered a short bark.

"Hobo, hush," the elderly man said gently. "They look like nice people, don't they?"

The dog wagged its tail, gave the man an adoring glance, then jogged over to sniff the tires on Melinda's car. The dog seemed intelligent and energetic, and she wondered if it recognized her vehicle. *I'm so glad you can't give me away*, she thought.

"You have some lovely eggs there." She offered the old man a smile that couldn't quite cover her confusion. The voice on the phone had sounded much younger than this man looked. "But we're here about the house, to meet Kevin."

The old man nodded but remained silent, a sea of emotions crossing his face.

Melinda wasn't sure what to think. Might he have dementia, or be hard of hearing? And where was Kevin? She came down to the bottom step and tried again. "Hi, I'm Melinda." She offered her hand and he responded with a dry, feeble grip. "And this is my dad, Roger."

"Horace," the old man nodded, finally offering a cautious smile. "Horace Schermann."

Roger and Melinda only had time to give each other a surprised glance before the metal storm door snapped open and a tall, slender man in his mid-forties leaned out. He had the same blue eyes as Horace.

"Sorry I didn't hear you knock at first, I was just cleaning up a bit. I'm Kevin Arndt."

Melinda eagerly shook his hand, relieved to solve at least one part of the puzzle. Even better, Kevin seemed calm and dependable. His light-brown hair was neatly trimmed, his glasses distinguished. His jeans looked nearly new, and clean. It was highly unlikely that Kevin Arndt staged rural rentals to lure unsuspecting urbanites to their deaths.

"I see you've already met my uncle." Kevin reached around Melinda and gently took the bucket of eggs from Horace, who gripped the railing tighter as he turned to mount the steps. Melinda and Roger pushed themselves against the side of the house to give the old man room, and Kevin held the door wide. "How are the chickens, Uncle Horace?"

"Pansy nearly pecked me again today, but I got her egg." Horace let out a smug chuckle. "A fine one, too. All of them look good today, no cracks." He carefully hung his faded cap on a row of iron pegs on the inside porch wall, revealing wispy white hair that was a bit shaggy on his neck.

"Well, there's plenty of chores to do every morning and night," Horace said, seemingly to no one in particular. "Chickens to feed, eggs to gather. Oats and corn to the sheep, they need to be watered. But Hobo keeps things running smoothly, he's always on the job." He carefully lowered himself down on a wood bench and began to slowly remove his boots, their bottoms caked in mud.

Kevin was friendly and Horace seemed more aware of his surroundings than Melinda had first suspected, but something didn't add up. Then she remembered what Diane had said about the Schermann brothers. Horace had to be in his eighties, at least. Was he living here all alone?

"Coffee's on in the kitchen," Kevin said gently. "Why don't you settle in with a cup and we'll be back in a minute."

Kevin gestured for Melinda and Roger to follow him outside, then made sure the storm door was latched securely behind him. They wandered over to the picnic table, which enjoyed the shade of another oak tree between the house and the garage.

"So if the house is for rent, does Horace come with it or something?" Roger inclined his head back at the porch. Kevin laughed, breaking the tension.

"No, unless Melinda's a nurse's aide. Sorry to seem so secretive about all this. I was trying to figure out a way to explain the situation without upsetting Horace."

Kevin leaned back against the edge of the picnic table. "I'll start from the beginning. Horace and my other uncle, Wilbur, lived here for years until Wilbur went to the nursing home in Elm Springs about a year ago. My mom, Ada, is their only sibling that lives around here and we've always been close to Horace and Wilbur. Horace is pretty spry for eighty-nine, still has his license, even. He's just shy with people he doesn't know very well."

"That explains why he was so quiet when he found us on his back steps," Melinda said. "I wasn't sure at first if he understood why we were here."

"Oh, he knows," Kevin sighed and rubbed the side of his face. "He just doesn't want to deal with all of this. You see, Horace fell two weeks ago. Says he was changing a light bulb in the kitchen and lost his footing, slipped off the chair. Nothing serious, the doctor said he didn't break any bones. But still, it scared us."

Kevin's shoulders slumped. There was both love and frustration in his voice.

"I'd told him to let me handle things like that, not to risk it. But he's stubborn. I've been coming down from Mason City every other weekend to help him around the farm, take him to town for supplies. Thank goodness for good neighbors, they keep tabs on him for us."

"It's tough seeing your older relatives decline." Melinda felt sorry for Kevin. He obviously cared for his uncle.

"My Grandpa Shrader worked behind the counter at Prosper Hardware until he couldn't get around, even with a walker. He had a hard adjustment to retirement. His work kept him going."

"Your family owns the store?" Kevin's mood brightened. "What a great place! Always glad to see it's still going. The community needs it. How's Frank doing? My mom said he had a heart attack."

For a moment Melinda couldn't believe word had traveled that fast. But of course it had.

"It's my wife's family that owns the store," Roger said. "Frank's doing much better, we're all thankful for that. So, I'm guessing Horace needs to go to senior housing somewhere, but doesn't want to go?"

"Exactly," Kevin sighed and shoved his hands in the pockets of his jeans. "Wilbur's ninety-two and is in the beginning stages of dementia, and Horace understands why Wilbur had to go to assisted living. But he sees Wilbur sitting around, looking out the window, and says that's not for him, he's got too much to do."

Kevin rubbed his hands together. "But now, something's come up. Wilbur's roommate is transferring next week to a place over in Charles City. I've convinced Horace to go for an extended visit, that Wilbur will be lonely when his roommate leaves. I'm not sure how this will play out, but I'm hoping once Horace gets there, he'll like it and maybe want to stay."

Melinda realized that if Horace's absence was to be temporary, at least at first, there was a chance to negotiate a short-term lease. But she could see how difficult this was for Kevin and tried to keep her excitement in check. "Actually, I only need a place for a few months. I was laid off from my job at an ad agency in Minneapolis and Aunt Miriam's asked me to help out at the store, just until Frank gets back on his feet."

A big grin spread across Kevin's face. He looked from Melinda to Roger and bounced up from the edge of the picnic table. "Well then, maybe you're the renter I'm looking for. We're hoping Horace will settle in at the home, but I don't know if he will or how long that might take."

Then Kevin hesitated.

"But there's another wrinkle to this plan."

"Oh my," Melinda's spirits started to sink. Maybe this *was* too good to be true. "Just how many wrinkles are there?"

"Depends, if you count all twelve sheep separately or as one flock." Kevin pointed over toward the barn, then gestured back at the chicken coop. "Same for the hens, I think there's eight of those. And then there's Hobo. He means the world to Horace. I wish I could take him, but he won't be happy at my bungalow in town."

Kevin crossed his arms and shook his head. "Horace says he'll only go if there's someone to look after the animals. We can't sell off the chickens and sheep until we're sure he's not coming home, that would break his heart. The neighbors are great, but requiring someone to come over twice a day to do chores is a lot to ask. Horace won't even consider that idea, as he says Hobo will be terribly lonesome if no one is living here. And I think he's right."

Melinda glanced around the yard. Tender green shoots were just starting to lift their heads in the garden, which Horace had carefully planted in rail-straight rows. It would need to be weeded and watered regularly. The outbuildings were sturdy, but she could make out small chips of peeling paint and worn shingles here and there, even from her spot near the picnic table.

If the house sat vacant and the animals were gone, this place would rapidly slip into the sad, tumble-down loneliness that marked abandoned farms all around the countryside.

And then there was Hobo. Hobo was going to lose his best friend. He didn't need to lose his home, too. She could see his kind brown eyes shining under the picnic table, as if he knew every word of the conversation. She crouched down and reached out to him, let him sniff her palm, then gently patted his head. "What do you think, huh?"

Hobo licked her hand and the funny white tip on his tail thumped once, twice, but he didn't get up.

"I know it's a lot to ask," Kevin's voice was low, tentative. Melinda could see Hobo's pleading look mirrored in his eyes.

She glanced again at Hobo and then at her dad, who gave her an encouraging nod. This wasn't what she had expected. It was complicated, difficult, a challenge. But wasn't her whole life like that these days?

"It's a lot of responsibility," Kevin warned as she got back on her feet. "I'd need you to be my eyes and ears out here. I'll bring all the feed down, you won't need to worry about that. The chicken and sheep chores aren't much in the summer, anyway. We'd like to keep the garden going," he looked over at the substantial plot, "but the animals would be the priority. The good news is, with all those contingencies, the rent would be low. How does one hundred a month sound?"

Melinda's eyes widened and she nearly laughed. "Are you serious? That just might be an offer I can't refuse." But then her shoulders slumped.

"I'm a town girl, grew up in Swanton. I love animals, but I've never taken care of anything other than a cat or dog. Are you sure I'm the one to take this on?"

"Look, I've only had two other calls," he leaned in conspiratorially. Melinda noticed her dad was hanging on Kevin's every word.

"One was a nice young couple, but the woman was scared of the sheep, believe it or not. The other was a bachelor, probably in his thirties, but he didn't seem very responsible. I didn't trust him to take care of the animals properly and I don't need rowdy beer parties going on out here."

He turned quiet for a moment, thinking. "If you decide you are interested, I'd feel fine asking you for only a hundred-dollar deposit. And just a month-to-month lease. The well water's safe and the natural gas tank's nearly full. There's cable and internet run to the house, although Horace doesn't have a computer so you'd need to hook up and pay for the wi-fi. We'd cover the rest of the utilities, just like now."

"This is a lot to think about. It's all come up so fast. But either way, let's go see the house. I have to admit I've been dying to get in there."

"I'll warn you, it's not fancy." Kevin started for the back porch, Melinda and Roger right behind. "And it's easy to let things slide when you're living alone, especially at Horace's age. But I'd get some help out here to clean before you'd move in. There's furniture, but you could bring whatever you want."

Horace's muddy boots were carefully aligned on a rubber mat just inside the door, his tan cotton jacket hung on a hook next to his cap. The three west windows above the brown-painted bench filled the porch with a cheery glow, even at this time of the morning. A double-door closet spanned the north wall. To the right, a wooden door with a square window in its top opened into the kitchen.

While the porch was fairly tidy, Melinda noticed several cobwebs in the corners of the white beadboard ceiling and a smattering of dried mud tracks on the painted gray floor. Through the kitchen door's window she could see Horace settled in what was probably his favorite chair at the table, looking south to the barn. He seemed so content, his slim legs stretched out, a chipped white coffee cup in hand. "What does Horace know about this, really?"

"I told him I'm hiring someone to live here while he's away, kind of like a pet sitter," Kevin whispered.

"He's hell-bent on coming home in a few months. For now, let's leave it at that."

* 6 *

Horace turned at the slight rattle of the kitchen door and beamed at his guests.

"Coffee's fresh, help yourself," he gestured at a cluster of mismatched coffee mugs on the dark-varnished wood table. A pile of tarnished silver spoons waited next to a blue plastic sugar bowl and a half-eaten package of store-bought chocolate sandwich cookies.

Horace probably didn't have much company. Melinda was touched by his simple efforts to make his visitors welcome, even if he had misgivings about why they were there. Roger profusely thanked Horace for his hospitality and took a mug over to the coffeemaker rooted on the beige laminate countertop. He glanced around the kitchen, raised an eyebrow at Melinda, and grinned.

The room was a tired mish-mash of items from the last century, a whirlwind of styles and colors. A dusty push-button light switch still there on the wall, next to the modern one. The white apron porcelain sink, which appeared to be original, was probably worth far more than all the appliances combined. A small window above the sink looked out into the enclosed back porch. The single-bulb glass shield over it was probably from the 1970s, but at least its design matched the lone light in the ceiling and the triple-arm fixture hanging over the table.

The pale-green wood cabinets wrapped around the room from just past the door, spanning the sink and turning the corner to support a tired electric stove resting along the north wall. Past that, a paneled oak door hinted at a staircase to the basement. The short stretch of cabinets on the east wall seemed like an afterthought, squeezed in between the basement entry and the open doorway into the dining room.

The wooden table parked in front of the kitchen's south-facing double window was square and solid, with thick, heavy legs that matched the dark stain on its scuffed surface. A squat, rounded mid-century refrigerator appeared to have been at home in the southwest corner for several decades, squeezed in between the windows overlooking the yard and the kitchen door.

Melinda reached for a cookie as she continued to study the kitchen. She could tell by the cabinets' thick sheen that they had been painted multiple times over the years. The laminate counters must have come from the most-recent remodel, which was at least twenty years ago. The walls were painted a tired light brown, the sort of color found at a recycling center where half-empty cans of paint were mixed and offered for a dollar a gallon.

But the strange color scheme somehow picked up the tones in the floor's flecked linoleum. Cheerful sage-and-cream checked curtains hugged the corners of all the kitchen's windows, and a handmade wooden shelf along the south wall was clustered with houseplants reaching for the sun.

"What did you think of the chickens?" Horace turned to Melinda with a proud look on his face. "They sure are a nice little flock, huh?"

"Well, I haven't made it over to the coop just yet," she hedged. Horace assumed they had been meeting the animals, rather than discussing his personal business. "But I'll be sure to see them before we go, OK?" She could see how much he loved this farm. It pained her to know he would leave it soon.

"We haven't seen the sheep yet either, Uncle Horace." Kevin patted him on the shoulder.

"Melinda wants to look over the house first. Then we'll be back for some of that coffee."

"Well, there's not much to see," Horace said in a tone that indicated he was far more excited for Melinda to meet his livestock. "House hasn't changed much over the years, haven't seen the reason to. But the barn roof got switched out maybe ten years ago, the sheds' roofs are in decent shape, too. They're all solid. Chicken coop's wire was replaced last summer. Don't have to worry too much about predators."

"What kind of predators?"

Melinda nearly dropped her cookie. She'd been trying to get a better look into the dining room, where a garish sky-blue wallpaper of swooping teal birds and forested vines threatened to attack the beautiful oak buffet nestled into the south wall.

"Well, we saw that cougar two years ago." Horace's eyes brightened as he leaned over the table toward Roger, eager to tell his story to someone new. But first, a dramatic pause. "Wilbur swore he'd heard this scream up in the trees on the far end of the windbreak the night before. I went out just before dawn to do chores, and I saw it with my own eyes, slinking off behind the chicken coop."

He turned and studied Melinda, waiting for her reaction. She could only nod, her mind racing. Surely there weren't cougars roaming around here? But then, the grove down at the creek would provide good cover, and a source of water ...

"There's an occasional raccoon out here, maybe a hawk," Kevin broke in, shaking his head at Roger, who took a hearty gulp of coffee to keep from laughing.

Horace still seemed to be in earnest. "You never know what might be running around out there. A neighbor over to the west saw a coyote last fall."

Kevin sighed and gestured for Melinda to move ahead into the dining room. An oval wood table with turned legs, far more refined but even older than the one in the kitchen, commanded the center of the room under an iron scrollwork light fixture rewired for modern electrical currents. Four chairs, their slatted backs carved with a delicate leaf pattern, gathered around the table.

"I'm not sure Horace is telling it straight," Kevin whispered once they moved away from the kitchen. "And you just got the condensed version. Sometimes when he tells that story, he's run off the big cat with his shotgun, but only after it charged him. The size of this alleged monster has ranged from three feet to eight feet long, depending on how likely it is his listeners will believe him."

"So he's trying to see how gullible I am." Instead of being offended, she found it clever. Horace was sizing her up. He didn't want to hand his farm over to just anyone.

"He hasn't had enough of a chance to get a read on you yet. Horace may come off as a simple farmer, but he's very intelligent. Could've gone off to Iowa State and studied engineering all those years ago, but money was tight. And really, I don't think he wanted to leave home." He gestured around the dining room and the adjacent living room. "Well, let's continue our tour of the main level. As you can see, it's filled with old-farm charm."

A large cased opening joined the two rooms. Warm summer light flowed in from the two south windows flanking the buffet, which was crowned with a long, narrow pane of leaded glass across the top.

The decorative diamond design was repeated in the two square windows in the living room's north wall, where they hugged a fireplace and brought in filtered light above the built-in bookcases set to each side. Melinda was relieved the twirling birds and vines didn't migrate into the living room, whose walls were instead coated in the same drab brown as the kitchen.

There was a graceful oval of beveled glass in the dining room's front door, which opened onto the screened porch that ran across the front of the house. A picture window in the living room also looked east, past the maple tree and down to the lilacs along the road.

"This house is really beautiful," she said, admiring the

warm, dark woodwork that carried into the living and dining rooms from the kitchen. "But I can see it needs updating."

The narrow oak floor planks in the dining and living rooms appeared to be original, but hadn't been varnished in years. A sagging, rust-toned velour couch was angled under the picture window, which was flanked by the same red-and-blue check curtains as in the dining room. Nothing coordinated with the puffy brown leather recliner rooted by the fireplace. The easy chair was across from a short cabinet that, surprisingly, supported a flat-screen television.

"Yeah, Horace's idea of decorating is making sure he has a good TV," Kevin shrugged. "And keeping his newspapers in order." One dining-room corner was stacked with boxes; another housed three-feet-high piles neatly tied at intervals with white cotton string.

Melinda pointed at the two doors in the west wall. "What's behind door number one? I can't wait to see."

"That would be the stairs. The second one is probably more interesting because it not only holds the downstairs bedroom, but the only bathroom on this floor." Kevin paused before turning the knob. "I'll warn you, I haven't been in here yet today."

The bedroom wasn't as cluttered as Melinda had suspected. Shirts and jeans were hanging in the tiny closet, a row of sensible shoes settled below. A few stray socks were flung on the top of a light-blue dresser wedged along the north wall, which held a single window.

An ornate iron bedstead fit along the west wall, next to the other window. The bed had been neatly made that morning, the crazy quilt worn but clean. And again, brown walls. "They must have gotten those buckets of paint for a steal," Melinda said.

"They might have even been free. It certainly looks it, doesn't it? I'm getting ahead of myself here, but if you ever felt like tackling some painting or other DIY projects, I'd be happy to pay for the materials. This house will have to be sold, eventually."

There was a narrow door in the southwest corner. Kevin peeked in, then gave a nod of cautious approval. "And now, for the smallest bathroom this side of the Iowa-Minnesota line. It was a closet until a few years ago, when Wilbur couldn't do the stairs anymore and we had it converted to a half bath. You'll need to check it out on your own, since there's barely room for one person in there."

"Oh, my." Her hands barely fit over the bowl of the sink, which was topped with a rectangular mirror that couldn't quite make the little room seem bigger. It was just a quarter turn to bump into the toilet.

"You don't have to worry about him falling in here, thanks to a grab bar and the walls being only about three feet apart."

She ducked out of the bathroom and followed Kevin back into the living room, where he opened the other door and gestured at the varnished stairs, which met a landing halfway up then doubled back to reach the second floor. A small dormer and window brought light into the stairwell, which had metal safety handrails bolted to its outside walls.

"Horace and Wilbur both slept up here, their whole lives, until Wilbur fell outside and broke his leg about three years ago. He moved to the downstairs bedroom then. Wilbur healed up, but his leg was never really right again. He needed a cane, then a walker, to get around. Then last year, his dementia started to kick in."

"I'm sorry." Melinda paused at the top of the stairs. One door went left, one right, and two more were straight ahead. Only the right-hand one was open. "Does he still recognize any of the family?"

Kevin lowered his head, his brow furrowed behind his glasses. "He knows Horace. And on good days, he recognizes my mom. We'd like Horace and Wilbur to have more time together before Wilbur can't remember his brother anymore. They both mean a lot to me, you know. My dad passed three years ago and they're the only older relatives I have close by."

He turned the iron knob on the door to the left and gave her an encouraging smile.

"This one would be your bedroom. See what you think."

The space was cozy and bright, painted a soft cream like the hallway. A double dresser with a mirror stood along the east wall, the bureau's surface empty but dusty. A small nightstand crouched next to it, as if unsure where it belonged. The west wall rose to a height of about five feet, then angled up to the ceiling. She peered out the west window and marveled at the reach of the oak tree over the picnic table, the neat rows of the young garden and the cozy chicken house beyond. The other view was of the north yard, punctuated by two sentinel evergreens surrounded by hosta beds. Past that, the windbreak marked the far border of the acreage.

"I like this room," she said, admiring the hardwood floors that appeared to run through the entire upstairs. "I'm hoping, though, that there's a closet behind that door."

"Absolutely. It's small but a walk-in one, with its own tiny window." Kevin yanked the door open and peeked inside. "There's a rod in here, some shelves below that. And it's empty. This was Horace's room for years, but it's been cleared out, mostly. As you can see you'd need to bring a bed, and whatever else you wanted."

Out in the hallway, he motioned to the two east doors. "The larger of these two rooms has the big dormer. It's full of stuff, been used as storage for years. The smaller one has just a window looking south. That was Wilbur's old room, and I have to say it's crammed with odds and ends, too. The bathroom's over here."

They went through the open door into a smaller room with just a west dormer and a roll-top desk. Through yet another door, Melinda glimpsed a white vanity that looked to have been made over from a dresser.

"I know, it's a strange layout," Kevin said over his shoulder. "This was the best place for a bathroom when indoor plumbing was added, being above the kitchen. But this space was too big for what my grandpa thought was a luxury. And he didn't want to lose the fourth bedroom up here, no matter how small it became. So they divided it up like this."

The bathroom held a white clawfoot tub, chipped but mostly clean, with a metal track bolted above it to hold the shower curtain. There was only one sink, but plenty of counter space on the vanity. The white-framed mirror above it was substantial.

The toilet was edged in by the south window, and the closet in this room had been filled in with floor-to-ceiling shelves. The floor was covered with what looked to be a remnant of the linoleum in the kitchen.

"I see why your grandpa designed it like this." She couldn't keep the smile off her face. There was something so welcoming about this house. "There's not one foot of wasted space, in here or anywhere else. And the little room would make a nice office."

Kevin looked pleased. "Washer and dryer are in the basement. The furnace and air conditioner are old, but still chugging along."

"Oh, I'm so glad there's air conditioning. I didn't want to sound like some pampered city chick, but I wasn't sure I could manage without it."

Kevin's face lit up. "So ... you might actually do it? You might take the place?"

Melinda was excited and scared, and happy and unsure. The desperation Kevin was trying to hide touched her heart. He loved his uncle so much and was obviously hoping she was the answer he'd been looking for.

"I don't know, Kevin, but I just might. Let me sleep on it tonight, think it over. It's a big decision, even if it's only for a few months." For some reason, she felt she could open up to Kevin even though he was practically a stranger.

"It's been crazy the past few days with Uncle Frank's surgery, but it's been good to be home, too. The last month has been so hard. I've been looking for work, but nothing's turned up," her voice began to waver.

"I've felt so, I don't know, disconnected from my life. But then yesterday, I decided to take the county blacktop over to Swanton, and then I saw your sign. I doubled back, came down this road, and this place sort of spoke to me. The house, the barn, everything."

Kevin smiled and pushed his hands into his jean pockets, then scuffed at the floor with his shoe. "I think I understand, I really do. I teach history up at the community college in Mason City. I love my work, my friends. But my partner, we broke up two months ago. He worked at the college, too, but then a job opened up out of state. He wanted to go, I wanted to stay. We were going to get married, even." She saw the tears in Kevin's eyes. "But not now."

He moved to the window to gaze across the driveway to where the sheep were wandering in the front pasture. "I don't know where my life is going, either. And when I look at Horace, at Wilbur ... who knows how much time either of them have left? Or any of us? Horace is willing to go stay with Wilbur, but he hopes to come home again. I can't take that away from him, at least not yet."

Melinda reached over and patted his arm. "Who knows how it all will turn out? Just take it day by day, week by week. That's what I've been doing lately. I guess I highly recommend it, since I don't know what else to do."

He laughed. "I've been doing the same, now that you mention it. Let's go see if there's any coffee left."

"How easy would it be, really, to look after the animals?" She tried to contain her excitement as they rounded the landing on the stairs. This idea was starting to feel right, but she had to be realistic about what she could handle.

"It's simple, especially this time of year. Put out some feed for the chickens and the sheep, make sure they all have water. I'll muck out the barn when it's needed. But they all spend most of their time outside in the summer."

He stopped at the door at the bottom of the stairs and lowered his voice. Laughter echoed from the kitchen.

"Hobo's easy to please. He just needs food, water, someone to spend time with him. I'm afraid, though, that he'll take it hard when Horace leaves. Think you can mend a dog's broken heart?"

"I think I might be able to try, for Hobo's sake. And Horace's, too. But first, I want to see if he has any more stories to share."

He did. Horace was giving an animated, blow-by-blow account to Roger of the time he chased an opossum around in the barn. "He was too scared to stop long enough to play dead!" His laugh was hoarse but hearty as he slapped a palm on the table.

He looked startled when Melinda came into the room, as if he'd forgotten she was there. Then he brightened. "Well, what do you think of our little place? Sure cozy, isn't it?"

"Yes, Horace, I really like your home. It reminds me of the farm my Grandpa and Grandma Foster had. You've done a great job keeping this place up." Something told her a little affirmation would mean a lot to someone like Horace.

His lined face broke into a wide smile. "Well, I do what I can. The place hasn't had much of what you ladies call 'decorating' since our mother died twenty years ago. Wilbur and I just tried to keep things wiped down and maybe sweep a little here and there. Kevin's been a big help to us."

Melinda poured a cup of coffee and looked for any sign of powdered creamer. She opened the cabinet above the coffee pot but saw only a box of dehydrated potatoes well past its prime. Surely there was more food in the other cabinets, but the starkness of the shelves made her heart ache.

"Oh, sorry, there's no creamer." Kevin noticed her puzzled expression. "But there's milk in the fridge."

It took her a moment to figure out that tugging down on its vertical handle was the trick to getting the vintage refrigerator open. The steel-grate shelves held only a half-empty gallon of milk, a porcelain bowl with a few carefully nested eggs, and one browning banana.

"Horace says he gets to the store in Prosper those weeks I don't come down," Kevin lowered his voice below the laughter coming from the table. "But I'm not sure I believe him." He reached for the milk and poured some into Melinda's mug, his mouth set in a firm line.

"When I take him shopping in Swanton, I stick extra items in the back of the cart because he keeps saying he doesn't need much. I worry what he's really eating, especially this time of year when the garden's not producing yet. He cans in the summer and fall, but he runs through much of his stash during the winter."

"I can see why you're worried," Melinda whispered, stirring her coffee and glancing back at Horace. "He's really at loose ends here. He seems to barely get by, and who knows how long he can sustain this?" She thought of the instability in her own life, how unsure she was of the future. But suddenly, thirty-nine didn't seem so old. She was young enough, healthy enough to make a fresh start.

The expectant look on Horace's face as she took the last empty chair at the kitchen table nearly brought tears to her eyes. He couldn't bring himself to discuss the situation with her, but he was obviously hoping she would say yes.

Maybe I can't do this, she thought as she stirred sugar into her coffee. *But even if I could, maybe I shouldn't.*

The smart thing to do was just say no, let Horace and Kevin down easy, stay at her parents' instead. What did she know about looking after a bunch of sheep and chickens, and a dog who probably wouldn't want anything to do with her? And working at Prosper Hardware? She hadn't had a retail job since college, and the long hours on her feet and the cranky customers hadn't been pleasant.

But she was tired of not knowing what the next day, the next week, would bring. She was searching for something to hold on to. This house, the animals, the garden, they weren't going anywhere. And they all needed her. So did Horace. So did Aunt Miriam.

Kevin was right about the house. It was dated, it needed work. But as she looked around, she could see how the kitchen had been, and how it could be.

Something felt right about how her father, Kevin, and Horace were leaning in around the table, laughing at some new story Horace was telling.

It wasn't just a few cups of cheap coffee around a scuffed kitchen table. There was a warmth in the room, a sense of stability, of family and friendship.

She turned to the sunshine streaming in the double window, admired the healthy grass carpeting the side yard, the robins chirping in the large oak at the side of the driveway. A peace settled in her heart and, for the first time in weeks, she felt a glimmer of hope.

* 7 *

Melinda enjoyed only a few moments of peaceful bliss at Horace's kitchen table before there was a staccato of barks outside and a brown-and-white blur zoomed past the kitchen windows. Kevin and Horace nearly knocked their chairs over in their rush for the back door. Horace was more spry than she ever would have expected, trailing only a few feet behind his nephew as they hurried down the driveway.

"Well, we might as well go, too," Roger grinned and set down his mug. "They may need a hand."

They rushed out to find Hobo in a face-off with one very indignant ewe on the far shoulder of the gravel road. The sheep divided her efforts between glaring at Hobo and sampling the thick grass sprouting along the edge of the ditch. Hobo danced and barked, but made no effort to chase the ewe or drive her back up the lane.

"He's not a herding dog, that's for sure," Kevin called over his shoulder to Melinda and Roger as he jogged back to the barn, reappearing a few minutes later with a small plastic bucket of oats. "And Annie doesn't take orders from anyone, even Horace. This isn't her first escape."

Melinda saw Horace down by the mailbox, waving his arms at the ewe and ordering her to "get along." Annie had no interest in his demands until she spied the grain bucket. Kevin let her get a mouthful, then shook the container and started up the lane backward, holding it just out of her reach. The ewe followed, slowly and casually, as if it was all her idea.

Hobo nominated himself grand marshal of the little parade, barking and turning occasionally to make sure the others were close behind. Horace, looking a bit winded, brought up the rear. Melinda and Roger joined the procession where the front pasture met the barn.

"How do you know which one is Annie?" she asked. "They all look the same to me."

"Oh, by her ear tag," Horace pointed. "See, all our sheep have green tags, but hers is No. 23. She's a feisty one. Was the smallest of a litter of triplets a few years back, when we still owned a buck and had lambs every spring. She wasn't about to let her brother and sister push her around. We gave her bottles, too, when she was small. So she got spoiled. Thinks she owns the place."

Melinda could tell that Horace secretly adored Annie, and the reminiscing seemed to restore his good humor. He asked her to "man the gate," which meant unlatching a wooden panel hinged between two fence posts and opening it at just the right time to let Kevin and a snorting Annie pass through. Some of the other sheep gathered to watch the commotion, then hurried into the barn with Kevin for an unexpected mid-morning treat.

Melinda waited until the hovering ewes disappeared inside before she slipped back through the gate. She made sure the panel was aligned with the post, then slid the metal latch over with a satisfying click. Horace was watching, and she wanted to do it right.

He nodded his approval. "Well, guess it's time to fix that fence. Melinda, could you run into the house and bring out that blue toolbox on the back porch? It'd save me a few steps."

It was as if she had passed some sort of test. In Horace's eyes, if she could manage the pasture gate, she could manage everything else with assistance from Kevin.

Roger offered to help Kevin and Horace repair the hole in the fence, which was discovered in a front panel just past the drive. Kevin said a quick fix would span the gap, at least for now, and suggested Melinda check out the garden and outbuildings while the repair was made.

"There's never a dull moment out here, as you can see. But if you do decide to come, I promise I won't expect you to fix fence."

Melinda fought back an unexpected urge to skip across the lawn, her grin growing wider as she marveled over the organized efficiency of Horace's garden. The chickens clucked curiously as she approached their run. Only two came over for a closer look at their visitor, and she wondered which one was the infamous Pansy.

Some of the birds were a lovely shade of rust, and the rest sported a mix of white and black feathers. She would have to ask Kevin about their breeds and how often she needed to gather eggs. There would be so much to learn, and so much to do. And she couldn't wait to get started.

There was another quick coffee break once the fence was repaired, then hearty handshakes all around. Melinda worked out her employment with Aunt Miriam that night, then called Kevin the next morning. He emailed her a lease outlining the details of their agreement, and she signed it and scanned it back from her parents' home office. Things happened quickly after that.

Linda, her former coworker at WP&S, had a niece at the University of Minnesota still looking for a summer apartment. Tonya was overjoyed to learn Melinda needed a subletter, and Melinda was overjoyed to learn Tonya's parents didn't blink at covering the full cost of the rent. Melinda got a set of house keys from Kevin, then gave Tonya spares for the apartment. In between visits to the hospital to spend time with Uncle Frank, she rented a small, pull-along trailer and began gathering what she needed to spend the rest of the summer in Iowa.

"Look at you," Cassie crowed one night as she and Susan helped pack totes to take to the farm. "Escaping the city for a few relaxing months in the country. What an adventure you're going to have. How many pairs of jeans might you need?" She gestured at the tall stack in the closet.

"Just grab those top three," Melinda called over her shoulder as she counted out a meager ration of socks and underwear into another pile. The horrified look on Cassie's face brought hearty laughter from Melinda and Susan.

"You know the rules," Melinda teased her fashion-obsessed friend. "Two totes of clothes, then one tote of house stuff per room, that's it. I'm going to streamline and simplify my life this summer. Besides, I don't want to make two round trips. So pack light."

"You sound like you're off to Oregon on a wagon train. Surely you'll need some cuter things, right?" She lifted out a watercolor-toned dress. Susan shook her head.

"I don't think the sheep would approve of that one," Susan reached around Cassie for a small pile of faded tee shirts. "Too colorful. It might startle them, and we don't want to give that Annie any ideas."

Melinda waved a worn sneaker at Cassie for emphasis. "I need pants, shorts, a few polos for working at the store. When you come for the weekend to visit, you can dress as chic as you like. Me, I'll be spending most of the next few months pulling weeds, scooping feed and waiting on farmers buying nails and cereal."

* * *

Only ten days after she spotted that sign on the side of the road, Melinda plopped the last tote of clothes on her bed and lowered herself to the comforter. She'd forgotten what a pain it was to move, to pack up clothes, books, kitchen gear and all the other pieces of your life and haul them to an unfamiliar place. Tomorrow was Tuesday, her first day at Prosper Hardware. If she wanted to get settled in at the farmhouse, she had to keep moving.

It was a good thing she'd been so strict about what to bring. It took only a few minutes to fill three of the six drawers in the bedroom's chest with most of her clothes. How grateful she was that Horace's old dresser was still in this room, and the nightstand, too. She and her parents had enough trouble yesterday angling her queen-size bed up those narrow farmhouse stairs. By the time the frame was assembled and the box spring and mattress tugged into place, she had only wanted to go back to her parents' house for a shower and a restful sleep in a made-up bed.

Tonight, her first night at the farm, was going to make all of this feel real. The house was so peaceful, so quiet, but it also reminded her how alone she was. She was used to living by herself, but there was always someone nearby, just across the hall or on the other side of the wall. Out here, distance was measured in miles, not feet. And it was more than a half mile to the nearest farm, back north over the creek.

She really wasn't alone, though. The chore list, also on the kitchen counter, was evidence of that. None of it seemed too complicated. But still, she'd feel better once she made the rounds this evening. The neighbors handling chores since Horace left Thursday had come again early this morning, before her arrival.

Kevin had made good on his promise to have the place ready within a week. A small army of neighbors and relatives must have made several passes through the farmhouse in just a few days, and she was impressed with the results. All the curtains had been washed and aired on the clothesline by the garden. The baseboards and wood floors were wiped down, the windows rubbed to a sparkle.

In the kitchen, the linoleum floor had been buffed and the cabinet doors and counters scrubbed. The stacks of newspapers and much of the other clutter had discretely vanished, with Melinda suspecting most of it was now stacked in the large upstairs bedroom used for storage.

She admired the clean-if-faded rag rug on the bedroom's freshly swept wood floor as she added a reading lamp to the nightstand, which fit nicely between the bed and the west window. The oblong rug, the perfect length to be rolled out next to a bed, had been waiting for her when she arrived yesterday. The blues, greens and browns in the striped runner picked up the neutral tones in her comforter. The windows in this room had been stark and nearly bare on her first visit, topped with only some tired vinyl roller shades. But someone had taken the time to dress them with white eyelet-trimmed curtains, and a delicate crocheted runner was draped across the polished surface of the bureau.

The dark varnish on the closet door stuck a bit as she turned the iron knob. There were just a few spare hangers dangling from the metal rod, and the iron hooks drilled into the wood strips on the perimeter were empty. She imagined how young Horace and his siblings would have put away their few overalls and dresses on those hooks.

"How did they ever all squeeze into this house?" she marveled as she hung up a few shirts and pairs of khaki pants. "I probably brought more clothes than they ever had new."

There was a thump and a roar outside the west window as the air conditioning unit kicked in, and soon a refreshing wave of coolness drifted out of the scroll-patterned iron vent in the oak floor. "I couldn't do this without you," she called out to the metal box down below. "I'm not as tough as you might think I am." Kevin's note said he had closed the house up again Saturday after the cleaning spree. She was to call if the air conditioner didn't stay on. It was mid-June, and the humidity was on the rise.

Melinda smiled as she watched Hobo scoot out from under the shade of the picnic table and visit the water bowl by the back steps. A few slurps and he wandered back to his favorite napping spot, pausing only long enough to study a squirrel chattering at him from the boughs of the oak tree. But he didn't bark, or try to start a chase. Kevin had warned her that Hobo would take Horace's absence hard, and to not expect too much from him at first.

"They've never really been apart," he said Thursday night on the phone. "And today, I had to split them up. I just hope Hobo will eat, that he won't give up with Horace gone. Oh, Melinda, I just hope we're doing the right thing."

Horace had his hard-side suitcase packed with a few changes of clothes by the time Kevin and Ada arrived Thursday morning. Kevin helped his uncle fill a cardboard box with some books, his checkerboard and a photo of Hobo that had been displayed on the fireplace mantel. The morning chores had been finished hours ago, but Horace, Kevin and Hobo took a walk around the farm while Ada straightened up the kitchen and made sure her brother hadn't left anything important behind.

Horace had warned the hens to not peck Melinda, and admonished the ewes to give her room when she brought their grain.

Hobo supervised while Kevin loaded Horace's belongings into the trunk of Ada's car, then Kevin and his mom took their time locking up the house to give Horace a few minutes alone with his beloved dog.

"I'll see ya soon, boy, real soon," Kevin had heard Horace say. "Melinda is coming to stay with you, and everything's going to be OK."

Once Horace was settled in the car's front seat, he launched into a rundown of all the things he longed to discuss with Wilbur, how happy he would be to eat meals with his brother again. And he was eager to show those other retired farmers how a game of checkers was really played. But when he turned his head away, Kevin saw the tears sliding down his uncle's weathered cheek.

Hobo sat at attention at the side of the driveway, his eyes mournful, as Kevin backed the car around in front of the garage and drove away down the lane.

"I could barely put the car in gear," he had told Melinda. "I don't know who was crying harder, Horace or me or my mom in the backseat. I managed to get myself under control by the time we got to the blacktop."

"You're doing the right thing for Horace, for Wilbur, too," Melinda had told him, in tears then herself. "And I'll take care of everything here, tell your mom not to worry. I'll just show Hobo as much love as I can."

But so far, Hobo wanted no more than a quick pat on the head. He spent most of his time under the picnic table, or in his doghouse. But some of the kibble was disappearing from his bowl, and Melinda hoped it was a sign he hadn't quite given up on life.

She took her bathroom tote across the hall. She stacked her towels on an empty shelf in the linen closet, reserving one hand towel for the tiny bath downstairs. The clawfoot tub gleamed, and a new white shower curtain slid on the rings above. She arranged her makeup and other items on the scrubbed vanity, then placed new aqua bath mats in front of the tub and sink.

"Upstairs, done!" She snapped her fingers as she made the turn on the stair landing and took the last steps down to the living room. She paused, admiring how perfect her beige chenille sofa rested under the picture window.

Her bed and the couch were the only pieces of furniture she brought from her apartment. The farmhouse was furnished, and the moving trailer was small. But the sofa really made the space feel like home, and it was worth all the tugging and pulling it took to get it there.

There had been more grunting and puffing to get Horace's old rust-colored couch wedged into his bedroom while still leaving enough space to reach the tiny bathroom in the back. It was apparent that Horace's sofa hadn't been moved in years, based on the piles of mysterious fuzz that had to be swept away from the baseboard and floor after she and her dad carried the sagging couch into the next room.

Horace's worn leather chair remained just where he'd left it, aimed toward the television. Melinda reached around the recliner, opened one of the glass-paned bookcase doors, and gently slid over a few titles on a lightly populated shelf to make room for some of her own books.

Her plastic bin for the living room also included her laptop and her favorite throw blanket. Surely it wouldn't be chilly enough to need it, but the lavender knit throw would look lovely draped over her couch. Three picture frames had made the trip wrapped in the blanket, and she took a moment to enjoy the photos as she put them on the mantel.

There was one of her with her parents and siblings, taken last summer. Another was a casual shot of Cassie and Susan from Melinda's birthday celebration in March. And then Oreo, lounging in his favorite corner of the beige sofa, curled up on the blanket Melinda now held in her arms. Wiping away a stray tear, she draped the throw over the couch and set her laptop on the dining room table. The internet connection had been turned on late last week, the wi-fi router looking comically out of place on top of the built-in buffet. Maybe tonight she'd have a chance to use it.

But first, lunch. They had stocked the refrigerator and a few of the cabinets with staples yesterday, trying to anticipate what she would want to eat in the coming week. During the lean years just out of college, she had become a master meal planner and coupon clipper. Those skills would serve her well this summer, as she was no longer a few blocks from a grocery store and would need to pack her lunch on the days she worked at Prosper Hardware.

She made a hasty sandwich and popped open a bag of chips, then considered both the dining-room and kitchen tables before sitting down in the kitchen, across from the double window. It was soon obvious why Horace preferred this spot. She could look out on the side yard, see the barn and front pasture and the fields beyond.

At least she didn't have to mow the expanse of lawn surrounding the house. There was a riding lawn mower in the machine shed, and Kevin had hired a neighbor named Nathan to come by once a week.

Some of the magenta peonies were still blooming along the south side of the house, and she had noticed a collection of white vases in the china cabinet in the dining room.

A clutch of flowers would be the perfect, final touch for the fireplace mantel. A few more totes needed her attention, and then it would be time to find a pair of scissors and select some blooms.

Melinda had cheated a bit on her one-box-per-room plan. She didn't need to bring anything specifically for the dining room, so that tote held her everyday dishes, some silverware and cups, and a selection of plastic containers. The kitchen box held her best skillet and her smallest and largest glass pots, some dishtowels and two cookie sheets that could double as pizza pans.

Horace's meager supply of dishes was tucked in next to the sink, with nothing stored too high or too low, and his few pots and skillets were wedged in a cabinet to the left of the stove. She decided to store hers off to the right. Most of the shelves were dusty and empty, but one had been carefully wiped down and a pouch of food set right inside the door. A note was taped to the front.

The bag of dog biscuits was nearly full. The scrawled, hesitant writing on the paper had to be Horace's.

Melinda, thank you for coming into our lives at the right time. It means so much to know you'll be here when I'm away. I'm sure you know what to do with these. Two in the morning, two at night. There is another bag down in the cellar, on the canning shelves. I buy them at the hardware store. Horace

She clutched the pouch to her chest, touched by the kindness in Horace's note. She could imagine him sitting there at the kitchen table, carefully measuring his words.

The last month had been a disoriented dream. Now her life had purpose again. She set the treat pouch on the counter and carefully removed the note.

"You came along just when I needed you, too, Horace." She slid the piece of paper under a rooster magnet on the refrigerator door so she could enjoy it several times each day.

She couldn't see past August, didn't know what was coming next. "But I'm here now," she said to the house, looking out to find the sheep grazing east of the barn. "Thank you for giving me a place to be."

The last tote was her laundry basket. She tucked her cleaning supplies under the kitchen sink, then headed for the basement steps. "This will be interesting," she said as she peered into the murky darkness below. Last week's tour, cut short by Annie's escape, hadn't included the cellar.

There was no light switch on either side of the basement door, but she found a chain dangling from a single bulb in the stairwell ceiling. It popped on, much to her relief, as did some other lights down below.

As she descended the wooden steps, their gray paint faded and peeling, her nostrils were hit with that musty yet somehow comforting smell unique to the cellars of old houses. It spoke of decades of hard work and memories. She always thought that the true essence of an old house lived its hidden corners, those spaces in the basements, attics and closets that were rarely disturbed, the forgotten items tossed there holding on to the past.

Horace's washer and dryer looked as if they'd seen many a heavy-duty cycle, but they were spotless and sturdy. And judging by the industrial cleaners lined up on the metal shelf above the washer, he knew his way around a muddy pair of overalls. A battered utility sink, slightly askew but bolted into the adjoining wall, hadn't fared as well. She was inspecting another wire shelf, jammed with bottles and tubes that appeared to be veterinary supplies, when she was startled by a banging noise coming from upstairs.

* 8 *

"Melinda? Are you home?" An unfamiliar female voice drifted down from the kitchen.

"I'm on my way up. Be there in a minute."

An elderly couple had already let themselves into the back porch and were peering in the kitchen door's window. But they smiled and waved, and the woman was holding a pie. Melinda suddenly felt at ease.

"We told Horace we'd come by to see how you're getting along. I'm Mabel Bauer, and this is Ed, my husband. We're just up the road, past the bridge."

"Oh, yes, of course. You have those beautiful peonies right along the drive. Come in, I'm still trying to sort out my things. That pie looks wonderful."

Mabel, beaming at the praise, set the pie plate on the counter. A vibrant scarf of greens and pinks protected her white curls from the summer breeze and humidity. Melinda noticed that while Mabel was wearing a faded pair of khaki capris, her berry-colored top matched her lipstick perfectly.

"It's strawberry. I just made the first ones today from our patch. The berries are a little early this year, so hopefully that means the season runs longer. Yours are a bit behind ours, I think, it will be another week before they'll be ready to pick."

Melinda was amazed at how Mabel could possibly know the current status of Horace's strawberry bed, but then

quickly realized her new neighbor had been peeking around
the yard before knocking on the back door.

Mabel gave Melinda an unexpected hug, and Ed grinned
and clapped her on the shoulder.

"It'll be good to have another young person in the
neighborhood," Ed said as he adjusted his red cap, then
removed it. He was all angles where Mabel was round. Ed's
iron-gray hair was cropped close, his forearms brown from
hours working in the sun. "Too many of us older folks around
these days. How's Horace doing? I know Thursday was the
big move."

Melinda wasn't sure what to say. Mabel and Ed meant
well, that was clear, but Melinda sensed Horace was a private
man and wouldn't want everyone in the township to know all
his business. "Kevin said he's adjusting well," she said
casually. "It's a big change, of course, but he and Wilbur are
happy to be together again, so that will help."

Ed nodded, seemingly deep in thought. Mabel and Ed
looked to be in their seventies, not so many years' away from
the decisions Horace was having to make.

"Glad to hear he's hanging in there," Ed said. "We've been
doing chores since he left. Wanted to come by and meet you,
see if you had any questions or needed any help. And Mabel
was over here the other day, helping get the place ready."

"Oh, yes, it needed a scrubbing, that's for sure," Mabel cut
in. "I don't know when those floors had been polished last.
And the curtains! They were fairly stiff with dust when we
pulled them down to be washed."

"Thank you so much for doing all of that," Melinda said
warmly. "I couldn't believe how the house was transformed
from the way it was just over a week ago. Horace was trying to
keep up, but I think it was tough for him to do on his own."

Behind her smile, her mind was churning. Should she
offer Ed and Mabel coffee and slice up the pie? Or was it all
for her? Where *was* the coffee, anyway? They seemed like the
sort of people who'd just make themselves at home if they
planned to stay. She'd just follow their lead.

"He's a sweet man. Wilbur, too." Mabel shook her head. "It's been hard on them, leaving this farm. They lived here their whole lives. Best neighbors you could ever ask for. I grew up on our place, Ed and I took it over when my parents moved to town decades ago. I remember coming over to visit Horace and Wilbur and their family even when I was small. Ada, their youngest sister, and I have been close friends since we were girls. She's Kevin's mother."

"Now Mabel, Melinda may not have time for a neighborhood history lesson just now," Ed jokingly rolled his eyes and Mabel playfully swatted at him. "She's got her hands full, unpacking and getting settled, figuring out the chores. How much experience you have with sheep and chickens?"

"None, I'm afraid." She might as well be honest. Her lack of knowledge would be clear soon enough. "My grandparents had a farm and I loved to visit. But I grew up in Swanton. We had a dog and a cat, and that was it."

"Well, that's just fine," Ed rubbed his hands together and gave her a kind smile. He was excited to show her the ropes. "Sheep are simple, and chickens more so. Do you have time for a few quick lessons?"

"You bet." She reached into a bin for the floral gardening gloves she bought last week. "Let me get my things."

"Oh, my dear," Mabel said gently. "Let's not use those, they're so lovely."

Ed was already rummaging through the porch closet and pulled out a dingy pair of yellow cotton gloves, the kind sold in a pack of ten. "These are pretty dirty, but that's the point."

Melinda, trying to hide her disgust, tugged on the gloves. Ed found a pair for Mabel, then took another for himself.

"We've still got a few chickens, gave up the cows a few years ago. Now that's work, milking twice a day," Ed said as they went down the back steps. "Haven't planted corn and beans for a decade. I'd rather putter in the garden or play with the grandkids than spend my days on a tractor."

Hobo, to Melinda's surprise and relief, came out from under the picnic table with a faint wag in his tail.

"Hobo, my friend!" Ed reached down to gently pat the dog's head. "How are you getting on, buddy? Let's go to the barn and see the sheep."

Hobo fell in step with Ed, and Melinda felt a lump form in her throat. In the country, you counted on your neighbors as if they were family. With the support and care offered by these two, she just might be able to keep her promises to Kevin and Horace.

"I don't know what to do about Hobo," she told Mabel. "He seems to like Ed. Maybe he should stay with you? I don't mean to impose, it just hurts to see Hobo so sad."

Mabel gave her arm a reassuring squeeze. "Horace and that dog were inseparable, that's for sure. But don't worry, Hobo will come around. He's happier here at home than he'd be anywhere else. Besides, our Sammy wouldn't want another dog on her farm. She's territorial that way. Do you know how Hobo got his name? It's a great story."

Melinda was starting to see that Mabel was full of information. "I'd love to hear it."

Ed was already to the barn, lifting the door's iron latch and standing aside to let Hobo run ahead. Mabel lingered in the grass just off the gravel drive.

"Three years ago, it was early spring ... a warm spell but still March, patches of snow on the ground, when the weather can't decide what season it wants to be. So, Horace and Wilbur came out one evening to do chores and they thought they heard a dog whimpering down in the lilac trees by the road. They hadn't had a dog for over a year at that time, Marty had died of old age. Anyway, they went down to see what the deal was and there was Hobo, maybe three months old. Someone must have dumped him out, there's no way such a little dog could walk far on his own. They called all around, no one was missing a pup. Or at least, they wouldn't admit it."

Mabel pursed her lips and raised an eyebrow. If she had any theories about who in the township might have let Hobo out at the Schermann farm, she was keeping those to herself.

"They made him a small hut out of a cardboard box and brought him in on the back porch, fed him scraps and milk as they didn't have any dog food around. About the second day, when they couldn't find out where the pup came from, Wilbur came up with that name. And Hobo's been here ever since."

"What a perfect name for a stray dog." Melinda smiled, imagining Horace and Wilbur discovering the puppy and scrambling to care for him.

They walked toward the open barn door, through which they saw Hobo happily accepting chin scratches from Ed.

"We came over the first day Hobo was here," Mabel went on. "Brought over some kibble. Horace and Wilbur said they were going to keep looking around for the pup's owner, but I could tell right off they were already hooked. Hobo came along at the right time. Wilbur and Horace were both devastated when they lost Marty."

Ed's appearance in the barn brought the ewes in from the pasture. The sheep nudged up to the feed bunks that lined their side of the aisle fence and let out a series of "baaaas" as they watched Ed play with Hobo and wondered when supper would be served. As Mabel and Melinda came near, some of the ewes backed up, hesitant. Melinda could see it would take several rounds of chores before she would be able to gain the flock's trust.

"Those must be the grain barrels over there?" She caught up to Ed and gestured to two fifty-gallon drums wedged along the aisle side of the fence. "Horace's got the tops weighed down with those bricks, I'm not sure why. Must be a pretty strong airflow coming in through the sheep's door to push the lids off."

For a moment Ed looked as if he was about to laugh. Then he realized she wasn't making a joke.

"I'd bet Horace has those on there to keep the critters out of the oats and corn," he said kindly. "Raccoons, probably, maybe an opossum or rats."

"Rats?" She froze in the alley and glanced around. She didn't want to meet an opossum out here, or a raccoon either, but she could probably scare one of those off with a scrap of wood or a pitchfork.

But the thought of rats, their whip-like tails slithering through the grain as they stuffed their creepy, toothy faces ... well, that was too much. Good thing the days were long in the summer, and she would be doing both morning and evening chores in the daylight.

"Oh, anytime you've got grain around, expect to have rats." Ed lifted the lid on one of the barrels and tunneled the scoop down into the oats, a sound that brought a chorus of excited bleats from the sheep. "Just keep the weights on and you'll be fine. The rats won't want to see you, either, so if they're around, they'll take off running when they hear you come in the barn."

As Ed shook the oats into the feed bunks, she gazed down the center aisle of the barn and wondered where the rats might hide.

The feeding area west of the main aisle was unused, with only a thin layer of stale straw covering the concrete floor. Too open, too visible.

A solid wall divided the barn in half. From what she could see through the open doorway, the back part of the barn had two rows of stalls down its center, each with a trough toward the middle.

The open space that made a U-shape around the pens included two closed pasture doors, one facing south and one west. The stairway up to the haymow was just on the other side of the supporting wall.

There was a small room just across from the gate into the ewes' area, its scuffed wooden door cracked open and hanging slightly askew on its iron hinges. It had a least one window, as there was faint daylight radiating around the door, but what else was in there? She felt her scalp start to prickle. "What's that room for, Ed?"

"Oh, that's the grain room, storage space. You'd put your extra oats and such in there, away from where the animals could get to it. But now, with just these few sheep, Horace leaves the grain out here in these barrels." He noticed her cautious expression and chuckled.

"You're right, that's the perfect place for rats to live, there or in the haymow. You're picking up on things quick. Be careful, though, if you go up there. Horace and Wilbur built those stairs to be sturdy and safe, but there's sure to be some holes or loose boards in the haymow floor."

"Well, I don't intend to go up there anytime soon." She crossed her arms.

For such a charming barn, there seemed to be potential dangers everywhere. That included the swags of cobwebs anchored in the ceiling's corners and spiraling out along the walls, swooping just low enough to let their residents enjoy pastoral views through the four-pane windows.

Ed glanced around, too, and lowered his voice. "Of course, there's spiders all over out here. They get really big in the summer. Huge. Their bodies can get as big as quarters, and their legs ..."

"Ed, really!" Mabel shot her husband an exasperated look. "We promised Horace we'd help look after things, not cause her to pack up her bags and run back to the city. Now, Melinda," she began in a soothing voice, "just sweep the webs off to the side when they grow too large. Spiders especially like open doorways, since they can catch more bugs in those. My personal rule is if the webs are low enough that a spider could jump into my hair as I walk under them, then it's time to get the broom."

Melinda wasn't afraid of a little bug here and there. Her apartment had spiders from time to time. But they were small, not these creatures that Ed described.

At least there shouldn't be cockroaches here. She hated those. They made her nervous, the way they seemed to anticipate her movements as she stalked them with a shoe. She could probably handle a few country spiders, as long as they stayed out of her way and out of her hair. There was one over by a west window right now, a fat beige one, too busy spinning to pay its visitors much mind.

"I'd already planned to bring out an old broom to chase off the rats," she sighed. "And I see there's some spare two-by-fours over there for backup. As long as I don't need a gun to fight off all these critters, I think I'll be OK."

Ed and Mabel exchanged concerned looks.

"Oh, no, don't tell me I'll need to be a crack shot, too. What else is lurking around here? Horace said something last week about some panther, but maybe it was really a bobcat? Kevin said he likes to exaggerate, though, and tell stories."

"He sure does," Mabel grinned, then grew serious. "But last winter ... well, Ed, should we even tell her? I don't want to frighten her unnecessarily ..."

"We saw tracks around our chicken house once last year, a day or so after Horace and Wilbur did."

Ed curled his fingers and pushed the tips together, his hands about three inches apart. "Big feet, rounded, like a cat's, not oblong like a dog's."

"But we never saw it," Mabel patted Melinda's arm encouragingly.

"The sun had melted the tracks some, they maybe weren't that big to begin with. Even if there had been a wild cat around, it would've moved on quickly, they can travel several miles a day. And it was winter, the snow was deeper than usual. A wild animal would never come around humans like that unless it was terribly hungry."

"Guess I'll have to learn animal tracks, too." Putting out feed and filling water tanks was apparently only a fraction of this job.

Ed shrugged. "I've got a rifle. Rarely use it, but it's good to have around. You have any trouble like that, you just call and I'll come over. In the meantime, there's always a shovel."

At least there was a hydrant in the barn, with a hose that ran to the ewes' water troughs. She wouldn't have to haul water for the sheep. But the chickens' water would need to be carried in a bucket from the hydrant next to the garden.

With Hobo leading the way, they crossed the yard to the chicken coop.

Mabel demonstrated the best way to distract the hens with their feed and then snatch the fresh eggs from the brooder boxes.

"You see, it's pretty simple," Mabel beamed as she handed Melinda the galvanized egg bucket. "Change their water once a day, twice when it's really hot, and that's it. They'll head for the shady parts of the run, closer to the windbreak, or come in here where it's cooler. And the wire run is nice and sturdy. These ladies will stay safe, no matter what might come sniffing around."

It sounded simple enough. But the hens had screeched unmercifully when the three strangers ducked into their coop. And one of the rust-colored chickens let out a vicious squawk and made a run at Ed's pant leg. Melinda cringed, but Ed just shrugged. "Always wear jeans at chore time. Long-sleeved shirts, too."

Mabel gave Melinda an unexpected hug as she and Ed got in their car. "Call anytime. Our number's on the pad there by the kitchen phone." They waved as they drove down the lane, Ed giving the horn a little toot.

Her neighbors' instructions and kindness were just the encouragement she needed. It would take a few days to win the trust of the sheep and the chickens, but the chores themselves weren't all that difficult. Prosper Hardware, however, was another matter. She had no idea how parachute in and fill Aunt Miriam's and Uncle Frank's shoes. But just as Mabel and Ed would help her with the farm, Bill and Esther would be at the store to offer their support and expertise.

"It's better to know exactly what I'm up against." As she glanced around the yard, she saw all the hard work it was going to take to keep this charming farm looking that way. They hadn't even discussed the garden, which looked as if it had been recently weeded. But it wouldn't stay that way for long. "I'll just find a way to get it all done, that's all."

And she couldn't wait to take it on.

She clasped her hands together, feeling the early-evening sun warm her back as she gazed down the gravel drive to the carpet of rising cornfields to the east. For the first time since she lost her job, she was excited about a challenge instead of feeling overwhelmed. This was her place, even if just for the summer, and she was going to find a way to keep it going for Horace's sake.

Hobo had ambled down to the road and was now stretched out in the soft grass on the driveway's shoulder. *He must be enjoying the early-evening breeze,* she thought, walking down to join him. Maybe he'd let her pet him again, as he had that morning.

"Hobo? Hey, boy," she called softly as she approached, her sneakers crunching the gravel.

Hobo looked up, and she was stunned to see the sadness in his eyes. He turned away and stared out at the road, first left, up the way Ed and Mabel had gone, and then right, down toward the next crossroads.

He put his head back down on his paws, his furry brown shoulders slumped as he let out a sigh.

Her heart swelled with concern for the poor dog as her eyes filled with tears. Earlier in the day, when he wasn't under the picnic table, she had assumed he was in the barn, using the little door cut in the front wall to come and go. But he must have been down here, instead. Watching, waiting for Horace to come home.

She carefully lowered herself into the grass next to Hobo, who wouldn't look her way.

"I don't know, Hobo, I don't know if he will," she sniffed, then gently placed her hand on the dog's velvet fur. Hobo didn't move.

"I know you miss him. I'm sorry you're stuck with me, instead. I'm sorry your best friend has gone away. I can't be him, Hobo, but I would like to try to help you."

She looked both ways down the road, just as Hobo had done, and was struck by how empty it seemed.

The tears were now rolling down her face, the confidence she'd gained through Ed and Mabel's encouraging words starting to fade. What would become of her, what would she ever do with her life after this? This was a break, a chance to get away from her normal life. But it was all temporary. It wasn't going to last.

"I know how you feel," she whispered, gently wrapping an arm around Hobo, tears falling into his fur.

"We don't know what's going to happen. But we will take this day by day, and do it together." At last, he turned his head and licked her hand.

☀ 9 ☀

A blinding shock of sunlight filled the car. Melinda hurried to yank down the visor, which didn't do much good because the sun was still low over the horizon. "And oh, is it early," she mumbled, turning east off the gravel road and toward Prosper. The dash clock showed 6:40 a.m., and the charcoal ribbon of asphalt was empty except for her hatchback.

"People with desk jobs somewhere haven't even left home yet," she sighed. But the local farmers were already done with morning chores and on to the rest of their days' tasks. She was, too. There would be no more sleeping in, no more lazy mornings with a bottomless cup of coffee and the paper. She had to be at Prosper Hardware at seven. Aunt Miriam wanted her to make sure the store was ready to open at eight, which was when Bill arrived. Esther came in at noon and closed the store at six. Unless there was some calamity, Melinda was free to leave at four.

And why wouldn't there be some sort of drama? There'd been plenty of that last night and this morning.

She had been a bit nervous about her first night alone in an old house, but had no trouble falling into a deep, restful sleep. That was ruined a few hours later by a sign she wasn't alone: the unmistakable "chireep, chireep" of a cricket hiding behind the dresser. She begged the insect to either shut up or leave the room, but the song went on.

She got up, flipped the light switch and confronted her foe with a shoe. But the little bug was too quick, darting behind the nightstand and then under the bed. She considered going downstairs to sleep on the couch, but decided to stand her ground and, after some choice words for her new roommate, managed to close her eyes again.

Three alarms woke her at 5:15 a.m. There was her clock radio, her smartphone and a wind-up clock she found in the drawer of the nightstand. But that was one too many. The vintage timepiece was a minute behind and so obnoxious that, still half asleep, she was startled by the racket and stubbed her toe on the nightstand while trying to turn off all her devices. She'd have to go to bed sooner, get herself adjusted to a new routine. And fast.

Hobo ate some of his breakfast, which was encouraging, but apparently he wanted her to sit next to him on the sidewalk while he slowly, slowly enjoyed his kibble. He allowed her to pet him and rub his ears during the meal, while her mind hurried ahead to how quickly she might be able to feed the sheep and chickens, get a shower and some cereal, and hurry off to town.

Mabel's idea to distract the hens with their feed was successful, and she was able to collect their eggs and change their water while they feasted. The ewes refused to come up to the inside fence while she was in the barn, but she wasn't sure if that was because they didn't trust her or because she was running around like a madwoman, racing the clock.

But then there was that noise in the barn, a skittering, scratching sound that made her heart jump more than when the old alarm clock clanged.

Some critter was padding around in the old grain room. At least, she hoped there was only one. Was it those rats Ed had warned her about? Surely those horrible creatures wouldn't come out while she was in the barn, frozen there in the aisle with the oat scoop in her hand. She was about to approach the grain room door, which was still open just a crack, when the scratching started again.

First across the floor, and then going up, up, up the boards of the wall. Her heart nearly stopped when the sequence repeated.

If there were two, there were surely more. The thought of a horde of rats baring their talon-like claws and swinging their stringy, hairless tails as they performed this feat of strength was too much.

The ewes, who had started to calmly chew their oats, erupted with bleats of surprise when she flung the scoop back in the oats bin and slammed the lid and brick on top.

"Good luck ladies," Melinda called to them as she ran out of the barn and double-checked the door latch behind her. "I'm out of here."

A knot was again forming in her stomach as she bumped over the railroad tracks by the co-op. A few pickups were already parked in front, most of them with an underbelly of gravel-road dust. She tried to comfort herself with the idea that these people, soon to be her customers, were of the no-nonsense variety. All she had to do was be friendly, direct them to what they were looking for, make small talk. It couldn't be that difficult to run the cash register. And Bill would be there, he could help customers find things until she learned the store.

"It's OK to be nervous. This is a big change. Besides, it's better than sitting around my apartment."

But the uneasiness remained as she cruised past City Hall and the front of Prosper Hardware, turning after the post office to come in the back side off Third. She didn't fit in around here anymore, and wasn't really sure she wanted to. Hadn't she spent the last two decades building her own, independent life? Then she remembered that awful morning when she cried on the floor of her apartment, Oreo's collar clutched in her palm, and how she'd decided to get on her feet and take things one step at a time.

"I'm doing that today, too." She turned into the gravel parking lot, and told herself she would handle whatever came her way as best as she could.

It was now seven. She took a deep breath and closed her eyes, tossed up a quick prayer for a good day. But even a so-so day would do.

There would be an hour to walk the aisles and get familiar with the layout of the store. She'd study the register's shortcut keys, maybe water the hanging baskets out front, make sure the floor was swept clean. And surely there wouldn't be a stampede when she unlocked the front door at eight.

Melinda stuck her key in the back door and nearly stumbled forward when it flew open on its own. Why wasn't it locked? Had someone broken into the store?

She stepped cautiously into the back room, mildly comforted by its sweet sawdust aroma. Bill had stacks of lumber piled around, projects he was cutting for customers.

Anyone could be hiding back here. This was worse than the rats in the barn; at least they might be the slightest bit afraid of her.

"Hello?" No answer.

She tiptoed to the steel door leading into the store, then remembered how badly it stuck. She wasn't going to be incognito for long. She turned the knob and pushed on the door with her shoulder. There was a scraping screech as it opened, but otherwise, silence. The early-morning sunlight beamed in through the spacious front windows, but the lights weren't on and there were shadows crouching in the back near the stairs.

She waited, her heart pounding. Then there was another unmistakable scent: coffee.

"Melinda?" A man's voice echoed from the front of the store, causing her to jump. Not only was someone here, but he was expecting her.

Then she sighed and started up the main aisle. Someone this friendly, and here this early and brewing coffee, wasn't likely to be dangerous.

A cheerful man who looked to be about sixty gave her a wave as he set out powdered creamer and sugar on the vintage wooden cabinet by the side window. A coffee maker, which may have been in that very spot on the metal counter for a few decades, was just starting to growl. The man's brown eyes were friendly but curious as he doffed his cap, which was embroidered with a seed corn company logo, and extended his hand.

"I'm August Kleinsbach, good to meet you." Melinda grasped his hand in a sea of relief and confusion. "Everybody calls me Auggie. I own the co-op."

"Oh, hello ... Auggie ... I don't mean to sound rude, but, well, what are you doing here?"

She didn't know what else to say. "I mean, I saw the co-op was already open when I drove by, and ..."

Auggie reached for a stack of chairs next to the wall and started to arrange them around the cabinet. He was obviously expecting company.

"Didn't Miriam tell you? Oh, sorry Melinda. She's got so much on her mind these days, what with Frank and all." He silently counted the chairs, hesitated, and set out one more. "The guys meet here in the mornings to talk over everything happening in Prosper and the rest of the world. We just let ourselves in."

Melinda started to wonder who else had keys to the store. Why did Frank and Miriam bother to lock up at all?

"I'm in charge of the coffee." He reached in an upper door of the cabinet for some mugs and spoons. "Sometimes we get lucky and one of the guys' wives sends along some cinnamon rolls or cookies. If not, we survive."

"What about the co-op?" It seemed a fair question, as Auggie could only be in one place at one time.

"Oh, Dan, my assistant, runs the shop while I'm here. We wrap up by nine or so. Don't worry, I empty the pot and put everything away. Heard about your job up in the city. That's tough. But you'll land on your feet, I'm sure of it. Folks from Prosper are made of iron, I always say. We always bounce back from anything."

That fact that Melinda wasn't from Prosper didn't seem to matter to Auggie, who was already off on another subject.

"We've got a little less than a month until the big Fourth of July festival. Some of the guys are on the committee, we've got some business to talk over this morning. We're always looking for volunteers, could use some more youngsters in the group. How about you give us a hand? Bet you'd have some great ideas."

Melinda wasn't sure which part to respond to first. She hadn't thought of herself as a "youngster" for many years. And her plate was already full. She hadn't even started her new job yet, and here she was nearly a member of a city planning committee.

But then, it could be fun. "Well, I might ..."

"Hullo!" Two more men popped in from the back of the store. The younger one, around Auggie's age, had a rounded face and graying brown hair. His crisp tee shirt sported the local high school's colors and mascot. He held the door for the older man, who was clad in a bright plaid shirt and spotless overalls and shuffled a bit as he came up the aisle.

"Hey, Jerry and George," Auggie raised his hand in greeting. "Melinda's opening the store today. It's her first day. Where's Doc?"

"He's out on a call, someone's horse is in labor. I'm Jerry Simmons." The younger man shook her hand. "I'm also the mayor of this fair city."

Jerry grinned at the surprise on her face. "As you can maybe guess, it's not a full-time job. Far from it. I was the principal up at the high school before the districts merged. I took the early-retirement buyout and now, I just spend my days helping out the great citizens of Prosper."

"That means he knows all the gossip," broke in the older man as Auggie roared with laughter. "I'm George Freitag. Glad to have you here. Frank will rest easy knowing you're helping out until he's back on his feet."

George squeezed her elbow with a weak grip that showed his age. He had to be at least eighty. "Can't wait to see Bill this morning, tell him about the chicken coop he cut for me. Took me a while, but I finally got it done yesterday."

"Oh, yes, Bill told me he was working on it. Where were your chickens living before?" *I never had this kind of conversation at my last job*, she thought.

"We've got an old shed out back that I had fitted with roosts and egg boxes. But the run wasn't sturdy. It was time to give the girls a better house."

Auggie settled into a chair with a mug. The coffee bar was apparently self-serve. "We should let Melinda get started. She's probably got a to-do list from Miriam."

The three men all looked at her expectantly. For a moment, she thought they wanted her to recite it.

"I just wanted to browse around a bit and get my bearings, maybe sweep the floors. It looked like the plants out front could use a drink."

Jerry stepped forward. "Watering can's under the front counter. Just fill it up in the restroom. I can do it, if you like. Saves you getting the ladder." He tipped his head over at the wooden one propped in the front corner.

"Wow, that would be great. I hope I can just figure out where everything is." Melinda hadn't expected anyone else in the store at this hour, but this was turning into a blessing. She would get all the help she needed, and then some.

"Won't be too hard," Auggie waved her worries away. "Pet supplies are in the second aisle, and that includes some farm animal stuff, too. Big feed bags are in the back, Bill handles those. You've got your groceries and housewares in the third aisle, gardening and seasonal in the fourth row, right there by the register."

He gestured at the refrigerated case behind him. "Perishables in there. Then the aisle on this outside wall, of course, has your hardware stuff, like tools, screws and so on. Clothing and related merchandise on the other side, and back by the stairs."

Melinda was impressed. "Sounds like you know your way around here." Maybe she was making this too hard.

"I worked here during high school, back when your grandpa and grandma still had the store. Then later, I moved over to the co-op. When it came up for grabs I was ready to buy it, thanks to what I learned at Prosper Hardware."

"This store's roots run deep in this area," George reached over to the cabinet's counter and added more powdered creamer to his mug.

He was clearly the elder of the group, and the others turned to listen, intent. "I remember coming here as a boy, especially on Saturdays when everyone came into town to do their shopping. That was a big to-do for me and my brothers and sisters. Back then, there were more stores to browse and people to watch, but my favorite spot was in front of that glass case over there, since it was filled with penny candy."

"Sorry the inventory has changed a bit," Melinda smiled at George, whose face had lit up over his memories. "But we've got some nice prepackaged, processed sugar." She made a grand gesture at the candy bars and sweet snacks that now took up just a portion of the display case inside the long front counter. Those treats were supplemented by packs of gum and small bags of chips.

George adjusted the glasses on his nose and peered over to the case. "You know what, I'll take a Snickers for the road when I leave. Just won't tell Mary, I'm not supposed to be eating that stuff anymore."

"See, Melinda, you've made your first sale." Auggie slapped his knee with his palm. "Nothing to it."

"Good thing you aren't taking delivery until later, George. I don't know how to run the register yet."

"I can help you with that." Bill came in from the back, tying on his tool apron as he walked. "I see you got Jerry watering the hanging baskets. Nice work. He's a master gardener, you know, got a green thumb."

"I may need his help, then. I'm renting the house out at the Schermann brothers' farm, and Horace planted a massive garden. I haven't had time to do more than a walk through and I'm not even sure what some of it is."

Bill didn't seem surprised by this bit of news, and she figured Aunt Miriam had told him all about her living situation. But Auggie and George looked up in shock from their coffee, and Jerry, who had just come back inside, looked like he might drop the watering can.

"You're taking over the farm?" George asked quietly but raised his eyebrows.

Auggie looked as if he wanted to say something, but was so shocked he couldn't get the words out.

"I'm just staying there for the summer, while I help out here," she shrugged and tried to keep her voice casual. This was breaking news. What she said, and how she said it, would be spread around the county by nightfall.

"Horace went up to the nursing home in Elm Springs the other day. Wilbur's roommate moved out." She rounded the counter and made a show of putting her purse on the shelf below and arranging the pens in the little bucket. "Kevin, their nephew, was trying to come up with a way to get Horace to go, too, at least for a while. Horace said he'd only go stay with Wilbur if someone was living at the farm, looking after the animals."

"And his dog," Auggie nodded, seeming to collect his thoughts. "He loves that dog."

"You're going to do it, Melinda?" She couldn't tell if the look on George's face came from shock or admiration.

"I'm going to try. It's only for a few months." She noticed the questions on the men's faces and decided honesty was the best approach.

"I grew up in Swanton and no, I don't have any experience with farm animals. But the chicken and sheep chores aren't much right now. And I'm spending as much time with Hobo as possible." This was directed at Auggie, who at last gave an encouraging nod.

"That's wonderful." Jerry, regaining his ability to move, set the watering can on the counter. "First, you're helping out Frank and Miriam, and now this elderly man."

His expression grew wistful. "I know how hard it can be to get an older relative to give up farming. I went through that with my parents just last year. They were over west of

Chariton and finally moved into a little house there. They love it now, but it was a hard transition."

"Mary and I came to town of our own accord," George lifted the cup balanced on his knee and took a satisfied sip. "But somedays I still drive out by the old place. A young couple bought us out, they're making some nice improvements to the house. I see their kids running around in the yard and I know we did the right thing. Besides," he brightened, "we brought our chickens with us. And Bill, that new coop is great, by the way."

"Glad it all worked out, George." Bill unlocked the register and counted the drawer, writing the total on a tablet that slid underneath. "I'll show Melinda how to run this thing and we'll be ready to open."

She quickly learned Prosper Hardware was either packed and busy, with people lined up at the register, or so quiet there was time to fix displays and just hang out with Esther and Bill. And she never knew what kind of request was going to come her way next.

Early that morning, she helped a woman pick out the right motor oil to mix with gas for her lawnmower. Then a gaggle of little kids rushed in after a special summer story time at the library, jostling each other as they chose candy out of the glass case. One farmer needed some medicine for his cows. It was something the store didn't carry and, after consulting with Bill, she sent the man down to the veterinary clinic. Several people dropped in for eggs and milk, and more came by to purchase lumber for various projects. She'd been glad to hand those customers over to Bill.

Melinda spent her lunch break on one of the iron benches in front of the store. As she sat in the shade of the store's awning, swigging her soda, she was struck by how different this view was from the one she had enjoyed for years from her favorite bench in the park across from WP&S. There, she'd been anonymous and blissfully ignored, able to let her mind wander as the crowds of office workers hurried by. Here, she was getting curious stares but friendly waves.

But she found herself enjoying the view from her bench and watching people come and go. Many of the vehicles in the next block were clustered in front of the Watering Hole. A faint fried smell drifted out each time the bar's front door opened. A handful of people went in and out of City Hall. She couldn't see down the street and around the slight bend to the co-op, but she assumed Auggie's shop was as bustling at noon as it was in the morning. The library seemed silent once story time was over, and she wondered what its hours were. She'd have to get a card and see what it had to offer.

It was hard to tell if the insurance office across from the bar was open. The building's front steps, however, were freshly painted a dark gray and the hanging flowers out front looked robust, as if they were being watered regularly. At the far end of Main, she spied a maroon truck with a metal tackle box parked in front of the veterinary clinic.

Doc must have returned from delivering that horse's foal. She supposed such a call would be routine for the town's longtime vet, but found herself anxiously wanting to know what happened. Maybe Doc would be there for coffee the next morning, and she could find out.

The day passed quickly and with no major upsets. She had just one moment of true panic when a customer rushed in looking for a certain size of lag screw.

Her communication skills served her well as, heart pounding but with a smile on her face, she guided him to the fasteners aisle and made general comments about the inventory, promising herself that she'd memorize the contents of the cubbyholes as soon as possible. It was a relief when the man spotted what he needed and thanked her profusely for her help.

She was really committed to this now, Melinda decided as she waved to the customer as he left the store, a tiny brown sack under his arm and the bells jingling above the door. A little friendliness would take her a long way, and the rest would come with time.

* 10 *

Melinda's legs ached from a long day on her feet, but she felt triumphant as she drove west out of Prosper that afternoon. For the first time in several weeks, she felt useful. She had a purpose, a reason to get up in the morning. She'd helped so many people, guided so many customers to what they needed. She had survived her first day, and she knew she could go back tomorrow and do it again.

But first, it was time for an icy glass of lemonade at the picnic table. As she neared her driveway, the sight of the white farmhouse winking at her through the windbreak made her smile. Even better, Hobo was waiting for her when she pulled up in the yard.

"Hey, Hobo," she patted him on the head as she hauled herself out of the car. "Everything go OK today? Did you keep the sheep in their yard?"

He touched her palm with his nose, but then tried to peer around her into the car, his brown eyes searching.

"I'm sorry, Hobo, he's not here. I don't have Horace with me." She crouched on the gravel and looked into his sad eyes. "But I'm here to take care of you. We're going to have a great summer. And ... I think I know what you might like."

She brightened her tone and Hobo tipped his head at a questioning angle. "Let me check in the kitchen and see if there's anything special in there for you."

A light blinked on the answering machine. It was Mabel, calling to say she was coming over Monday morning to show Melinda how to can strawberries. Angie was coming, too, another neighbor. Melinda wasn't going to be lonely this summer. And she wasn't going to be bored, either.

She poured a glass of lemonade and added some ice, then reached into the cabinet near the stove for the package of dog treats. Hobo was waiting on the steps with just the slightest wag in his tail, as if he knew exactly what she had fetched for him. She shook some of the snacks onto the sidewalk, and Hobo snatched them up. A few happy slurps from his water bowl and he flopped down, content, in the cool dirt under the picnic table.

Melinda sat on the north side of the weathered wood table, which allowed her a sweeping view of the fields stretching past the barn. She glanced at her phone, which she'd brought outside with the intention of going through messages, but didn't feel like scrolling through it just then. She had constantly been on her phone at WP&S, online or texting, "plugged in," as everyone liked to say.

But now, stretching her legs under the picnic table, she thought of how much time and stress had gone into keeping up with every text, every message the moment it came in.

Sitting in a cubicle texting people who were just across the room wasn't really being connected. She'd had more face-to-face conversations during her first day at Prosper Hardware than in probably an entire month at her last job, and had been so engaged in her work that she rarely glanced at her phone.

Many of those conversations were about the weather, or Uncle Frank's health, or which aisle held the cereal. All of them were with strangers, but the friendliness shown by the customers made her feel welcome.

Melinda felt her shoulders relax as she watched the ewes, who were clustered in the front pasture. Some of them seemed to be sniffing around for the freshest, newest grass they could find; others were happy to stuff their faces with whatever was in reach. She leaned over the table's weathered boards and tried to see down the lane to where her dad, Kevin and Horace had mended the fence. It looked sturdy enough to her unskilled eye, but what about the rest of the perimeter?

She should walk the pasture line all around, check for broken wires or gaps that might beckon the sheep to break out. And find tools in the basement she could use to fix fence if she had to. And, of course, ask Ed how to do it.

The chickens were clucking and scratching in their run, picking up grubs and making little inroads in the dirt. Melinda could make out one strutting just inside the screen door. She wondered if that was Pansy, patrolling her turf. How would she ever tell them all apart? Unlike the sheep, the chickens had no ear tags. She had managed so far to distract the hens long enough to pop the eggs out of the nesting boxes, but wondered how long her luck would last.

Kevin said he was trying to get out of Horace a list of people who bought eggs on a regular basis, but didn't have it yet. There weren't too many, Kevin assured her, but she didn't know when the kitchen phone might ring and there'd be someone on the line, wanting to stop by for a dozen or two.

Still thinking about fences and her lack of skills to fix them, she realized the wire panels that made up the chicken yard would need to be checked regularly, too. The last thing she needed was more animals on the loose or a predator getting in.

The chicken coop looked solid but it could use a fresh coat of paint, she decided, smiling as she thought about how cute the little shed would be with some improvements. Of course, the other outbuildings could use paint, too. And the garage, whose boards were a faded, dull white.

She swiveled around to look at the house. Its comforting lines would be even more lovely with a freshening up. Another coat of white paint, maybe some shutters on the windows. A muted green would be nice ...

She rubbed the side of her face. "There's not enough hours in the day, and not enough cash in my wallet for any of that," she said to Hobo, who thumped his tail in the dirt. "Besides, this is really Horace's place. And yours, too."

But there was one task that Kevin had asked her to tackle, and that was the garden. Lemonade in hand, she wandered over to the plot northwest of the house, wondering how she could at least keep Horace's handiwork alive, if not thriving. She found herself tightening her grip on the glass as she evaluated the plot from one side to the other.

It was substantial, maybe three times the size of her parents' garden in Swanton. It was obvious that Horace had poured hours of his time and energy into designing and planting the plot. She could imagine him crouching on the fresh earth, patting his seeds and plants into rod-straight rows, with Hobo right beside him, supervising.

The recycled popsicle sticks on the rows' ends were scrawled with the names of plants that she knew well. There were carrots, onions, potatoes, then several short stretches of pumpkins that made a square patch of their own on the far northeast end. Those wouldn't need much tending.

But then there was a sign for "pole beans" and two rows of sturdy plants that were only a foot high, and no poles in sight. She'd have to ask Kevin about that. Then more than a dozen tomato plants, still short and tender, each clinging to a wire cone. But they were surrounded by round, fence-panel cages that were at least five feet high and two feet across. Surely they wouldn't get that big? What kind of tomatoes were they, anyway? There were no tags to tell her.

Then peppers, and what looked to be a few rows of sweet corn stretching to the sky along the back edge. Next were clusters of plants with elephant-ear leaves that she recognized as rhubarb. Finally, on the western edge of the plot, were the rows of strawberry plants.

They were robust and healthy, just as Mabel had predicted, with heavy clusters of glowing fruits peeking from under their canopy of leaves. She couldn't believe how many strawberries there were, hundreds of them ready to be picked, even though the birds had apparently been enjoying some, too. She noticed a rotting berry in one dirt path, smashed and buzzing with flies, and wondered how many neighborhood raccoons were out here after dark, frolicking in the moonlight as they stuffed their jaws with berries.

How wonderful of Mabel to come over and help harvest these for Horace. Melinda didn't want his hard work to go to waste. She snapped a large strawberry off its stem and took a bite. She was surprised at how sweet it was and ripe all the way through, not like the strawberries in the grocery store that were larger but sometimes lacking in flavor.

"Tastes like summer," she told Hobo, who was sniffing around the water hydrant on the south edge of the patch. There was a snaking pile of green hoses in the garage. She had to get them hooked up and ready. And there were bird feeders in the oak tree by the driveway, their visitors visible from the double window by the kitchen table. She'd need to check for birdseed or stock up at the store.

There was so much to do, so much life at the farm. And more critters that she hadn't met yet. Melinda shuddered as she eyed the barn door that opened into the yard, remembering the thumping and scratching noises that had come from the grain room that morning.

Then she pulled herself up short. Like George said, she had taken on quite a lot, probably more than she could have ever imagined. But she was in charge of this place now. Her job was to live here and look after everything, and everyone, for Horace and Kevin. It would be a long summer if she felt a wave of dread every time she opened the barn door.

Her pulse pounding, she marched up to the back porch, through the kitchen and down into the basement, tugging the light chain with a quick flick of her wrist. A tired broom rested in the corner of the coal room, its worn straws spread out like a hoop skirt. But it would do. She didn't see any rat poison and she was secretly relieved. She didn't want to harm anything, just show them who's boss and send them packing.

Hobo met her at the back porch steps, sensing that something exciting was about to happen.

"Let's do this, Hobo." He ran ahead and was waiting when she reached the barn door and slid the latch open.

As nervous as she was, she knew this was like a scene out of a bad horror movie, the clueless woman armed with only a broom as she stepped into the shadows to face an unseen foe. She had never been squeamish about disposing of a mouse caught in a trap. But these rats would be bigger, more cunning. Maybe the broom wasn't going to be enough. She tugged a length of lumber out from behind the grain barrels, the scraping noise bringing one of the ewes to the open pasture door to check if supper was being served early. Then more of the sheep came across the grass, snuffling and poking their noses around the door frame, like they didn't want to miss what might happen next.

"I'm here to take care of you," Melinda called over to the sheep. Hobo was at attention, staring at the crack in the grain room door, his ears alert. "All of you. Don't you worry, Horace is gone but I'm here."

And I feel ridiculous stomping through the barn with a broom in one hand and a scrap of wood in the other. At least if this ended badly, Hobo and the sheep couldn't spread news of her failure across the township.

Nobody would know. Unless she needed to call for an ambulance. Melinda rolled her eyes. She'd left her phone on the picnic table.

She paused in the aisle, listening. There was a scratching sound in the grain room, then a crunching noise. At least that morning, the critters had been on their way out. Whatever was in there now seemed content enough to stay put. She moved closer, deliberately making her footfalls louder as she approached the door.

"I'm coming in!" she yelled, feeling foolish and frightened. She clenched both the broom and the board in her left hand and put her right palm, fingers shaking, on the ragged door.

Then, a scurrying noise. They were running across the room, away. She took a deep breath and shoved the door in, just in time to see a gray tail disappear through a broken board in the left wall above a shelf filled with metal toolboxes. Two grimy square windows let in only a bit of the late-afternoon sun.

When her eyes adjusted she saw the room's corners were stacked with rusting farm implements. The dented tool boxes on the shelf looked like they'd been opened fairly recently, as they weren't as dusty as the junk in the corners.

Hobo stepped forward to inspect a colorful sack, slashed open from top to bottom, resting in the middle of the floor. He nipped a few bites of its contents and sauntered out of the room. Melinda peered at the label on the side of the bag.

"*Cat food?* Horace seems to like animals, but I can't believe he'd leave food out for the rats."

The rip in the bag was pushed wide and a depression in the kibble showed it was being eaten, and obviously not all by Hobo. The gray tail she'd seen in just one blink, she now recalled, had been sort of fuzzy, not hairless the way a rat's would be.

There was a white sheet of paper on top of one of the tool boxes. She held it up by the window.

Melinda, two cats came here last month. Don't know where from. They don't seem to want names, but one is gray and white and the other orange. Hadn't told Kevin they were here, wasn't sure they would stay. They drink out of the sheep waterer. I put food out 2x a day, and they come when I leave. Left the bag out so they'd get fed until you found them. Horace

"Two cats, gray and orange." Melinda saw claw marks in the weathered wall boards near the ceiling, then another hole. "They come up and down from there, go into the haymow. Or through the back wall into the lambing stalls."

Hobo padded back in and gave her a puzzled look, as if he wondered when she would get on with chores.

"Keeping secrets, huh?" She rubbed his head. "Here I thought you were home alone with the sheep and chickens all day, but you've got two friends." She set the broom and scrap of lumber in a corner. "Guess this broom's just going to be for sweeping, at least for now. Let's see if we can find them."

With Hobo leading the way, they passed through the opening in the wall that divided the barn into north and south sections. The far end had more of the same paned windows that faced east and west, the south sunlight casting a warm glow on the rows of stalls.

She was glad Horace and Wilbur had built those stairs to the haymow years ago, as she couldn't imagine using the crude wall ladder covered with cobwebs in the north part of the barn. The thought of having to swing herself from the ladder to the haymow floor through the adjacent trap door made her dizzy.

Hobo was eager to lead the way to the stairs, then hurried off to sniff the haymow's corners and angles. The faded-summer smell of hay greeted Melinda as she mounted the steps, the brightness of the south end of the barn replaced by this shadowy cavern above. More of the four-paned windows were visible high up on the north and south walls of the haymow, and beams of late-afternoon sun made puddles of light on the floor.

While most of the loft was vacant, there were stacks of rectangular hay bales on the north side of the barn, near the trap door. One corner on the south end held a similar fort of straw, its bright yellow bales glowing in the diffused light. Either pile would be the perfect hiding place for cats.

The thick floor boards were sturdy, probably twelve inches wide, but she had to watch her step. In a few places the boards were cracked or rotten. Here and there were holes just big enough for her foot to slip inside.

"Or for a cat to squeeze through," she said to Hobo, who had circled back to help with the search.

"Here, kitty," she called, walking from one end of the loft to the other, but was met with only silence. They could be tucked behind the bales of straw and hay.

Or, in the time it took her to find her way into the

haymow, the cats could have scooted back through the lambing stalls and slipped out the open pasture door.

They don't seem to want names, Horace's note had said. All she'd seen was one gray tail. That cat had made a break for it the minute it heard her approaching the grain room. It didn't act like it wanted human companionship.

This was one more challenge to add to her list, but Melinda thought she might be up for it.

"Kitties, I will see you later," she cooed to the apparently empty haymow, as Hobo had already padded back down the stairs. "You'll come around. You'll see."

* 11 *

Her first weekend at the farm was going to be full of work. And sticky with strawberry juice. After attending church with her parents in Swanton, Melinda pulled herself away from a relaxing Sunday dinner and headed home to start crossing items off the to-do list given to her by Mabel. She had no idea how to can strawberries, but saw it was going to be quite the assembly line based on Mabel's instructions.

First, she had to clean up three dozen jars, mostly pints but a few quarts. Then there were the metal rings to be scrubbed and rinsed, and quickly rubbed dry so they wouldn't rust. The new lids and the old graniteware canner also had to be washed.

Horace's canning room in the basement was impressive in its size and inventory. There must have been two hundred empty jars crowded on its shelves, along with a few dozen that still held produce from the previous year. The graniteware canner was gathering dust on a spacious metal table whose top was a faded red and pockmarked from decades of use. Next to it was a gas stove that was probably from the 1950s.

She approached the pale green monster cautiously, wiping down its top and front with the same soap and bleach solution she used on the table. The plan was to use the old range to boil and sterilize the empty jars, then transfer them upstairs to be loaded with berries and processed on the kitchen stove, which was modern by comparison. She didn't want to go anywhere near the gas range with a lit match, and decided to let Mabel handle the beast in the basement.

Sunday evening, with Hobo tagging along, she dragged what seemed like every available pot and pan out to the strawberry patch and started picking. She kept at it until it grew so dark she couldn't see to pitch the berries into the pans and was going on touch, her hands covered in juice and the sweet aroma clinging to her hair and clothes. The back porch floor was lined with buckets of berries by the time Melinda, tired but satisfied with her efforts, trudged upstairs to take a shower and collapse into bed.

Monday morning found her sore and slumped in Horace's favorite chair at the kitchen table, staring out at what was yet another fine June day. She'd confidently promised to make lunch for Mabel and Angie but now, as she absentmindedly scratched the mosquito welts on the backs of her hands, she had no idea where to start.

Mabel was bringing one of her famous coconut cakes for dessert, so that was covered. There was some leftover chicken in the refrigerator for sandwiches, and some random vegetables still fresh enough for a pasta salad.

She wished she could gather what she needed from Horace's garden, but it was too early in the season for all but a few varieties of lettuce.

She had always loved to entertain and was known among her city friends for her comfort-food dinners as well as her impromptu cocktail parties. But her simple menu would have to do for today, as would the sorry state of the farmhouse. She had scrubbed the kitchen counters, stove and table already that morning, and washed two kettles and the few remaining serving bowls that could be used to process the strawberries.

But she sighed as she glanced into the dining room. While Kevin's cleaning crew had made the old house sparkle as much as they could, there was no doubt that the wallpaper was faded and the windows could use some new curtains.

Melinda hadn't had time to dust since she'd moved in just a week ago, and some of her totes were still stacked here and there. Not exactly how she'd like to have the house for her first official guests.

"It's not like Mabel hasn't been here before. And Angie is surely wise to the realities of farm living," she reminded herself as she pawed around in the silverware drawer for the largest stirring spoons she could find. She chopped the veggies and shredded the chicken. There was barbecue sauce, plenty of bread and, of course, strawberries. Although she'd probably be tired of looking at them, much less eating them, by the end of the afternoon.

The pasta salad was nearly ready when she heard two short barks from Hobo and a knock at the back door. There was an ancient doorbell on the front porch wall, but it had become obvious that her dad was right. No visitor was going to enter through the front of the house.

"We're here and ready to work," Mabel called as she burst into the kitchen, balancing her purse strap on her forearm as she carried a cake safe with both hands. Melinda had almost expected her neighbor to be in shades of pink to fit the day's theme, but Mabel was in a faded navy tee shirt and worn jeans with sneakers.

A younger woman with copper curls smiled and waved from behind Mabel. She was carrying two canvas bags that looked to have more mixing bowls in them. Melinda was pleasantly surprised to see that Angie was probably in her late twenties. She recalled Ed saying he was glad to have more young people in the neighborhood.

"I'll take that cake." She reached for the round aluminum container in Mabel's arms and set it in the last vacant spot on the counter. "I'm so glad you both could help today. You must be Angie." The younger woman quickly set her bags on a chair and shook Melinda's hand with a firm grip that said she was as no-nonsense as Mabel. Melinda liked her already.

"That's me. Nathan, who's been mowing the lawn here, that's my husband. I was so excited when Mabel said she was coming to help you can strawberries and asked me along," Angie's hazel eyes sparkled. "Our patch is newer, only two years old, and we won't get a whole lot of berries yet. And I wanted to meet you. The whole neighborhood's talking about how you moved down from the city to help Horace out, and to work at the hardware store."

"Why am I not surprised?" Melinda laughed.

Mabel let out a chortle and started to take the mixing bowls from Angie's bags. "You got that right. News travels fast when there's not much news to start with. Anyway, I'd promised Horace I'd get over here and help you with the berries. He and Wilbur have spent years tending that patch, and there's nothing better than home-canned strawberries in the dead of winter."

Angie went back out to the car. "She's getting the extra jars we brought," Mabel eyed the heaping pans of berries that were now set around the kitchen. "Looks like we may need them. You've must have been up half the night picking all these. Thank you for getting that part done. It's going to get hot today, and these old bones aren't so good at crawling around in a strawberry patch."

"I was sort of surprised when you first said that we were going to can the strawberries." Melinda got out small paring knives for stemming berries and set the pasta salad in the refrigerator.

"My mom and I used to get them from Grandma and Grandpa Foster's farm, but we froze them instead."

"Frozen berries are certainly good, and I'm partial to them myself." Mabel started to line up bowls on the kitchen table. "These take more sugar and a little cooking time, and then there's the canning, but Horace loves them this way. It's the way his mother always did them," she said with a smile, "and who are we to tell an old man he has to change?"

Angie appeared in the kitchen door's window, her arms full with a heavy box of jars. "I also brought extra sugar, so we don't run out," she nodded over at one of the canvas bags. "And the lemon juice."

"Lemon juice?" Melinda wrinkled her nose. "Doesn't that make them too sour?"

"Not if you use the right amount of sugar," Angie set the bottle of lemon juice next to the stove. "It adds extra acid, makes sure the strawberries don't spoil."

Mabel patted Angie on the arm. "My mother never used lemon juice in her canned berries, and we all survived. But there's always something new to learn."

"Nathan and I are trying to grow and can as much of our food as possible," Angie told Melinda. "Come August, it'll be nearly an all-day project for weeks, seems like, to get it all done. We farm full time," she said, as if to answer the question Melinda was about to ask.

"We have two little girls, Emma and Allison. Nathan and I met at Iowa State, even though I grew up only about twenty miles from here. Isn't that funny? Anyway, we milk cows and do some field crops, too, mostly corn. So, how are you getting by, Melinda? This must be a big change for you."

"For sure. But I'm looking at this like it's my summer vacation. It's great to be back closer to my parents, who live over in Swanton. And I'm getting plenty of exercise working at the store and looking after the animals and the garden."

"We'll make a farm girl of her yet." Mabel surveyed the kitchen and walked over to the clean jars lined up on the counter. "If you've got any cooking pots left over, I'll get these jars boiling in the basement so they're ready to go."

"You've got a separate canning stove." Angie was impressed. "That will be handy come August."

"Well, Horace has one, but I haven't attempted to light it. Mabel says she not afraid of the thing, so I guess I'm going to let her do the honors."

"No worries, ladies, I have one at home that's similar "Now, if you've got some matches ..."

Melinda reached into the cabinet above the wall-mounted phone and handed the scruffy cardboard box to Mabel. The younger women huddled at the top of the stairs as they heard Mabel cross the pitted concrete floor into the back room.

"Think we're too close in case that stove blows up?" Angie cringed. "I've got a gas one at home, but mine's only three years old, stainless steel."

"I'm not sure anywhere is safe," Melinda muttered, wishing she'd insisted they only use the kitchen stove. "If it explodes, this house will shoot sky high and come back down as nothing but tinder. But in that case, I might as well go, too, rather than have to explain to Kevin why I let a woman in her seventies light a stove that's almost as old as she is. Let's back up, at least."

There was a faint scratch and a quiet "whoosh," then an "a-ha!" from Mabel echoed up from below. She grinned as she topped the stairs, puffing just a bit, whether from excitement or exertion or maybe both.

"We've got heat, girls. I'll fill these pots with water and jars, and then let's get started on those berries." Then she looked at Melinda. "My dear, you don't want to wear *that*."

Her tee shirt and shorts were faded but clean. She noticed then that Angie's pants carried faint splatters of old paint and her knit top had a hole in it near the hem.

"Strawberry juice is nasty to get out once it sets in. You'll want the oldest things you've got," Mabel suggested as she loaded empty jars into a stockpot. "And we'll need newspapers for the table, counters and the floor."

Once Melinda changed and the newspapers were spread over every surface, they set up an informal assembly line. Melinda washed and drained the berries into a clean pan. Angie took the pan to the kitchen table, where Mabel was set up with a paring knife in one hand and a bucket by her feet. With a few flicks of her wrist, Mabel lopped off the tops of the berries and sliced them in half and then half again. The chunks of fruit plopped into another pan on the table.

Once all the berries were washed, Angie and Melinda joined Mabel at the table with their own knives and buckets. Mabel eyed the mounds of sliced berries, calculating their volume, then filled the canner with water and cranked up the electric kitchen stove.

The rings and the new lids were stacked in a small pot of water and put on to heat. Then several cups of berries, their juices already starting to run, were measured into a kettle. When it was half full, sugar and lemon juice were added.

"Melinda, you can stir that until it's just about to boil," Mabel handed her a large spoon. "Once it does, turn it down to medium-low and give it about ten minutes, make sure the sugar is dissolved. We'll get the jars ready."

"I think I can handle that." Melinda took up her place in front of the stove. "We're not adding pectin, right, since this isn't going to be jam?"

"Exactly," Mabel nodded and gave her a wink. Melinda felt her confidence grow. This really wasn't so hard.

"Where can I get an old cookie sheet for these jars?" Mabel asked. Melinda gestured to one of the lower cabinets and Mabel, with some clanging and banging of metal, tugged out a dark-shaded pan that had seen better days. "Wow, Horace must not bake much. But this will do."

The sparkling, sterilized jars, steaming from their bath on the basement range, were lined up on a stack of clean towels on the counter nearest the kitchen stove. Mabel used a funnel to fill the jars with the strawberry mixture while Melinda followed behind and wiped the rims with a damp dishcloth, set the steaming-hot lids on top, and screwed on the metal bands until they gave a little resistance. Angie lifted the rack out of the canner, which was now growling and filled with a rolling boil of water, and used tongs to place the jars in the metal rack. With two thick potholders, she carefully lowered the basket into the canner and set the lid securely on top.

"And now we wait." Angie nodded with satisfaction and set the alarm on her phone. "Let's get another stack of towels ready for when these come out of the canner."

They had two canner loads of pint jars done by noon, stemming and slicing mounds of berries and sterilizing more jars and lids while each batch processed. The jars cooling on the counter's bed of towels started to "ping," announcing their lids had sealed.

"The best sound you can hear on canning day," Mabel told Melinda as they sat down for lunch at the kitchen table. The newspapers were splattered with red stains and Melinda's hands were dotted with bright blotches. Her ragged tee shirt, which she was unconsciously using as an apron, wasn't going to be good for anything other than canning in the future, but she didn't care. The jars on the counter glowed like rubies, proof of the women's hard work.

Angie took a bite of her pasta salad. "What's in this dressing? It's fabulous."

"Well, it's a secret blend of ranch dressing and whatever spices are in the cabinet. Today, that's just salt and pepper and a little celery seed."

"This hits the spot." Mabel wiped her hands on one of the paper towels Melinda had hastily handed out as napkins. "The perfect lunch for canning day. I always say, the day I put up strawberries is the first real day of summer, no matter that the calendar says we've got another week until the solstice."

"We'd better get back at it." Angie gathered the paper plates. "Looks to me like we've got about a week's worth of berries left."

Once the last jars were down in the canner, the women began to wash up the sticky-sweet bowls stacked around the kitchen. It was nearly four o'clock before the mess was cleared away and it was time for some dessert. Melinda put the last of the cooked berries in a bowl in the refrigerator and, just before Mabel and Angie headed for home, they sat down at the cleared kitchen table for slices of Mabel's famous coconut cake, doused with strawberry sauce.

"This cake is amazing," Melinda raved as she scraped the last of the coconut crumbs and berries out of her bowl. "I'll need that recipe, Mabel."

"I'll bring it over soon," Mabel sighed and stretched her legs under the table. "We did great work today, ladies. Just look at all those jars."

"Be sure to load up whatever you want to take home." Melinda waved her spoon at the counter lined with rows of glowing jars. "There's more than enough for Horace and myself to enjoy. But I think when more berries come on, I'll just put them in the chest freezer in the basement."

"Just wait," Angie raised an eyebrow. "Once the canning bug bites, you'll be firing up the stove again in no time."

"Well, actually, I noticed there's a rhubarb patch out there," Melinda said casually, but she was already hooked. Now, every row, every plant in the garden was full of potential. "It crossed my mind that some strawberry-rhubarb jam might be worth a try."

Angie's face lit up. "Just call and I'll come over. We have until June 25th to cut rhubarb this season. Then we need to leave it alone so it grows back next year," she added after seeing Melinda's puzzled look.

"I pull my rhubarb, and pull it by the end of June," Mabel glanced sideways at Angie, then smiled.

"But that's a debate for another day. It's nearly chore time. Melinda, if you're still trying to win over the chickens and sheep, all you have to do is give them those strawberry tops. They'll be your friends for life."

* 12 *

It took a few more days, but Melinda began to settle into her new routine. She still needed an alarm each morning, of course, but one was finally enough. She was up early, seeing every sunrise for the first time in years. Morning chores were followed by dragging the hoses up and down the garden rows, watering the plants on a rotation she designed with Jerry's guidance. Then off to Prosper Hardware, then back to Horace's for a second round of chores and dinner.

But while the garden thrived, so did the weeds. They seemed to sprout up everywhere the moment she turned her back. On many evenings, she donned a battered straw hat she found in the porch closet, pulled on her new floral gardening gloves and went out to battle the invaders. A folded towel helped spare her knees along with her jeans, and an application of bug spray kept at least a few of the pests away.

Pushing a dented metal bucket ahead of her, she crawled up and down the rows while Hobo sniffed the tracks he found in the garden dirt or lounged next to the hydrant. Her back ached and her pretty gloves quickly became dingy, but Melinda didn't care. For the first time since she walked out of WP&S, hugging her cardboard box, she felt a sense of satisfaction about how she spent her days.

Working at Prosper Hardware was more fulfilling than she expected. She had loved her old job and the creativity and camaraderie it offered, but there had been too many hours spent in endless meetings about customer demographics and media trends. But now, she made people's day-to-day lives easier, and she could immediately see the effect her efforts had on customers. Bill and Esther proved to be good friends as well as supportive co-workers, and Melinda found herself looking forward to the gossip around the coffee pot before the store opened.

Hobo was always waiting by the garage to greet her when she came home, but the cats remained aloof. The orange one was fluffier than the gray-and-white one. She was lucky to catch a glimpse of them peering down at her from the rafters at chore time. She bought them a set of sturdy food and water bowls, hoping to win them over. But neither cat would come down to eat until she left the grain room, then the sound of their munching echoed from behind the door while she fed the sheep.

She stuffed the cats' open bag of food in a large trash bag and took it inside the back porch, placing it next to Hobo's kibble. She had yet to meet any rats or raccoons in the barn, and the tracks Hobo traced in the garden were thankfully small, but she didn't want to tempt any unwanted visitors by leaving food unsecured.

The sheep were beginning to trust her, helped along by the coos and tentative forehead scratches she offered along with fresh water and grain. They now answered with an enthusiastic chorus of "baaaas" when she called them to come into the barn. The chickens also learned her voice and no longer rushed for the far corners of the run when she came through their gate. One of the rust-colored hens, however, seemed to be looking for chances to peck at Melinda's legs. She decided that one had to be Pansy, and kept watch out of the corner of her eye for any sudden, darting movements.

There were more eggs than she could eat or give to her parents, and she was thankful when Kevin emailed her a list of Horace's regular buyers. One couple came by the next night and took two dozen off her hands. Kevin said she could keep the money, but these were Horace's chickens and it didn't seem right. She pinched the dollars and coins into a glass jar and set it in the kitchen cabinet above the phone.

Melinda didn't have much free time. But when she did, it was relaxing to sit out at the picnic table or on the front porch swing, watching the fireflies dance across the lawn as the sky deepened into a violet dusk.

When thunderheads puffed up to the west or the humidity drove her inside, she stretched out in Horace's easy chair, surfing his impressive collection of cable channels or reading. Melinda had brought along a few favorite novels and some titles she had yet to begin, but she was curious about the selection at the Prosper Public Library. Her expectations were low, but it surely had more to offer than the dozens of Westerns and thrillers stocked on Horace's shelves.

The library, just across the street from Prosper Hardware, was only open for a few hours Wednesdays through Saturdays during the summer months. Melinda took her first internet bill to work one day so she could stop in on her lunch break to sign up for a card.

The library's picture window illuminated the paneled checkout desk and a small alcove for coats and hats, but left the rest of the space in those cozy shadows that seemed to be reserved for libraries and bookstores. The lights were on, as was a radio behind the counter, but no one was at the desk.

Melinda wandered through the stacks and came upon the children's story time area and what was apparently the media center: a wooden work table topped with two computers. There looked to be a small meeting room in the very back, but the glass window between it and the rest of the library was dark.

"Hello?" Melinda still saw no one else in the library.

"Over here, I'm in here. Sorry, was taking care of some of my other duties," a woman called out from an entryway that opened into the front room of City Hall next door. She popped into the library, adjusting her glasses and shifting a stack of papers from the crook of her right arm to her left.

"You must be Melinda. I'm Nancy Delaney, Prosper city clerk and librarian all rolled into one. Jerry and Miriam told me you were back for the summer. How wonderful that you're able to help out over at the store." She paused, then laughed at the amazed look on Melinda's face.

"We so rarely have anyone new in town," she explained, as Melinda began to laugh, too. "So I guess the odds were overwhelmingly in my favor."

"So glad to meet you." Melinda admired Nancy's stylish, razor-shaped bob. Her dark brown hair was shot through with streaks of gray. "I've been wanting to stop in and get set up with a card."

"Oh, absolutely." Nancy settled in on the high stool behind the polished oak counter. "Great, you've got a piece of mail with your current address, a photo ID ..."

She reached in a drawer for a new library card and activated it with a scanner. "Believe it or not, we only went digital two years ago. I'd love to upgrade those computers in the back, but the budget's nearly nonexistent. However, we do our best to get in the new books, especially fiction." Nancy gestured at a display rack by the front door. "See if there's anything over there that catches your eye."

Fifteen minutes later, Melinda walked out into the sweltering afternoon with her arms wrapped around two books. One was historical fiction from Nancy's display of recent arrivals. The other was an aged title on the basics of gardening discovered on a back shelf. As she crossed Main Street, Melinda once again felt that exhilaration she'd experienced as a child visiting the library in Swanton. Books could take you anywhere you wanted to go, and she couldn't wait to get home and turn those first pages.

"Nancy keeps this city running," Jerry told her the next morning as they were preparing for the coffee group's arrival. Auggie was out of town, so Jerry nominated himself as the set-up and tear-down committee.

"She's the city's only full-time employee. Handles the accounts and the bills. Takes minutes at the council meetings.

Oversees the library, with the help of a part-timer and a group of volunteers. We've got probably ten years before she'll retire, thankfully. It'll take that long to find a replacement."

Melinda did the math and guessed that Nancy was in her mid-fifties. "I found her friendly and super sharp. I can certainly see her being capable enough to keep all the plates spinning."

The back door creaked and John Ogden came in, offering Jerry and Melinda a tired wave. Prosper's only veterinarian carefully rubbed the soles of his work boots on the floor mat before ambling up the aisle. He sighed and lowered himself into a chair then removed his navy cap, the gray of his stubble-short hair seemingly at odds with his wiry, strong frame. Doc, as everybody knew him for miles around, looked like he'd been up for several hours already.

"We were lucky to hire Nancy, back when I was on the council," Doc said. "She'd been down in Des Moines, wanted to move back closer to her family in Hampton after her divorce, have the kids near the grandparents. She had the right degree and didn't balk at obtaining her library certification after our longtime librarian retired a few years back." Doc yawned and gratefully accepted the steaming mug handed across by Jerry.

"Late night or early morning?" Jerry asked.

"Got an emergency call at four-thirty, of all hours," Doc muttered. "Cow had her head stuck in a fence, must have been there for quite a few hours last night. Just a few minor lacerations, didn't need stitches. Took us longer to get her untangled than treat her wounds. I'm starving but there's not time to run home before my first office call at eight. Melinda, are there any packaged muffins back in the grocery aisle?"

"Sorry," she checked the row but shook her head. "Got some granola bars, though."

"That'll do. Here," Doc fished a five out of his wallet. "Many thanks."

There had been snacks at only one of the coffee gatherings in the two weeks Melinda had worked at Prosper

Hardware, but she hoped to become a regular contributor. Angie was coming over that weekend to show her how to make strawberry-rhubarb jam, and she planned to bring in a jar next week for George's birthday. The preserves would be perfect slathered on some fresh baking-powder biscuits.

She didn't want to get her hopes up about the jam. She had Grandma Foster's biscuit recipe down, but her first attempt at using rhubarb had been anything but sweet.

First, there was the dilemma about whether to cut or pull the stalks. Melinda wasn't sure if she should follow Angie's or Mabel's advice, so she did a little of both. The rhubarb pie recipes she found online seemed easy enough, but the amount of sugar they called for made her gasp. Surely she could ease up on it and the pie would still be good. Her parents were coming over for dinner, and they were trying to eat healthy.

The crust browned beautifully and she was proud to set the pie on the dining room table, but the looks on Roger and Diane's faces as they took their first bites told the truth. She forked into her own slice, determined to give it a try. The sharp, bitter taste brought on a coughing fit that had her reaching for her water glass. Even worse, the filling was what could only be described as gooey yet crunchy. Horace's oven apparently ran overly hot, and the bottom crust had burnt before the rhubarb cooked through.

Trying to salvage even a little of her efforts, Melinda dumped the pie into a bowl, rinsed off the rhubarb pieces and carried them out to the chickens. The hens took only a few pecks before they shook their feathers and strutted off with indignant clucks, leaving her hard work in the dirt.

The strawberry-rhubarb jam, however, was a success, thanks to Angie's expertise. Melinda was so pleased with the results that she vowed to make another batch on her own before the rhubarb season came to an end. The afternoon also gave the women a chance to get to know each other better.

Melinda found herself in awe of Angie's kitchen skills and was impressed by the goal she and Nathan had to add an organic vegetable delivery service to their farming operation.

Angie in turn was fascinated and entertained by Melinda's stories about her life in the Twin Cities.

The morning of George's birthday, Melinda hurried to make sure she was the first one to arrive at Prosper Hardware. She arranged the jam and a platter of biscuits on the sideboard, setting out napkins, small plates and plastic knives. Then she began to tidy the store as usual, picking up where Esther had left off the evening before.

She was sorting the display of nails and screws when she heard mumbled conversation and then the squeak of the back door. It was George and Doc. She just called out a "hello" and continued with her work, waiting to see their reaction.

"What's all this?" George stopped, his eyes growing wide.

"I heard somebody is turning eighty-two today," Melinda said. "And I don't think it's Doc."

"Are you sure it's not Auggie?" George laughed, but she could tell he was pleased. "Those biscuits look wonderful. You made them yourself?"

"I like to bake now and then," she offered, setting down a pack of nails and joining the men at the sideboard. "Now that I've been here a few weeks, I promise to start contributing to the morning snacks once in a while. Have a seat, guest of honor. I'll get your coffee. Lots of creamer, right?"

"I'll make you up a plate, George," Doc said, slicing a biscuit and piling the halves with preserves. "Is this homemade jam?"

Melinda tried to keep her grin in check, her voice casual. "Just made it the other day, strawberry-rhubarb. That's just some of the leftovers I had in the fridge."

"Well, I think I speak for the others when I say we'll be happy to sample anything you want to bring in," Doc said, passing George his share and then getting his own biscuit and coffee. Melinda went through the line next, then Auggie arrived with Jerry right behind him. It wasn't long before only one biscuit remained on the platter.

"Bill's lucky he'll be here soon, if he wants any." Jerry wiped the crumbs off his hands. "I haven't had strawberry-rhubarb jam in years, it's not something you can get off the shelf at a store. Actually," he turned to Melinda, "I know you're busy, but I've got a favor to ask."

"Sure, I'll try. Your expertise has helped me keep Horace's garden going. What is it?"

"Well, you know the Fourth of July festival's coming up and it's the biggest event of the year. Most of the plans are done, but we need help getting the word out. Nancy and I were talking about it yesterday, and she's swamped."

He hesitated for a moment. "Might you be able to put together a press release? Our city website isn't much to speak of, but the info could go there, too. Maybe you'd have some new ideas to get the word out?"

She might as well say yes. Auggie had mentioned the festival planning committee on her first day at the store, and she'd forgotten all about it.

It was clear her friends wanted her input, and her mind was already running ahead to all the possibilities.

"Sure, why not?"

"You know, I could use a little help, too," Doc ventured. "Now, this you'd get paid for."

Jerry started to chuckle. "No, I'm serious," Doc said. "I always drive my truck in the Fourth of July parade. I've been meaning to get some new signs made up for it. My son was going to do it, but he's busy with baseball right now. What do you say?"

Before she could respond, Bill came in from the back.

"That reminds me. We need to do something for the parade, even if it's just a vehicle with signs, like Doc. Miriam and Frank always handle that and with everything going on, I just thought of it now. And we'll want to have special store hours during the festival, maybe offer something to draw people in to shop."

Melinda sighed but found herself smiling. "Oh, dear. Doc, let me know what your ideas are about the signs. Bill, let's talk to Esther when she comes in at noon. And Jerry, I guess you'll see me at the next committee meeting. When is it?"

That's how, two nights later, she hurried home from the store to do chores and gulp down some leftovers. Hobo was puzzled when he saw her rush out again.

"Don't wait up," she called over to him. "I may be home late." *So much for the quiet country life,* she thought as she backed around the car and headed down the driveway.

* 13 *

Property owners along Main Street unfurled flags and set out patriotic decorations in the days before Prosper's Fourth of July festival. The hanging baskets in the tiny business district were in full bloom, and a group of volunteers scrubbed the park benches resting up and down the sidewalks.

While an air of excitement and anticipation spread throughout the town, a range of emotions filled Frank and Miriam Lange's Victorian house on Cherry Street. The family was thankful Frank was finally able to come home, which allowed Miriam to drop her daily seventy-mile round trip to Mason City. She was now able to come by the store a few times a week to settle the books, but Frank couldn't be left alone for long.

At least, that's what Miriam said. Frank disagreed.

"I'm supposed to rest, but I don't need to be hovered over twenty-four-seven," he grumbled to Melinda one night when she stopped by their home with a hamburger casserole and a large container of fresh-picked strawberries. "I've read every magazine in the house and all the puzzles have been put together at least once. Thank goodness there's plenty of baseball on TV."

Uncle Frank was pale but despite his complaints, he was glad to be home. His doctors warned Frank he wouldn't be returning to work anytime soon, a directive that had him discouraged and grumpy. Prosper Hardware would push him to spend too many hours on his feet and provide too much stress for someone recovering from heart surgery.

"Am I glad you're here," Miriam whispered to Melinda as she washed the berries in a colander at the kitchen sink. "Frank's driving me crazy because there's so little that he can do. That man's worked ten hours a day since high school, first at that grocery over in Swanton and then at Prosper Hardware once we were married."

Miriam flicked her paring knife in swift strokes as she sliced the berries. "That store is his life; mine, too. I miss it. I miss the people and the comings and goings and hearing all the news."

"Well, don't worry. I'll keep you updated on all the gossip," Melinda wedged her casserole into the refrigerator. From the look of its cramped shelves, Frank and Miriam wouldn't run out of donated meals for quite some time.

"Bill and Esther have taught me what I need to know, and they handle the rest. Maybe you could arrange for some of Frank's buddies to come by when you need to get out for an hour or two? You'll need to find some way to let off steam. When we have a crazy day at the store, I go home and pull weeds in Horace's garden. But then, even when we don't have a crazy day, I still have to pull weeds."

Miriam gave a short laugh, then sighed.

"I'll take your help as long as I can get it. I'm starting to think Frank may never be able to go back to work, at least not full time. But I don't know how he'd ever accept retirement, especially since I'm nowhere near ready to hand the store over to anyone else, I'm only sixty-three. What will Frank do with himself if he can't run Prosper Hardware?"

Then Aunt Miriam answered her own question. "He'll drive me nuts, that's what he'll do."

Melinda saw her chance to bring up an idea that she, Bill and Esther had been discussing for a few days now. The two-day festival would bring visitors from miles around, and the more that came into Prosper Hardware, the better. Along with special discounts on certain merchandise, they had come up with the idea of hosting an open house.

"Aunt Miriam," she began hesitantly, "what if Frank could come back to the store, if only for a few hours? It would boost his spirits and give him a chance to personally thank people for all their support."

Miriam blinked but didn't immediately shoot the idea down, so Melinda plunged forward.

"Bill and Esther and I were thinking it would be great to have Frank there on the Fourth of July, as sort of a 'welcome home' celebration. We'd make him a comfortable spot by the register, bring in some lemonade and cookies. Nothing too extravagant. We know Frank wouldn't want to feel like some kind of sideshow act."

"I think he'd go with a circus theme if it gave him a chance to set foot in the store." Miriam considered for a moment, then nodded. "I love that idea. We were just talking last night about how much it's meant to both of us that people have called, or sent flowers, or brought food. The refrigerator's full, as you can see, and there's more baked goods coming in every day."

Miriam got comfortable in one of the chairs, motioning for Melinda to take the opposite one. "I'm sure you've got this all worked out in your head. Let's hear the plan."

She was right, of course. Melinda's mind had been working overtime since she joined the festival committee.

"I think we'd run a short 'thank you' item in the newspapers, and include the time and date for the open house." She ticked the fine points off on her fingers.

"Maybe plan it for the two hours immediately following the parade, when the most people will be in town. Bill's going to put the signs from last year on his truck for the parade, and we can make something simple to attach to them reminding people about the open house. We could make a large card from poster board and have everyone sign it for Frank."

It was hard for Melinda to contain her excitement about the festival, now that she had joined the planning committee.

Most of the events were the same year to year, but she had discovered that promoting the celebration was where committee members felt they were falling short. It was a perfect fit for her skills.

"Did you know that Jerry started a Facebook page for the city two years ago? No one has had time to work on it, so it's been just sitting there. I'll be posting items about the festival there and also on the city's website. The press release about the celebration goes out in a few days. I'd include the store's open house in that, just like all the other activities in town. What do you think?"

Aunt Miriam's answer came in the form of a big hug.

"I think I've got the best niece anyone could ask for. Frank was really down the other day when the doctors said he couldn't ride in the back of Bill's truck in the parade. It'll be too hot and humid. But this way, Frank can still meet with people for a few hours, inside where it's cool. I'll get busy making cookies and will get the lemonade, too."

"And I've got more news."

Aunt Miriam rubbed her temple but tried to smile. "It's not a job offer already, is it? Because I'd hate for you to have to go back so soon. I mean, I know that is your home now ..."

"It's not that," Melinda shrugged. "I've been looking, but there's just not that much out there to apply for, anything I'd really want. Besides, my subletter isn't moving out until the third week of August." She saw her aunt's shoulders relax.

"My news is that Cassie and Susan are coming down for the weekend, the one after the Fourth of July. Kevin said if I wanted to take on any painting projects, he'd provide the supplies. I know it's not my house, but the living room and kitchen are in desperate need and I'm itching to take it on."

"I'm so glad your friends can come for a visit." Miriam selected a covered dish from the refrigerator and set the oven to preheat. "Prosper will be a big change from what they're used to."

While Melinda was excited to see Cassie and Susan again, she felt a little nervous about their visit. "Cassie is a city girl through and through, but at least Susan is from a small town in western Iowa. She'll feel more at home than Cassie will."

"Well, I'm sure you girls will have a great time. You deserve a break, honey, even if it includes painting someone else's kitchen." Miriam winked, then reached for a divided container on the kitchen counter. "Well, I better get these pills in to Frank."

Melinda busied herself cutting slices of angel food cake for supper, her mind on her friends' upcoming visit. Susan and Cassie wouldn't turn their noses up at the weathered farmhouse or mock the deepening "farmer's tan" on her forearms. Both of them had been so supportive of her "adventure," as Cassie loved to call it.

So, what was it, then? Melinda paused with the serrated knife in her hand.

She was the one who was changing. She hadn't been away from Minneapolis for quite a month yet, but it felt like much longer. Her old job and her former life there seemed distant, and not just because they were a three hours' drive away. Would she feel as close to her friends as she had before?

She missed Minneapolis, of course. But she had to admit she was happy here, more content than she expected to be. She found herself coming in the back door of Prosper Hardware in the mornings with a sense of happy anticipation, wondering who she might meet that day and what funny or odd request would come from a customer.

While she had a circle of close friends in the city, she now realized she really didn't know that many people. Here, everyone was connected somehow.

Melinda was even more surprised by how much she enjoyed caring for Horace's menagerie. Watching the sheep graze in the pasture and the chickens waddle about brightened her day. The cats were a challenge, but a rewarding one. And then there was Hobo. She still sometimes found him sitting at the end of the driveway in the evening dusk, watching for Horace. She would drop everything and go down the lane to sit with him for a while, wrap her arm around his plush brown fur and scratch his ears. But the other night, he had astonished her by joining her for a walk up to the creek bridge. She couldn't imagine Horace had roamed very far, but she was honored to be Hobo's substitute walking buddy and told him so.

"It'll be interesting to see how Hobo reacts to having company," Melinda said as Miriam came back into the kitchen with an empty water glass in her hand and a grim look on her face. Frank hated taking his medicine and made sure everyone knew it. "I'll need to put fresh sheets on Horace's bed downstairs and tidy up Wilbur's old bedroom upstairs, too, and make up that bed."

"Well, you girls could just make a regular slumber party of it," Miriam said as she put the casserole in the oven. "Spread out downstairs, sleep on the floor in the living room. That'd be fun."

"Oh, I don't know about that." Melinda laughed, knowing that in some ways, she would always seem young to Aunt Miriam. "I'm stiff enough from pulling all those weeds in the garden and being on my feet all day at the store. A soft bed's what I require, and Susan and Cassie, too. Especially since I plan to put them to work painting."

"Well, I've got more work coming, too." Aunt Miriam smiled and reached for the stack of cookbooks resting on a high shelf. "This open house is going to take more cookies than will probably fit on the counters of this kitchen. But the fun question is, what kinds should I make?"

* 14 *

The Fourth of July dawned warm and muggy, and Melinda feared the skies might literally rain on Prosper's parade.

She couldn't believe how many people were already in town when she drove in just before seven. Main Street's parking spaces were roped off as part of the parade route, but the elementary school's parking lot and the side streets' curbs were rapidly filling with vehicles.

As she angled into a lucky parking spot just down from the veterinary clinic, she was filled with excitement and a little trepidation. Her family had been coming to the Prosper Fourth of July celebration for decades, and it remained one of her fondest childhood memories. Since she moved away for college and a career, she had missed some of the annual festivals, instead choosing to attend a balcony cookout or a backyard celebration in the city. She hadn't been to the festival in more than five years and wondered if it would feel different, now that she was ...

"What am I, exactly?" She put the car in park, the sun already beating hot and steady through the windshield. "A resident? Not really. An employee? Yes, but only temporarily. A local? Well, I guess I am, for now."

Doc appeared from behind his freshly waxed maroon truck, wearing a maroon-and-white "Prosper Vet Svcs" jersey. "He's really taken my marketing advice to heart," Melinda marveled as she returned Doc's wave. Just last night, she had finished painting the plywood signs to hang on his truck. It had been only been a few hours of work but her little project had gone well, and she again had that feeling of accomplishment when a request came together for a client.

Doc rubbed his hands together and peered expectantly into the back of her hatchback. "It'll be hot this afternoon, no doubt, but the rain should hold off until tomorrow. At least, that's what Auggie says."

The Prosper co-op had served as an official weather station for more than seventy years, a series of gadgets mounted on a wide ledge outside one of the office windows. The company's storage room held temperature and precipitation logs going back even further, to the early 1900s. Auggie had proudly taken on those duties when he purchased the business decades ago, and enjoyed sharing his forecasts with anyone who would listen.

"Let's hope Auggie is right." Melinda reached in for the signs. "You know this is an important day when the coffee klatch is canceled."

Doc laughed, then whistled. "Well, look at these. I'd say they were worth every penny. By the way, I've got your check in the office."

She circled for a few minutes to find a parking spot closer to Prosper Hardware. The sweet, yeasty smell of the pancake grill set up in the Prosper Methodist Church parking lot followed her to the store's back door.

"I got extra ones from the bank over in Swanton yesterday. Today's always the highest volume day of the year," Bill called over his shoulder as he set up a folding table for the open house.

They planned to serve Miriam's cookies, waiting in plastic containers in the back room, from the sideboard's counter, and put the lemonade and ice water on the table. Miriam was bringing a padded folding chair from home for Frank.

"How did it go last night?" Melinda asked as she set her purse behind the counter. Prosper Hardware had remained open until eight on the first day of the festival. She had stayed until five, and Bill, who had come in later than usual yesterday morning, helped Esther close.

"Crazy busy. Couldn't believe it was a Thursday. Most of the activities didn't start until six or so, like the softball games over at the school field, but it was crowded in here the whole time. I hear the food vendors over at the city park were pleased with their sales last night. The beer tent was packed, and the band played until midnight."

Parade watchers were already lining up their lawn chairs along Main Street. Some of the seats were empty, but Melinda knew their owners had staked out prime places before walking over to the pancake breakfast. Seating was first-come, first-served, but no one would be rude enough to shove anyone else's chair out of the way. Latecomers would settle for sitting on the curb or standing behind the chairs.

Her parents were going to the pancake breakfast before coming to Prosper Hardware. Diane thought they should stake out a spot in front of the store with their chairs, but Roger cautioned that plan could backfire.

"You know that's a prime spot, honey," he had said the other night when Melinda was at their house for dinner. "Might look like favoritism, being that your family owns the store and all. Could rub someone the wrong way."

"I get that everyone knows Mom," Melinda had said, "but does everyone recognize your lawn chairs, too? It is that serious of an offense?"

Diane had sighed and patted Roger's hand. "Let's just plan to watch the parade from the doorway of the store, just to keep the peace. Besides, Miriam will need our help setting up for the open house."

Melinda spent the next hour straightening displays and polishing the counter. The flower baskets had received an extra soaking yesterday afternoon, as there would be too much congestion out front this morning to wrangle the ladder and watering can along the sidewalk. Bill double-checked the restroom was clean and stocked then stationed himself upfront to help customers, as Melinda would be busy working the register. A steady stream of people came through once the store opened, many of them purchasing sodas and snacks.

While Bill took a turn behind the counter, Melinda filled a bucket with small American flags on sticks to hand out in front of the store. She'd been inspired to place an order when a merchandising catalog turned up in the store's post office box. The flag's wooden poles were flat, more like popsicle sticks than dowels, and for a small fee she'd been able to have "Prosper Hardware" printed on one side.

She toted the galvanized tub out the front door and began offering the flags to passerby, reminding them to stop at the open house after the parade. Most of the adults were dragging lawn chairs, coolers and children, and accepted the flags with at least a polite smile. It was the kids, however, who really appreciated the tokens. Already in overdrive from the day's building excitement, they whipped the little flags in the air, whooping and shouting. Hundreds of people were starting to jam the sidewalk up and down Main Street, and the supply of flags was rapidly being depleted. Melinda decided to switch tactics and offer the flags only to the littlest revelers.

"That was fast," Miriam came in from the back, wearing a red-and-blue tee shirt and grinning from ear to ear, just as Melinda brought the empty bucket inside. She could see how being at the store energized her aunt.

"I had no idea how many to order. I got us a hundred, and they're gone already."

She pushed the bucket behind the counter. "Just look at all these people. I remember when I was a kid, how huge the crowd was. I've been thinking that maybe everything just seemed larger because I was younger then. But the sidewalks are just packed. And here comes Mom."

Diane fanned herself as she came in the front door. Melinda suspected her dad was still over at the church breakfast, helping himself to the last of the pancakes.

"No one has a good count, but I know Jerry always estimates at least a couple thousand people attend the parade every year," Diane said, checking her watch. "And they'll be starting any minute now."

It wasn't long before the blare of a fire truck siren echoed down Main Street, causing the revelers to glance away from their conversations with friends and neighbors and hurry to their seats. The giddy anticipation of the crowd was infectious, and Melinda hurried out to stand in the shade of the store's awning and peer down toward the co-op. The parade route started and ended at the elementary school, with the procession following Oak to First, then turning on Main. Once they reached the corner by Doc's office, the entries would turn on Fourth and back to the school's parking lot.

"Here they come!" shouted a little boy in front of the store, his mother grabbing the back of his shirt as he tried to leap out to the curb.

Members of the local veterans' organization started off the parade, stepping smartly in their pressed uniforms as the flags in their hands listed in the humid air. Then Prosper's one fire truck came into view, lights whirling and siren blaring. It had been waxed and polished until its chrome threw off blinding glints from the late-morning sun.

Parades were an opportunity for small town emergency crews from miles around to show off their vehicles and gear, and it was tradition for the hosting community's rig to lead the way. Crew members toting cherry-red buckets dropped candy into the hands of the eager children along the street.

Close behind came Jerry, nearly unrecognizable in a pressed button-down shirt, riding in a convertible and waving to the crowd. He gave Melinda a thumbs-up and she waved back. Then the notes of the National Anthem drifted up Main Street, and parade watchers scrambled out of their lawn chairs and removed their hats. Members of the local high school's marching band, wearing black shorts and purple tee shirts, came into view.

Marching bands from three other schools were also in the lineup, along with entries from dozens of businesses and community groups. Some participants simply walked the parade route, carrying signs or banners and waving to the crowd. Others had spent countless hours building floats and polishing their vehicles. Doc pulled by in his veterinary truck, the metal tackle box in the back gleaming and the signs Melinda had painted tied to each side. He tooted his horn when he approached the store.

Members of Swanton's Jaycees handed out even more candy to the children. The crowd roared as a group of Shriners circled their motorcycles in an intricate maneuver in the street. A local trail club, the horses flashing patriotic ribbons in their manes and tails, high-stepped down the parade route. A dozen elementary-school kids in patriotic costumes, with their parents walking along behind, piloted their big wheels in random patterns.

The procession lasted nearly forty-five minutes, longer than Melinda expected. She smiled as she went back into the store to make the final preparations for the open house. So many times as an adult, the anticipation of revisiting something from childhood outweighed the actual event. It just wasn't the same, or as great as one remembered. But it was now obvious that the Fourth of July in Prosper was still as special as when she was a little girl.

Miriam had ducked out before the end of the parade to drive the few blocks home and bring Frank over for the open house. Soon Bill and Frank were coming up the aisle from the back, with Frank determined to move under his own, slow power and Bill trying to act as if he wasn't serving as a medical escort.

"Miriam's parking the car. It's the one day of the year where parking's at a premium in this town," Uncle Frank told Melinda. "Almost felt like I ought to knock at the back door on the way in. Haven't been here for a month. Don't think that's happened in all the years we've run the store."

Frank was decked out in a red-and-blue plaid shirt and khakis, with his gray hair combed across to stubbornly cover his receding hairline. He looked happy, but rather pale. Melinda was concerned, but reminded herself that this was probably the most strenuous activity he had attempted in weeks. He just needed to regain his strength.

"Let me help you." She met Frank and Bill at the far end of the counter and offered her arm, a gesture which Frank pretended to wave away then gratefully accepted.

"Forgot how long of a walk it is from the back lot to the front of the store," he said, a little out of breath as he sank into the padded stool set by the counter. Bill came down from the upstairs office with a glass of ice water and a coaster.

"Thanks, Bill and Melinda," Frank wiped his brow and leaned his arm on the oak counter. Melinda thought she saw a few tears in his eyes. "Oh, it feels so good to be back. You don't know how I've missed this place."

Frank took a grateful gulp of the water. "How was the parade? Jerry was at the front I suppose, waving like the president." Uncle Frank and Jerry had been friends for decades, but Aunt Miriam told Melinda there was always an air of competition between them that she had never quite figured out.

"Yes, he was master of ceremonies, as always," Melinda said, then changed the topic. "Now, anything else you need?"

"The pork producers are firing up those grills over in the city park. That wonderful smell hit me as I got out of the car."

He leaned in close. "How about one of you run over there and get me a tenderloin or two? Pickles and mustard, hold the ketchup."

"Very funny, Frank." Bill started for the front of the store, when two more customers had just wandered in. "Miriam already told me all about it. You're not supposed to have any fried food. I don't know how you are going to make it, but you're supposed to be eating healthy from now on."

"Oh, come on," Frank whispered to Melinda, glancing to the back of the store. "It'll take her a while to find a parking spot with that crowd. You can run out quick and be back before she notices, just hide it upstairs for now ..."

"It's getting steamy out there," Miriam said as she came in from the back, a thin sheen of sweat on her forehead.

"I'm parked at the end of Third, practically in the corn field on the edge of town. Melinda and Diane, would you bring the cookies up from the back? I left them on the cutting table when I dropped Frank off."

She turned to her husband, worry on her face. "I see you made it up here by yourself. I hated to just dump and run, honey, but we've got to hurry."

Before he could answer, she gave him a knowing smile. "And I've got a nice grilled chicken salad in the cooler for our lunch. Wouldn't hurt me to drop a few pounds, too." She turned to Diane and Melinda and lowered her voice. "I can always run out and grab something else later on, maybe a funnel cake ..."

"I heard that!" Frank turned and widened his eyes at his wife. "I've got a feeble heart these days, but I'm not deaf."

Miriam must have packed cookies into every food container she owned, Melinda decided as they brought the packages up from the back room. There were peanut butter cookies with chocolate stars, sugar cookies with patriotic icing, then chocolate chip, oatmeal, and more.

Frank put a hand on her arm as she came by, then snapped open the lid on a stack of M&M and walnut cookies. "I'll take one of those, thanks." He winked at Melinda, who started to give him a warning.

"Oh, no worries," he said. "These are baked, not fried. Miriam never needs to know."

"The store looks great, Melinda." Diane arranged pitchers of lemonade, dripping with condensation, on the folding table by the vintage cabinet, whose counter was loaded with cookies. Melinda had blanketed both surfaces with patriotic tablecloths and draped some bunting over the top of both the front windows.

"Thanks, Mom. It's just sort of tossed together, but it will work. Besides, Frank is the real attraction. He seems overjoyed to be back here, if only for a few hours." Frank had a dreamy smile on his face as he nibbled at his cookie while Miriam was out of sight, running an errand upstairs.

"He's been down, stuck at home for a month," Diane said. "Maybe if this goes well, he'll feel more comfortable getting out and about. Just because he can't work behind the counter at the store, doesn't mean he has to stay at home all the time."

The bell above the front door jingled and an elderly couple came in. The woman gave Frank a hug, and the man clapped him on the shoulder.

"This was the right thing to do," Miriam said to Diane and Melinda before heading over to greet the couple. "Look at his face. This will really boost his spirits."

It didn't take long for the aisles of Prosper Hardware to fill with people. Not only did all of them want to see Frank, but they were willing to stand in line to get their few moments with the guest of honor. Both Frank and Miriam glowed as they chatted with old friends, neighbors, and longtime customers. Many of the visitors seemed to know each other, and they were shaking hands and catching up while they waited their turn.

Diane went to the refrigerator upstairs for more jugs of lemonade and water as Melinda tried to keep the cups full. Bill ran the register and Roger bagged purchases. Esther, who had just arrived, went to work stacking more cookies on trays.

"Melinda!" A woman's voice caused her to look up from the cups she was filing. "So good to see you!"

She turned to see a woman about her age with short brown hair and a friendly face. There was a boy holding her right hand and a little girl on her left. Melinda smiled, stalling. She couldn't put a name with the face. Who was this?

"I'm Jen Fuller. Well, Jen Collins these days." The woman nodded at her kids. "We were in debate together, remember? Junior year, when we did that radio play at state?"

"Oh, yes, of course. How are you? It's so good to see you." Melinda grinned, hoping she sounded enthusiastic enough. She felt a pang of guilt that, even with those clues, she only vaguely remembered Jen.

Actually, she had been a senior when Jen was a junior, so she wasn't in Melinda's class. Even so, shouldn't she remember someone she was in an activity with in high school? But it seemed so long ago.

"I'm great, wonderful, actually. Working as a nurse up at the hospital in Mason City. Wasn't in Frank's wing, though, when he was there last month, so didn't see any of you then."

Jen took two cookies off a tray, gave one to each of her children. "My husband, Steve, and I live here in Prosper, over by the school. He's a sheriff's deputy, works for the county. How's Minneapolis? I heard you're working in public relations. That must be so exciting."

Melinda was taken aback for a second. News spread fast around here, but not to everyone. Of course, Jen wouldn't have known. She could answer honestly, or she could keep the celebratory vibe going with an evasion or two.

"Oh, it is." She handed a glass of lemonade to the girl, who paid her back with a shy smile. "Well, I'm more in marketing, actually. But yes, it's wonderful. Very creative."

"Well, I'm so glad you were able to get away long enough for the holiday weekend. I'm sure it means a lot to your family to have you here." Jen took a second lemonade for her son. "We're off to the carnival in the park. It was good to see you!"

"You too, Jen, have a great time!" She waved as Jen ushered her children to the door.

Melinda automatically passed out cups of lemonade to more visitors, but her mind kept wandering back to her conversation with Jen.

She'd always prided herself on being direct, on not sugarcoating things. But life had been easier before, or at least it seemed that way compared to what had happened in the last two months.

Other times when she returned home and ran into someone she knew, it had been easy to respond. She'd been proud of her job, her independence, her life in Minneapolis. Maybe she wasn't married yet, and she didn't have kids, two things people back home always asked about.

But she'd had her career to fall back on in those conversations, and talk of what she was doing professionally often brought smiles of admiration and interest from people around here. It had been enough.

But now ... what did she have? Her brow furrowed as she filed more glasses and handed them out with a smile plastered on her face.

Yes, she had her family and friends, a place to live. Two places, if she counted her apartment and Horace's farm. But she felt vulnerable, unsure about her future. She had been so busy preparing for the open house that she hadn't considered the possibility of running into someone she knew, that someone might start asking questions. And she no longer had an easy, cheerful answer to give them.

* 15 *

"Well, I sort of lied to a bunch of people today," Melinda told Angie that evening as they sat on a curb across from the park.

There was a freshly grilled burger in one of her hands, and an iced tea in the other, so things were looking a little better. She had hurried home after work to get chores done in record time, squeezed in a fifteen-minute nap before she showered, changed into a clean blouse, shorts and sandals, and headed back to Prosper.

"So what happened?" Angie was trying to keep her bratwurst's juices in the bun, rather than on her hands.

They were waiting for Nathan, who was taking the girls over to his parents' for the evening, giving the young couple a much-needed night out. Angie had insisted Melinda come with them to the beer garden and listen to the band that was now tuning up down the street.

"People at the open house started asking me what I was doing, where I was working these days." Melinda took a satisfying gulp of her tea. A breeze had picked up during the late afternoon, but the air was still hot and muggy.

"Oh no, that's the dreaded question," Angie rolled her eyes. "You're thinking, 'What do I say? Do I even care what they think?'"

Angie was in good spirits and the most dressed-up Melinda had ever seen her, with her dark-auburn hair pulled up in a bun and a little makeup on her face, wearing a pale green sundress.

"Exactly." Melinda pulled her legs up close, out of the way of a group of kids pedaling bicycles down the street.

"I hadn't thought about it until now, really. I guess I assumed the word was out. Prosper Hardware seems to be the epicenter of this town."

"That, and Auggie's office at the co-op."

"Then today, I ran into someone from high school at the open house. I really didn't remember her, which was bad enough. But she started gushing about how exciting my life must be in Minneapolis, and I didn't have the nerve to correct her." Melinda started to scuff the concrete curb with the bottom of her sandal.

"It was too easy to fake it and act like I was just here for the weekend, as she assumed. Then more people came up and asked me the same thing. I figured, if they hadn't heard the real story by now, why bother with the truth?"

She took another bite of her burger, and chewed slowly. "I wonder now, though, if they'll hear otherwise and know I lied. It's not the end of the world, I know, but I'm normally not one to make up stories to save face."

Angie nodded as she sipped her soda. "I get it, really, I do. Just in a different way. I've got an economics degree from ISU, but Nathan and I got married the summer after we graduated and came right back here to farm with his parents and start a family."

Her face clouded for a moment. "I'm not sorry about the choices I made, but you should see the pitying looks I sometimes get from college friends the few times a year I see them. I'm a stay-at-home mom, shoveling manure while some of the other girls are getting promoted into corner offices."

"I guess it just caught me off guard," Melinda said, touched that Angie would be so honest about her situation. It reminded her that she wasn't alone in dealing with other people's expectations. "You know, sometimes I still wonder how I messed up at work, why I was laid off. I don't feel like as much of a failure as when it first happened, but those feelings sometimes come back, and when I'm least expecting them. And today they did."

"Well, I'd say the Twin Cities' loss is our gain," Angie gave Melinda an encouraging smile, then stood up and stretched. She waved to Nathan, who was coming up the street. "You're guaranteed to run into more people at the beer tent. Let's get our story straight. You're just visiting, right?"

"Sounds good to me. And if they know I'm working at Prosper Hardware, let's just say I took some time off from my regular job to help out. I want to have a good time tonight, just put it all out of my mind."

"That's even better. It'll get you points for being a great niece, on top of keeping the questions to a minimum."

The beer garden was packed, with people crammed around the picnic tables and spilling out into the park. Melinda couldn't believe she was nervous, but she was. It had been years since she'd attended this part of the Fourth of July celebration, and she remembered too late that it was basically one big high school reunion. Forget about the wonderful chance to see old friends and reminisce about the glory days. Reunions were when all the measuring sticks came out.

"Here," Angie handed over a plastic cup of beer. "It's not a glass of moscato, but it's fresh from the keg and it's cold." She smirked. "I think this could be fun. We'll have you looking like Mother Teresa before the night is over, rushing in to save the family business in its hour of need."

"You're putting quite the spin on things. Maybe you should get into marketing. But I'm not sure I'd recommend it as a career these days."

More revelers were pouring into the beer garden, from people looking barely old enough to get a wristband to others Melinda guessed had taken their grandkids to the parade that morning. The band jammed away at a set list that was a mishmash of old-school rock and current country hits, but it seemed to be the perfect backdrop for the crowd, which was animated but not rowdy.

"I see they've got security tonight." She pointed to a county sheriff's cruiser parked just outside the park.

"I doubt there'll be much trouble," Nathan said, "just a few ugly drunks and maybe one fist fight over who has the coolest truck. The good news is, only in a town like Prosper can you have this many people crammed together and just need one cop."

Melinda scanned the crowd for any faces she recognized. A few people looked familiar, but she wasn't sure enough to approach anyone. Angie stepped away to say hello to someone she knew, then quickly elbowed back through the crowd, her head bobbing to the music.

"There's a whole group of people from Swanton and Prosper over in that corner, come on!"

Melinda was soon on her second cup of beer and started to relax. It was a beautiful night, she was in a comfortable place with new friends, and as Angie started to make introductions it became clear no one was going to ask too many questions.

The combination of a warm night, a festive atmosphere and a seemingly endless supply of cold beer made for instant friends. She was repeatedly hugged by people she didn't know and more than a few she remembered from high school. One of her second cousins was there, and began sharing memories of visiting Prosper Hardware as a little girl.

How good it is to see some of these people, she thought. *Maybe they aren't a part of my life today, but they're part of my past, a shared past. I should make a better effort to stay in touch.*

"I gotta go," Angie tapped her arm and nodded toward the portable toilets lined up at the edge of the park. "If I want to get back before the fireworks, now's the time. Need to come?"

Melinda realized she did. They walked across the lawn in the deepening dusk, the grass swishing under their feet. A trash bin along the way smelled of sour beer and grease. "I'm glad I'm not the one that has to clean this up tomorrow," Angie wrinkled her nose. "The Swanton Jaycees certainly earn their donation from the city every year. Imagine how fragrant that will all be by morning."

Melinda stifled a yawn. How was she this tired, and before ten? In the city, she and her friends would just be going out at this hour.

"Melinda!"

A tall man with a big grin was approaching, a petite blond a step behind. Again, she started scanning her memory bank. He looked familiar, but she couldn't place him.

"Hey there! I'm Adam. Adam Greenvale," he responded to Melinda's blank smile. "I think I was a grade ahead of you in school." Angie was about to step in with a "hello" when suddenly, Melinda remembered.

"Oh! Yes, it's good to see you." Adam had once lived down the street from her family. She remembered him as a bright, inquisitive child who grew up to seemingly have it all: class president, captain of the basketball team, one of the most popular guys in school. He'd gone out East for college. She couldn't recall which one, but knew it was the kind of place with stately brick buildings covered in ivy and portraits of presidential alumni in the halls.

"So, where are you these days?" He extended his hand with a practiced-yet-easy smile, radiating a complacent confidence. "What are you up to?"

"I'm in Minneapolis, been there since college." Melinda had been reciting this script for nearly three hours already, but still couldn't believe how nonchalant she sounded. Of course, a few beers hadn't hurt, either. "I'm in marketing. How about you?"

"Twin Cities, huh? Nice place, but we're in Chicago. Oh, this is my wife, Caroline."

Melinda had started to wonder when he was going to introduce the bored woman in an all-white cotton dress, her pale blonde hair artfully arranged in an aggressive-yet-casual topknot. Like his wife's curated outfit, Adam's seersucker plaid shirt and pressed khaki shorts leaned in the direction of New England clambake, not small-town beer tent.

It was the kind of look that appeared casual but actually took hours of shopping and effort to pull off. And money. Melinda knew it well, but she'd given up on that long ago. Caroline gave a half-hearted wave and delicately sipped her beer, her eyes wandering off into the crowd.

"I'm in investments." Adam shoved his hands in his shorts pockets and rocked on his heels. "Investment banking, actually. Caroline's in law school, Northwestern. We've got a condo not far from the lake, a great place. Will probably move up into something better in a few years. How about you?"

The ball bounced into Melinda's court. She could keep this up all night. Angie was smirking behind her beer cup.

"My marketing work is really on the creative side of things, working with some of my firm's major clients." She matched Adam's casual tone note for note.

"In fact, they're so well-known we're not supposed to talk about them in public, it's confidential. But anyway, we've got a dynamic crew, some of the best and brightest. And I've got the most darling pre-war walkup in Uptown." This she directed at Caroline, who suddenly seemed to be listening to the conversation. "Oak woodwork, built-in bookcases, a butler's pantry. They just don't make them like they used to, do they?"

"I'm remodeling our condo." Caroline managed a vague smile. "We prefer a more contemporary look. Vintage is darling, but I think it's sort of had its moment."

"That's great, Melinda," Adam cut in quickly, keeping his voice smooth.

"Glad to hear you're doing so well up there. We've thought about moving back, closer to home, once the kids come. Minneapolis might do. It's smaller, of course, and I'd hate to leave my company, it just topped a *Forbes* list. But sometimes you've got to sacrifice for the family, you know."

Melinda felt a hot pinprick of rage in her chest. Adam was a snob. His wife was worse.

Of course, they could stoop so low as to leave Chicago if duty called, transfer their real estate investments to the backwaters of the Twin Cities. How noble of him to consider dropping one executive position for another just like it.

She was sick of this. Sick of pretending, sick of making everything sound good, sound great. This was her life, and she needed to own it. To hell with what anyone else thought.

"You might want to rent my vintage walk up, then," she said acidly, matching Caroline's insincere tone. "Just to see if Minneapolis suits you, keep it as a weekend place. I may not have it much longer. Because if I don't find another job, I'll be out on my ass at the end of November."

Angie nearly choked on her beer. Adam and Caroline's serene smiles began to fade. *Excellent*, she thought. *For the first time since I ran into him, he's speechless.*

"That great firm I worked for? They canned me. Laid me off two months ago. Packed up my desk for me like I was a five-year-old. Then they gave all my accounts to a twenty-five-year-old."

"Wow, Melinda, I'm sorry to hear that." Adam looked confused but maybe just a bit sympathetic.

Melinda was on a roll, though, and couldn't stop. Didn't want to stop.

"It's a good thing my uncle had that heart attack last month. What a break, you know?" Her voice was getting louder, but she didn't care. "Because of that, I was able to get my aunt to hire me on at the hardware store. Oh, and I'm squatting in this old farmhouse with a bunch of sheep and some chickens, a dog and some cats."

She'd just implied all the animals were living in the house with her. Whatever.

"The one old guy's been in the home for over a year and it's too late for him, but the other one might come back. Then, I could basically be homeless."

"That's ... great you have pets," Caroline blinked. "How ..."

"Not so great, no, not really. One sheep stomps her foot every time I get in with them, and the chickens try to peck me when I take their eggs. The dog? He's depressed. And the cats run the other way when they see me coming ..."

She paused long enough to take a deep breath. The tears were pricking at the backs of her eyes, but her head felt clear. The clearest it had been in some time.

"I'm Angie. It's nice to meet you." She stepped forward and all but forced Adam to shake her hand. He seemed unable to move. Then, she turned to Caroline.

"I like your dress. I spend a good deal of my time in a cow yard, so I don't wear white much anymore. Laundry day's tough as it is, I'm sure you can imagine." Caroline shifted her feet and brushed at her hair with her free hand, ready to bolt.

"See you around," Angie gave a little wave. "Enjoy the fireworks. Let's go, Melinda." She grasped Melinda's arm and started to pull her away.

"Wow. Damn. That was ... I don't know what to say." Angie began to giggle and leaned over, started laughing so hard she couldn't walk for a moment. "You knocked the smug right off his face. And Caroline ..."

"I think she really thought the animals lived in the house with me." Melinda began to giggle, then gasped and wiped at her eyes. "I didn't mean to say it that way, it just came out. Maybe I should invite the sheep in, it's cooler in the house than in the barn."

"You could put the chickens out on the front porch," Angie took up the idea. "Can't you see them, nesting on the porch swing and lounging in the screens, the breeze ruffling their feathers ..."

"Why not?" Melinda sighed. "Oh, but I do feel better. That felt good."

They got in the shortest line at the portable toilets, Angie still laughing so hard that Melinda hoped her friend could hold on long enough to take her turn inside.

"How tragic to have to give up Chicago for Minneapolis someday," Melinda said sarcastically, then sighed.

"It's just as well I spilled the beans. All it would take is for Adam's mom to run into my mom, and he would hear the truth eventually. And then I would look as evasive and fake as he is."

"Wow, was *he* full of himself." Angie crossed her arms. "I was about to make a snarky comment, but you beat me to it."

"OK, so I exaggerated some, but you know what? So much of what I said was true. Really true." She put a hand to her face. "Angie, what am I going to do?"

A boom echoed across the park, and a roar of approval drifted over from the beer garden, where the band had taken a break for the sky show. "Whooo!" yelled an obviously drunk man in the next line.

"You're going to give it time," Angie pointed at Melinda. "And in the meantime, enjoy these fireworks."

She gazed up to see the first burst of light explode across the sky, ribbons of green and red and blue raining down over Prosper. Each blast echoed through her, pushing out all the fear, at least for now. And her spirits rose a little more every time a shower of sparks appeared in the darkness.

* 16 *

"I envy you, Melinda." Cassie stretched her tan legs under the picnic table, flexing her feet in the silver open-toed sandals Melinda and Susan had suggested she leave at home.

"This place is so peaceful, so serene. And you even have cell service."

"Wireless towers are everywhere these days," Susan reminded her, then took a satisfied sip of her white wine, which Melinda had poured into foam cups discovered in one of the kitchen cabinets. "Remember how many we passed on the way down, along the interstate?"

"The cell towers and the wind turbines sort of broke up the monotony of the drive," Cassie said. "I'm glad that you don't have any of those turbines nearby. There's something startling about seeing so many at once, especially when they are rotating. Almost makes you dizzy to watch them."

"Well, I've got enough work for both of you this weekend to make your head spin." Melinda passed Cassie her cup. "I'm glad Aunt Miriam gave me tomorrow off so you could come down and help. Horace won't know what to make of his spiffed-up house. I bet it's been decades since anyone's taken a brush to those kitchen and living room walls."

It was Friday night, and it seemed like the first time all week Melinda had a chance to really relax. Prosper Hardware had been especially busy, and then there was the cleaning frenzy to get the house ready for guests. In addition to scrubbing the kitchen and bathrooms, she had spread fresh sheets on the downstairs bed and also the one in Wilbur's old room upstairs. Both spaces got a thorough dusting, then stalks of purple phlox and yellow daisies from the cluster of perennials on the west side of the house were arranged vases for both rooms.

The hesitant crawl of Cassie's Escalade on the gravel and the blinker that came on long before the driveway announced her friends' arrival. That was followed by a series of excited barks from Hobo as he danced by the garage, eager to serve as the official greeter. Melinda was relieved that Hobo didn't check inside the vehicle for signs of Horace, and hoped a weekend filled with visitors and activity would put him in high spirits.

Any misgivings she had about reconnecting with her old friends vanished the moment they stepped out of the car. Their smiles, hugs and laughter told her that distance and circumstance didn't matter. She put their overnight bags on the back porch bench and then, with Hobo leading the way, gave them a tour of the farm.

Both exclaimed over its potential, and Susan seemed especially enamored by its charm. The cats refused to appear, but a few of the more social ewes lined up for forehead pets across the fence.

Cassie was taken with the chickens and asked if she could go into their run and pet them, misreading Pansy's agitated pacing as a sign of friendliness. Susan quickly put a stop to that, then winked at Melinda and suggested Cassie could collect the eggs in the morning if she wanted to get closer to the hens.

Dusk would come on soon, but Melinda was determined to enjoy a peaceful evening around the picnic table until the mosquitoes drove the three women inside. Susan and Cassie had stopped for dinner on the way down, so all Melinda had to do was pour the chilled wine, rip open the bag of tortilla chips and dump the salsa in a bowl.

"There'll be plenty of time for painting tomorrow. And Sunday, too, if we can't get it all done in time for dinner tomorrow night." She reached over to light the citronella candle on the table. "I've been on my feet at the store all day and you've had a long drive. Let's just take it easy. What's new up north?"

Susan heard most of the other people laid off from WP&S hadn't found jobs yet, either, then added it had only been two months and Melinda shouldn't give up. Cassie rolled her eyes over a gallery opening she attended last week. It was a work thing for Jim's law firm, she said, and apparently the art had been secondary to the displays of wealth offered by the attendees.

Melinda wasn't sure if the event was really that pretentious or Cassie was just trying to be kind, downplaying the glamorous circles she moved in while Melinda fed sheep and pulled weeds at Horace's.

Susan laughed at Cassie's scathing critiques of some of the other women's dresses, but Melinda could barely work up a smile. Everything happening in Minneapolis seemed like it was worlds away.

She glanced down at her roughened hands and scuffed sneakers, then over at the thriving garden and Hobo lounging on the sidewalk.

"Melinda, are you OK?" Cassie reached over and grasped her hand.

"I don't know," she sighed. "I don't know what I'm doing here, sometimes. I'm living in the middle of a cornfield, I never seem to get all the dust out of my hair or the dirt out from under my fingernails. I can hardly remember what it's like to get up in the morning and put on stylish clothes," she gestured at her tee shirt and knit shorts, "and go to work in an office filled with computers instead of lumber and nails and, well, milk and eggs."

"You sell eggs at Prosper Hardware?" Cassie blurted out, then darted her eyes over to the chicken coop.

"Yeah," Melinda said, trying not to sniffle. Was she really

going to cry about this? "But not from Horace's girls. The kind that come on a truck."

Then she started laughing. "Listen to me. What has happened to my life? What am I doing out here?"

Susan came around the picnic table and squeezed in next to Melinda, wrapped her arm around her friend. "You, my dear, are helping your family. You're giving an elderly man the peace of mind he needs to spend time with his brother before it's too late. And you're saving that sweet dog over there from total heartbreak."

"Look, anyone would feel turned inside out in your shoes." Cassie set down her cup and leaned in. "And those ..." she glanced under the picnic table, "well, never mind. I know this has been hard for you. You loved your job, and you were good at it. It's been a terrible loss, one that will take time to get over." Melinda could only nod, as the tears were now rolling down her cheeks.

"I wouldn't last one night out here by myself," Cassie went on. "And you've made it, what, six weeks? You've kept this place going, look around at all you've done."

"I just get so overwhelmed sometimes. The store is interesting, but it's more challenging than I expected. And the other night there was a terrible thunderstorm, so much lightning and wind. The power was out for nearly an hour. I hurried down to the basement with a flashlight and just sat there, alone in the dark, worrying about the animals and if they were safe."

"Well, I don't know much about sheep," Cassie gestured over at the ewes enjoying a few more nibbles of grass before sunset. "But they seem smart enough to me."

Melinda gave Cassie an incredulous look.

"OK, maybe they aren't that smart," Cassie hurried on, "but they know to go inside the barn when it rains, right? And the chickens, they've got their own cute house over there. And you said there's a little door on the barn for Hobo, right? And I can tell he is a very smart dog." Hobo thumped his tail, thanking Cassie for her compliment.

"I'm just so glad to see both of you." Melinda took a deep breath and sat up straighter. "Everyone has been so kind, and it's good to be close to my family again. But until you drove in the yard, I hadn't realized how lonely I've been sometimes."

Cassie got up, motioning for Susan and Melinda to join her. "I know you said not to wear these open-toed sandals and I'm already wishing I hadn't, as the mosquitoes are starting to attack. But I'm feeling reckless tonight."

She started off past the back corner of the house and Melinda and Susan followed, exchanging wary glances.

"I think we need to have a look around out here," Cassie said cheerfully as she gazed up at the house. "This place needs more than what we can do in a weekend, but you're being here allows this old house to still feel like a home."

"Cassie's right." Susan rubbed Melinda's back. "You've done wonders by just being here. And you must be such a blessing to Frank and Miriam, and the whole town, too. It takes a lot to keep a locally owned business going these days."

"OK, OK, I'm not sure I've single-handedly saved the great city of Prosper from economic ruin. But, well, I've had many people tell me they're glad I'm here."

"And this garden over here looks wonderful." Cassie marched over to the plot and stretched out her arms. "Just look at this, it's huge. Those tomato plants are growing right out of their cages. These carrot tops look, well, fresh and green. And those things in the third row, next to that fence ..."

"Green beans." Susan rolled her eyes. "Those are beans."

"Well, yes, the beans look ... healthy." Cassie grinned. "I'm not much of a gardener, obviously, but even I can tell you're working miracles here. All this green stuff would be brown if you weren't here to water and weed and, well, whatever else it is you have to do."

"That mostly covers it. Lots of weeding. And bug patrol."

"Bug patrol?" Cassie took a step back.

"The green hornworms on the tomatoes are the worst," Melinda told her. "Kevin said Horace squishes them between his fingers and feeds them to the chickens." Cassie's eyes widened in disgust. "But I can't deal with that. I've been swatting them into a little bucket of lawnmower gas and when they're dead, I throw them over the fence there. Mabel, my neighbor, suggested that."

"Sounds kind of dangerous." Susan crossed her arms. "Flammable materials and all that. You're making some interesting friends out here."

Soft shadows were beginning to gather around the edges of the yard. The hens, who earlier were clucking and scratching in the dirt, started to settle on their roosts in the chicken house. One dove called from the windbreak, and an answering "cooo, cooo" came from the evergreens on the north side of the yard.

"Speaking of new friends," Susan said as they turned back toward the house. "I've brought something that should help us meet up with those two cats you were telling us about. Let's go in and I'll show you."

A cool blast greeted them as they came in through the kitchen. Melinda was relieved the cranky old air conditioner rumbled on, especially since she had guests. Susan unzipped her duffel bag and started to rummage inside.

"I took Penny in for her checkup the other day and told the vet about your cats." Susan lifted out a tiny glass jar. "He said if anything could bring them around, it would be this."

"Is that what I think it is?" Cassie snatched the jar and held it up to the light. "Are you serious, Susan?"

"Baby food!" Melinda rolled the jar over to see the cherub-faced newborn on the label. "Chicken and gravy, huh? I can't imagine the cats turning this down."

"Dr. Baxter said this is what rescue groups use to win over ferals. You offer it on a spoon, and the smell is so tempting that most of the kitties eventually set their fear aside for a taste. It takes time, but they associate the treat with the person offering it, and that's how you win their trust."

"I'd love to get closer to them. I can verify both are males, but that's about it. They take off the second they see me coming. Unless I have their food bucket."

"How did they get here?" Cassie looked out toward the barn, as if the cats might appear. "What did Kevin say?"

"He was shocked when I told him they were here." She carefully set the jar on the dining room hutch, as if it held diamonds instead of chicken and cornstarch. "Horace left an open bag of food and a note on the shelf, saying the cats just showed up one day. And," she paused dramatically, "that they don't seem to want names."

"Horace sounds like a character." Susan reached back in her duffel for her pajamas and toothbrush. "How's he doing?"

"Kevin says he is happy to be with Wilbur again, and he seems to like the nursing home." She shrugged, hoping Kevin's assessment was accurate. "But then, he expects to come home eventually."

"Well, he sure will be in for a surprise when he does come back," Cassie said. "We can do a lot with a few gallons of paint." She glanced around the dining room at the bluebirds darting along its walls. "Although I can't imagine he's a fan of this wallpaper. It doesn't exactly say 'old bachelor farmer.'"

Susan shook her head. "I suppose that Horace and Wilbur's mother found it fashionable back in the day. I'd say it's at least fifty years old."

"It was hard to pick colors that would compliment these twirly birds." Melinda shook a finger at her friends' expectant faces. "But that's a surprise for tomorrow. I'm beat."

"I think it's time to turn in," Cassie yawned. "I suspect you country folks get up early?"

"Seven is fine. I'll be up before that and have the chores done and the coffee on. This rustic B&B only has two rooms available. I'll let you two fight over the accommodations."

Cassie reached for her carry-on and rolled it toward Horace's bedroom. "I hear this one has a private bath."

"I'd love to snoop around more upstairs, so Wilbur's old room suits me just fine." Susan gathered her duffel and purse, then paused to admire the living room's fireplace and bookcases before turning for the stairs. "This house is amazing, Melinda, truly it is."

* 17 *

A brief thunderstorm rolled through just before dawn, washing away the heat and humidity. Melinda was greeted by a refreshingly cool breeze when she went out to the barn for morning chores, the sun's rays already bending across the fields and glinting off the raindrops still clinging to the oak trees' leaves.

"It's perfect painting weather, isn't it?" she said to Hobo as she washed out his water bowl at the garden hydrant. The house's windows could be opened and fans stationed around the first floor, reducing the paint fumes and allowing the walls to dry faster. "We couldn't have asked for a better day."

The chicken coop was cool inside, still full of shadows at this early hour. She shooed the ladies away long enough to snatch up six eggs and arrange them in the bucket on her arm. Scrambled eggs would be perfect with the cinnamon streusel coffee cake she was about to pop in the oven.

Susan was sitting at the kitchen table, lost in thought, and dressed for the day in a ragged-hem tee shirt and worn shorts. A faded headband held her strawberry-blond hair off her face. Melinda knew Susan well enough to know she was hatching some sort of plan.

"You know, why don't we try to at least scrub down these kitchen cabinets today? I know we don't have the time to paint them, even though they desperately need it."

"I was thinking that very thing yesterday." Melinda reached for a large crockery bowl and began dumping in flour for the coffee cake. "The new wall paint will make the cabinets look worse if we don't. We'll see how far we get."

"Cassie's in the shower." Susan had already started the coffee pot and now motioned for where to find the mugs. "Want me to start scrambling those eggs? It must be heavenly to walk outside and help yourself like that."

"It is, except a couple of the hens get broody and don't want me to take their 'babies' sometimes. I thought it was best to gather the eggs myself this morning, despite Cassie's interest doing it herself." Susan nodded in agreement. "There are some regular egg buyers, and I've been trying to keep up with their orders. Kevin said I can just keep the money, but I'm saving it for Horace."

"This is a sweet deal you've got here." Susan gestured around the kitchen with a fork in her hand, then began whipping the eggs with a little milk. "This kitchen can't decide which decade it wants to be from, but it's charming. That paint you picked out will really make a difference." She gave Melinda a sly look.

"You'll just have to wait until after breakfast. I'm starving, and our master painter hasn't yet arrived."

Cassie was proof of the old saying to not judge a book by its cover. Back in college, long before the designer handbags and luxury vehicles, she worked summers as a painter for a Twin Cities house restoration company. Melinda had gratefully put Cassie in charge of purchasing the right cleansers to scrub the farmhouse's plaster walls and choosing the best painter's tape to protect the substantial oak built-ins and woodwork.

That had left her with the exciting-yet-daunting task of choosing the paint. Kevin suggested she aim for neutrals, but told her to pick whatever she thought would look best.

She finally settled on a warm white for the kitchen, so soft it was the color of melted vanilla ice cream. Hopefully that shade would magnify the light coming in the south windows, and provide a better backdrop to the pale-green cabinets than the drab brown now on the walls. The bluebirds in the dining room guided her choice for the adjacent living room, and it took several samples brushed on the plaster to get the color just right. There, the brown would be replaced by a pale gray with sky-blue undertones.

"These are the perfect shades!" Cassie exclaimed when Melinda pried the lids off the first two paint cans. "And I'm glad both have the primer built in. Do you have enough so the kitchen can get two coats?"

Melinda nodded. Susan gave her a high five. "I can't wait to get started. It's going to be beautiful."

With the paint colors no longer a mystery, the friends lingered over third cups of coffee and second helpings of streusel coffeecake. Melinda's spirits soared as she looked around the kitchen, her doubts from last night long gone. How great it would look with just a few simple changes.

"We'd better get started," Cassie finally said, breaking up the chatter and laughter. "Let's tackle the living room first. With all this beautiful woodwork, it might take us longer to prep and tape the walls than roll on the paint."

Susan quickly washed the breakfast dishes while Melinda and Cassie lifted the sofa, Horace's chair and the television stand away from the living room's walls and draped plastic drop cloths over the furniture and across the oak floors. Melinda wrangled a stepladder up from the basement and Susan took down the faded curtains and removed the rods, flooding the downstairs of the house with even more light.

"Ladies, we've got our work cut out for us here," Cassie said as she filled buckets with hot water in the kitchen, adding cleanser to two of them. "Melinda, how about you man the rinse sponge while Susan and I start scrubbing this grime off. I bet there's layers of fireplace smoke and country dirt on these tired brown walls. No wonder Horace chose that color."

Cassie was right. The room seemed to come alive as the years of residue were wiped away. Melinda opened all the downstairs windows, including those in Horace's room. The green-growing breeze coming in off the fields soon mingled with the nose-tickling scent of the cleanser.

"Smells like a fresh start in here, if you ask me," Susan told Melinda as she swapped out a water bucket filled with murky suds.

They took a quick coffee break as the living room walls began to dry. Cassie suggested they tape off and paint the living room before lunch, as it would take all afternoon to scrub the spacious kitchen's walls and cabinets, then give the dull walls their first coat of the cream paint. That would leave time tomorrow to paint the kitchen again before Cassie and Susan left for Minneapolis.

The kitchen cabinets were coated with a greasy film that gave the women sore forearms by the end of the day, but the scrubbing revealed the once-drab doors and drawers to be a cheerful celery green.

The living room was, as Susan called it, "a revelation." The soft blue-gray paint brought out the reddish undertones in the dark oak woodwork, and there was no longer a jarring color difference between the living and dining rooms.

"I don't even want to hang those ugly old curtains back up in here." Melinda gestured at the red-and-blue checkered panels draped across Horace's dresser. "Maybe a nice, subtle stripe in blues and greens would complement both rooms ..."

"That's always how it goes." Susan folded her arms and admired their handiwork. "One project leads to another. But now, even the bluebirds look more at home."

Melinda had planned to treat her friends to steak dinners in Mason City, but they were all too tired to get cleaned up and drive more than half an hour just to eat. After only sandwiches and chips for lunch, they were starving.

Instead, Cassie defrosted some chicken in Horace's grumbling microwave while Melinda brought out the round charcoal grill hiding in the garage. She would have to baste the chicken often with Italian dressing, as there was no time for a marinade, but hoped the result would be nearly the same. She cut up carrots and potatoes and onions, making foil packets to put on the grill, while Susan chopped up a salad with lettuce and early veggies from the garden.

The potato packets made a pile of peelings that Cassie was about to toss in the garbage can, but Melinda waved her away. "The sheep love those, it's their favorite treat. I'll take them out later."

"I'll do it." Cassie's face lit up. "We haven't had much time to see the animals up close. They won't bite, right?"

"Nope. Just toss the peels and they'll come running."

"She's really getting into this country thing," Susan said as the back porch's storm door banged shut. "She told me earlier today that she could almost see herself out on a farm, living the simple life."

Melinda shook her head. "I doubt Jim wants to give up his law practice to become an organic farmer. But I guess a girl can hope."

Only a few minutes later, a muffled yelp and three frantic barks drifted in through the kitchen windows.

Melinda rushed out to the back porch and spotted Hobo with his paws up on the pasture fence and the ewes clustered inside. But no Cassie.

"Are the sheep out?" Susan hurried to join her, shading her eyes from the early-evening sun.

"Worse. I think Cassie's in. Do you have your shoes on?"

They raced across the yard, Hobo turning to meet them as they came near the fence. The frightened ewes were jumping back and forth, bleating nervously, shoving each other out of the way to get at the vegetable peelings. Cassie, her paint-splattered limbs now also covered in dirt, was curled up in the middle of the pack, holding her hands over her head and yelling, "go away, get away!"

"Cassie!" Melinda ran to the gate and let herself through. "Are you OK? What are you doing? Back sheep, back!"

At the sound of Melinda's voice, the ewes turned away from Cassie. A few of them started to amble toward her, hoping she had more treats. The vegetable bowl had been kicked away nearly to the barn.

"You said to just toss out the peelings!" Cassie struggled to her feet, wiping at her arms and legs. "You said they'd just lap them up. Why are they attacking me?"

Melinda sighed. "I didn't mean for you to go in the sheep yard. You just throw the stuff over the fence. But it's OK. They're just overly excited."

"That one over there ripped the bowl right out of my hand." Cassie pointed an accusing finger at one of the ewes, who was searching the trampled grass by the barn for any remaining peelings. "She knocked me down, then her friends closed in for the kill."

"That's Annie. She's bossy and greedy. But she won't hurt you, nor would the others. You are OK, right?"

Cassie nodded, then sniffed. "Do I smell smoke, or am I hallucinating from a head injury?"

"The chicken!" Susan called over her shoulder as she ran for the house. Hobo, sensing Melinda had Cassie under control, bolted after Susan.

Melinda sighed as she saw Susan lift the grill's lid and a black cloud bloom above the grate. "I hope you like your chicken well done." She glanced down at Cassie's open sandals and cringed. "Do your feet hurt? We'll need to make sure you didn't step on a nail or ..."

"Oh, no," Cassie groaned as she examined the bottom of one of her no-longer-cute shoes. "You girls were right that I should have left these at home. I think they're OK, though. My feet, I mean. The sandals, well ..."

Melinda recognized the pungent odor of fresh sheep manure. "You should consider yourself lucky." She laughed, then helped Cassie over to the gate. "That stuff is in high demand for garden fertilizer. We could scrape it into a baggie and you could take it home for your rose bushes."

"No thanks. Let's just eat. I don't care if it's cooked or raw or whatever at this point."

Sunday morning again dawned bright and clear, and the women made quick work of giving the kitchen's walls a second coat of paint. The soft vanilla hue provided a unifying backdrop for the random mix of fixtures and furnishings. Inspired by the facelift, Susan volunteered to scrub down Horace's tired stove until its chrome trim was mirror-bright.

Then Cassie reached into her suitcase and handed Melinda a fresh set of burgundy-and-tan check dishtowels and pot holders. Melinda took Horace's burnt, ragged pads down from the pegs above the stove, and arranged one of the new towels on the gleaming bar of the oven door.

"It's perfect." She blinked back a few tears as Susan and Cassie beamed. "It's like this old house is coming alive again."

"All it needed was a little paint," Cassie said.

"I'm not sure if it's the paint or the painters." Melinda gave each of her friends a hug. "It's probably been some time since this place was full of people and laughter. By the way, I'll be sad to see both of you go."

"You come up for the weekend, anytime." Cassie motioned Melinda and Susan into the living room. They still needed to set the furniture back in place and hang the curtains. "I think I might even like to come back here again, as long as I stay out of the sheep yard."

Cassie rearranged the kitchen counters while Susan and Melinda created chicken salad out of last night's leftovers. Beaming with pride, Melinda asked Susan to go into the cellar and bring up a jar of the canned strawberries, which were poured over dishes of vanilla ice cream for dessert.

"This is wondrous." Susan wiped strawberry juice off her chin with one of the paper-towel napkins Melinda handed around. "Even more amazing is how many jars of it you have down there."

"Well, Mabel and Angie know their way around a kitchen. I learned from the masters."

Sometimes, when she'd had a hard day at Prosper Hardware, she went down to the basement just to admire the rows of ruby-hued jars, encouraged by the hard work and friendship they represented.

Susan stretched her arms above her head and twisted in her chair. "I'm going to be sore tomorrow. When did we get so old? But before we go, I think there's one more task on our to-do list." She jerked her chin in the direction of the barn.

Melinda grinned and got up from the table. "I'll get the baby food."

"Never before has a little jar of mashed-up meat been so exciting." Cassie reached for her sunglasses. "Do you think they'll come to us?"

"If this stuff is as addictive as Susan says, we might have a chance," Melinda said, "but I can't promise anything."

She had seen both cats that morning. The orange one had at least turned at the sound of her cooing, but wouldn't double back to see what she wanted. The gray-and-white cat simply took off when it heard her enter the barn. Their kibble and fresh water would be set out in the grain room either way, and they knew it.

Hobo barely looked up from his sunny spot on the sidewalk as the ladies passed. After two days of excitement, he was ready for a rest.

"Maybe this isn't the best way to go about it, all of us going in the barn together," Susan said in a low voice, as if the cats could hear her.

"We'll just have to stay relaxed and not stare them down," Melinda said. "I'll call them and we'll see what happens."

The barn appeared to be vacant, as the ewes were lounging in the south pasture. Melinda's repeated calls of "here, kitties!" were met with silence. The cats could be anywhere, hunting in the ditch or even up by the creek, or napping in the cool shade of the windbreak. Or ...

"Let's check the haymow, just in case," she said in a near whisper as she beckoned Susan and Cassie over to the stairs. "Step quietly." She took the lead and peeked over the edge of the haymow floor, then motioned for Susan to hand her the jar and plastic spoon.

"Hey," Melinda said softly, "want a snack?"

The gray-and-white cat had been asleep on the stack of hay bales but now had his head up, watching. Melinda tipped the open jar toward the cat, whose nose started to twitch.

"Are they there?" Susan whispered.

"The gray one is," Melinda whispered back. "I think he might come to me. He's sniffing the air. Maybe he'll want to see what's in this jar."

Suddenly there was a thump below them in the grain room. Then two orange, furry ears poked up out of the space where the haymow floor met the west wall, not three feet from Melinda's post on the stairs. Then, two golden eyes were watching her and the jar in her hand, the orange cat easing his way up into the haymow. The gray cat remained alert but didn't come any closer.

She scooped the blended chicken and held the spoon out, reaching as far as she could without stepping forward. The orange cat hesitated at first but then padded across the floor, tail down, and sat about a foot away from the spoon.

Melinda waved the spoon slightly back and forth. "Come here, kitty," she cooed. The orange cat leaned forward as he evaluated her, as well as the treat.

"Should we go?" Cassie whispered from where she and Susan were crouched on the stairs. "Are we scaring him?"

"Just stay there," Melinda breathed. "I think going down the steps would startle him."

A few more hesitant steps forward, and then the orange cat lifted his left paw. He tapped the side of the spoon and then peered under it while Melinda fought down her laughter. His inspection emboldened the gray cat, who jumped down from the stack of hay bales and inched forward, crouched so low he was almost crawling on his belly.

Slowly, cautiously, the orange cat touched the baby food with his nose and then tried to bite down on the plastic spoon. Once he tasted the chicken, his shoulders relaxed and he began to lick the spoon clean.

For a moment, Melinda thought the gray cat might join his friend. But then there was a rustling in the rafters, and two starlings began to squawk. The orange cat jumped back and the gray cat ran for the hay bales. Before she could refill the spoon, both were on the far side of the haymow.

Susan and Cassie were beaming. "Who knew farm life could be so exciting?" Cassie clenched her palms together. "That had more drama than any novel I've read lately."

"Just call her the cat whisperer," Susan said, reaching up to take back the jar and spoon. "You'll win them over yet. They know you and are starting to trust you. It'll just take time, and a great deal of patience."

"I hope so," Melinda sighed, "but they aren't exactly the snuggly type." She was encouraged by this small step of progress, but it also made her wistful and sad.

She still missed Oreo terribly, and here were two kitties living right in Horace's barn. She wished she could give them both a pet, sit on the back porch steps with one in her lap and one at her feet. Maybe they didn't want anything from her but food and shelter, but she had to keep trying.

"It won't be easy," Cassie declared as the three friends clomped down the wooden stairs. "But I think you're up for this challenge. You've practically got a Noah's Ark going on here, what's a few more animals to look after?"

* 18 *

Early mornings became Melinda's favorite moments in the garden. The summer air still held some of the night's coolness as the sky turned from lilac to mauve and, finally, a pale blue. Hobo was always her assistant, waiting nose-on-paws at the end of the next row, his tail thumping slightly as he eyed the water gushing out of the hose, the dirt spraying as she moved from one plant to the next.

Maybe he just wanted to be at hand the moment she was ready to dish out his breakfast, but she could see there was more to it than that. Hobo always watched her with a light in his brown eyes and what could only be a smile on his face.

Melinda could think out here in the garden, really think. She could survey the growing fields, feel the fresh breeze and hear the chirps and chortles of the birds as they began their day. She often found herself humming as she checked the progress of the tomato plants, their still-green fruits hanging thick and heavy inside their cages.

According to Mabel and Jerry, the first tomatoes should be ripe in a few weeks. The peppers, green beans, and sweet corn would soon follow. It wouldn't be long before she could reap the rewards of her weeks of hard work.

Cassie and Susan's visit had brought her a reassurance she hadn't realized she was seeking. Something about having both sides of her life come together for even a few days gave her a sense of peace, of balance. Seeing the farm and the animals through her friends' eyes reminded Melinda of how much she had already accomplished this summer.

The past few months had been hard, full of change and uncertainty, and the challenge of letting go of the old and trying to embrace the new. There had been loneliness, too, but she could see now that most of that had lifted once she left Minneapolis.

She didn't miss those long, dreary days when she wandered around her apartment in a fog, trying to find her way back into a life that was already gone. Every time she met up with friends, or went to the grocery store, or walked over to the park by the lake, she had hoped to somehow magically be herself again. But it never felt the same.

Prosper didn't quite fit, either, but it was a welcome change, a chance to catch her breath, figure out what she wanted to do next. Her life here had purpose, and there were skills to learn and people to meet. Her new friends seemed to find something in her that they admired. Still smarting from the loss of her career and torn away from the anchors of her day-to-day life, she just wasn't sure what that was.

"Maybe it doesn't matter what they see in me, or that I can't yet see it in myself," she said to Hobo one morning in late July as she watered the pepper plants. "It's enough to know that they care, isn't it?" She slid the garden hose over to a tomato cage and set it the dirt long enough to reach over and scratch Hobo's ears.

"I just wish your kitty friends were as social as you are. You tell them I want to be friends, OK?" He let out a happy whimper and rolled over for a tummy rub.

She'd tried at least once a day to tempt the cats with baby food, and had been delighted when the gray-and-white cat had finally joined the orange one in taking a few licks off the spoon. But the moment she tried to touch one of them, both cats scattered.

Even so, they just happened to appear when she was outside, keeping their distance but stationing themselves so they could observe her activities. If they were willing to give up some of their time in the haymow and the fields to at least be in her presence, she was going to call that progress.

"I know Horace said you two don't seem to want names," she told the cats that morning, "but I'm going to make an executive decision."

The kitties were sprawled out in the ferns on the north side of the garage, pretending to nap while they waited for their breakfast. But Melinda could feel their eyes on her as she moved down the rows.

"Fluffy-orange cat, I'm going to call you Sunny. And gray-and-white cat, you are now Stormy. I know you aren't gray all over, and your gray isn't very dark, but it's better than naming you Partly Cloudy."

Sunny blinked at her declaration, as if he might be listening, but Stormy just stretched and rolled over.

"If we're going to hang out together the rest of the summer, we've got to be on a first-name basis around here. Isn't that right, Hobo?"

He gave her what could only be an agreeable look, then hurried to the other side of the garden. She was about to move the hose down to reach the last of the plants, and he didn't want to miss anything.

That afternoon, the pleasantly warm day morphed into the steamy, sweltering weather Iowa is known for that time of year. Phantom water puddles, always just down the road, began to appear on the blacktop under the blazing sun.

While the stifling humidity was tiresome for people and animals alike, the crops and gardens loved it. Melinda could almost see the corn growing in the field across the road, and the garden seemed to expand in height and volume overnight. Horace's neat rows of tender, spiky plants had evolved into a wild tangle of vines and stalks in the last month and now threatened to overtake the garden's walkways. She began carrying a roll of twine and scissors in her pocket each morning, checking for trailing plant shoots and tying them to their fences and cages.

The few puffy clouds in the sky drifted lazily along, and the flags at Prosper's post office and in front of City Hall sagged in the stagnant, humid afternoons. Main Street was quieter than usual. Bill said activity in the little town wouldn't pick up until just before school started in August.

The heat lost some of its punch in the evening but even at firefly time, Melinda could still work up a sweat just relaxing at the picnic table with a large bottle of water.

"I say, today's the day," Auggie said Friday morning as the men gathered around the vintage sideboard at Prosper Hardware. "We're overdue for some thunderstorms to roll through. This weather's got to break sometime. It's so hot, I don't know how I can continue to drink this coffee."

"You know, Auggie, they do have iced versions these days," Melinda suggested as she came inside with the watering can.

Jerry was out of town, and she had been carrying the ladder out to water the flower baskets every morning. Yesterday the blooms were so droopy by late afternoon that she gave them a second drink before going home.

"That would be too fancy for me. All those syrups and stuff they put in those drinks? Takes longer to make the coffee than gulp it down."

"What's your prediction, then?" Doc settled in his chair.

"Hard to say," Auggie hedged. "Days like this are ripe for severe weather to break out. We could get hail, high winds, even a tornado. Might hold off until sunset, though."

Doc nodded, concern showing on his sun-weathered face. "It's been too hot and humid for too many days. The air just doesn't feel right." He lowered his voice.

"I was out at the Emmersons' farm this morning, right around sunrise, for a cow having trouble giving birth. She came through fine, but it was the other cows that gave me pause. They were pacing, anxious, mooing more than usual. The Emmersons have horses, too, and those horses were jumpy and on edge. Made me uneasy."

The group fell silent. George rubbed his chin.

"I've seen that before, but not very often. People who say animals are dumb have no idea."

"And it wasn't just the livestock." Doc stared into his coffee mug. "Will Emmerson said he had this sense of foreboding, like something was wrong. He thought a storm was coming."

"Melinda, better make sure that weather radio under the counter has fresh batteries," Auggie said. "I remember one time when I worked here in high school, we had a bad storm roll through. Your grandpa and grandma hurried everyone into the basement."

Melinda could only nod and glance to the back, where she could hear Bill's table saw already whirring through an order. It gave her comfort that Bill, like Doc, was a member of Prosper's volunteer emergency department. "I hope you're wrong, Auggie. And you, too, Doc. And George."

"And Will Emmerson's cows," George said, trying to lighten the mood.

"And the cows," Melinda managed a laugh. "And the horses, and Will Emmerson himself. If it makes any of you feel better, Horace's sheep didn't seem the least bit concerned this morning."

Nearly every customer that day asked if Auggie had made a prediction and wanted to know exactly what it was. But not everyone believed his forecast.

"I've known Auggie for years, and he's not always right," said Glenn Hanson, the town's postmaster, as he paid for a sack of nails and a bag of charcoal. "The whole thing could blow past us. Me, I'm grilling out tonight, after I put in some more work on my deck. Besides, we're close enough to the river. Twisters won't cross rivers."

The woman in line behind him rolled her eyes. "That's an old wives' tale, Glenn, that stuff about rivers."

"I'm telling you, my grandpa swore by it. He said ..."

Melinda quickly reached for the woman's purchases and began to ring them up. "Let's just hope Auggie is wrong." She gave each of them a soothing smile. "Stay safe tonight, OK?"

Esther was puffing and sweaty when she arrived just before three. Business had been so slow the past week that Miriam had told Esther she needn't come in at noon. "The light's starting to change. Melinda, I don't have to ask if Auggie predicted a storm today, he'd be a fool not to. When's it supposed to hit?"

"He just said maybe by sunset. Is he really that good? I can't tell you how many people have asked."

"I'll say this," Esther tucked her purse under the counter next to Melinda's.

"He's just as accurate as those TV weather people. It might start to blow before you get home. Everything secure out at the farm?"

Melinda thought for a moment. "Horace and Wilbur don't have patio furniture, just that old picnic table, but it would take a tornado to blow that heavy thing over. Hobo can get into the barn, as can the sheep and the cats. The chickens, too, can get inside. I didn't leave any windows open on the house. It's been way too hot for that."

Half an hour later, the sunlight began to fade. Bill came through from the back just as the weather radio began to blast warning tones for a tornado watch.

"I'll take Miriam's flower baskets down, just in case." He reached for the ladder that was still propped in the front corner of the store. "Auggie might be a bit off on the timing, but my prediction is he'll get his storm."

Melinda followed Bill to the front door. A dark mass of clouds loomed behind the co-op, approaching from the southwest. Nancy Delaney was folding the flags she'd just removed from the pole in front of City Hall. She waved to Bill and Melinda and hurried across the street, a sudden gust of wind whipping her skirt.

"There's been a tornado over north of Fort Dodge," Nancy said, shaking her head. "Pretty bad, I think. The whole cluster is coming this way."

"I'll check it out on my phone once we're done out here," Bill said. "I'm guessing Tony knows about this?" Nancy

nodded. Tony Bevins was the town's fire chief; although he
lived in Prosper, he worked at a bank over in Swanton.

"I just spoke to him," Nancy said. "Jerry's still out of
town, of course. I know Glenn is already gone for the day. I'll
take the post office's flags down, too."

The light changed again, dimming to a sickly greenish
shade, as Bill passed the last flower basket to Melinda.
Another gust rolled down the street, but this time the air
within it was icy cold. Melinda shuddered, her pulse racing
and goosebumps rising on her arms. She'd seen enough
severe weather growing up to know any quick temperature
change could mean damaging hail, or worse.

"I don't like this, Bill. There's two customers in the store
right now."

"I'll tell them to stay with us until this blows over." He
snapped the ladder closed. "Let's get inside and get them
away from those plate-glass windows."

Esther looked up, worried, as they came in. "Weather
radio's gone off again. Tornado warnings west of here." One
of the customers, an elderly man, hurried to the front
windows to look out as Esther shook her head at Melinda.

The young woman standing at the counter started to
wring her hands. "My parents live over in Swanton." She
wiped tears from her eyes.

Melinda squeezed her arm. "Mine, too. I'm sure they're
heading for the basement."

Bill opened the front storm door for one last look before
latching it securely and cranking the deadbolt on the oak
interior door. His face was grim.

"Wind's blowing from the west, then from the north. The
clouds are starting to rotate. Let's go to the basement."

An inky blackness fell over the town, and rain suddenly
began to slide down the front windows. Bill reached behind
the counter for two flashlights and handed one to Melinda,
then the group started for the stairs.

The lights flickered and the store went dark. The young
woman whimpered and reached for Melinda's hand. Melinda

felt a fluttering in her stomach and pressure building in her eardrums. The weather radio's tones made everyone jump.

"This is a tornado warning for Hartland County. Spotters have indicated a large funnel west of Swanton, moving northeast, with winds estimated at more than 120 miles per hour. Hail the size of golf balls has been reported with this storm ..."

"See, it's going to miss Swanton," Melinda said to the woman, who could only nod.

"But we're next in line," Esther muttered.

They fumbled their way down the stairs, the flashlights' beams bobbing along the stone walls. The slightly moldy smell of the basement was strangely comforting. It was a reminder that they were below ground, with a sturdy two-story brick building between them and the storm.

Bill gestured for everyone to crouch along a wall. There was a deep rumble of thunder, then a wailing screech in the escalating wind. Melinda felt the hairs on her arms and the back of her neck stand up. Eerie, menacing noises filtered down the stairwell, along with a series of rattles and vibrations that stopped as suddenly as they had started. The group waited in the silence, unsure what might happen next.

After a few minutes, Bill stood up. "Might as well go back upstairs, sounds like the worst is over."

Melinda was amazed to see everything was where it had been just minutes before. A spider-web crack created by a hail stone now ran across the front storm door, but the store's plate glass windows were unharmed.

"Thank the Lord," Esther pushed her palms together. "We've been spared. Oh, what a relief. Frank and Miriam have been through enough as it is."

Bill slid back the deadbolt and the group stepped cautiously out of the store. Small twigs littered the sidewalks and lawns along Main Street. A few larger tree limbs were scattered in the road. The young woman surprised Melinda with a hug and then ran for her car. The elderly man, however, seemed more interested in surveying the scene.

There wasn't much else to see. But the hanging baskets across and down the street had been tossed from their light poles and smashed on the sidewalk, and were now only sad lumps of black soil and bedraggled stems.

"I'm glad you took our flowers down, Bill," Esther sighed. "Miriam worked so hard on those. But if that's all that's been destroyed, I'd say we all are pretty lucky."

A few people stepped out of the Watering Hole and began gathering up downed tree limbs in front of the bar. Nancy appeared in the front door of City Hall and ran the flags back up the pole. The grinding squeal of a chain saw echoed down Main Street as Bill peered toward the co-op.

"It does look like there might be more limbs down over that way," he said. "I think there's even a tree down by the corner of Main and First, hard to tell from here. I hope that next round of rain holds off or bypasses us so people can clean up."

While the sky wasn't as black as before, it seemed closer to twilight than four-thirty and more threatening clouds were bubbling up to the west. Melinda helped Bill gather and stack broken branches while Esther swept the last of the sidewalk's debris away with a broom. Then Bill's phone rang.

"Hey, Tony. Well, it's not too bad here, really, it could be much worse." He was reaching for another tree branch, then froze. "So, one did touch down. Where?" He looked at Melinda, his expression turning grim. "Anyone hurt? Wow. Yeah, I'm on my way."

Melinda's heart began to race. She could feel her pulse pounding in her neck. Bill put a hand on her shoulder.

"There was a tornado west of here, tore things up pretty bad. Several farms were hit hard, there's serious structural damage and somebody's trapped inside a collapsed house."

"Oh, my God," she gasped. "Where is the worst of the damage? I have to get home. I have to go right away!"

She barged through the front door of the still-darkened store and lunged over the counter for her purse, Bill and Esther right behind.

"Tony didn't say for sure, just that it's a few miles west of Prosper." Bill tried to sound reassuring. "Twisters can hopscotch around, touch down here but not there."

Melinda could only nod, tears burning under her eyelids. What if Horace's had been hit? The house could be damaged. And the animals ...

A horn honked out front and Doc pulled up. Bill ran out and leaned in the truck's window, then Doc drove away. "Doc says every first responder in the county's been called out. I need to go, now. Esther, can you close up?"

"Absolutely, don't worry about the store. I'll call Frank and Miriam and let them know everything's OK here, the power's out, is all. You go, both of you."

Melinda frantically dialed Angie's cell. "She's not answering." She tried Ed and Mabel's house; the line beeped and beeped but didn't ring through. "I can't get Ed and Mabel, either."

"Their phone is probably just out." Esther gave her a hug. "Watch out for downed power lines on the roads, there'll be wind damage even away from the tornado's path. You be careful, now."

Melinda pushed through the back door, which hadn't yet snapped closed from when Bill ran out just a minute before. Her hands shook as she cranked the ignition and turned onto Main Street.

All through town, children gathered up twigs as adults worked in teams to lift and drag larger limbs out of the way. An ancient tree had tumbled over and now blocked First Street, leaving a sad void in the yard of one of the town's historic homes.

But the Prosper co-op looked the same as always, its tower unscathed and stretching to the heavy clouds lowering overhead. Melinda tried to calm her nerves.

"It could have been much worse, just like Bill said," she whispered as she bumped over the railroad tracks. "Word spreads fast after something like this. It's possible that the damage isn't as bad as what we heard."

She had traveled nearly two miles before she spotted a power pole snapped off at its base, the black electrical cable snaking through the weeds at the edge of the field. The next few poles were leaning this way and that, the power lines snapped and drooping dangerously close to the county highway. The nearby acreage appeared to be intact, only a few soggy shingles resting on the front lawn.

But Melinda gasped when she passed the next farm, its silo crumpled as if smashed by a large hand. Part of the house's roof had peeled away and the pasture fence was splayed into the grass. She slowed her car to a crawl, sliding over the center line to skirt a mangled hunk of metal siding in the road.

Two agitated pigs and a yapping dog circled in the ditch, followed by an exhausted-looking woman. The dog darted out on the blacktop and Melinda stopped, powered down her passenger-side window.

"Is everyone OK here?" she called to the woman, who caught the dog by the collar and made an apologetic gesture.

"We're all right, thanks." The woman came up to the car. "Some building damage but that's all. What a nightmare, the sound was something I'll never forget. But we've got lots of help here and more coming." Melinda noticed several pickups and a car in the driveway. Large plastic tarps were being unloaded out of the back of one of the trucks.

"I wish I could stay to help, but I haven't been home yet."

"Where's that?"

"West of here two miles, then south. There's a collapsed house somewhere, have you heard anything about that?"

The woman shook her head, then put her hand to her cheek. "No, oh no, how awful, I hadn't heard that. We've been outside since it happened. Saw some fire trucks and an ambulance go by here about ten minutes ago, though. I hope you make it home OK."

Melinda powered up the window, her heart pounding in her ears. She'd seen the fear on the woman's face when she said where she lived.

Tears began to spill down her cheeks. "I have to get home. Please God, I just have to get home."

Her car crept over the rise before the next intersection. She gasped, unable to believe what she was seeing.

The cornfield to the left, which has been leafy and vigorous just that morning, was completely flat, its downed stalks all pointing northeast. On the other side of the road, the soybean plants were no longer in orderly rows but twisted and tossed about in the churned-up black earth. There were flashing lights down past the crossroads, a vehicle blocking the road. In the gathering gloom, she could just make out the county sheriff's logo on the side of an SUV, and a man wearing a neon-yellow vest bunched over a rain poncho.

She slowed to a stop and lowered her window. The officer leaned in, his face scrunched against a sudden spray of rain. "Ma'am, I'm sorry, but we've got the road closed up ahead. You'll need to turn around, head back to the state highway."

"But I live here!" She could barely get the words out, alarm rising in her voice. "I, I have to get home, I've got animals out there. They ..."

The deputy gave her a sympathetic look then glanced over his shoulder. There was a hazy black cloud about a half mile down the blacktop, an angry scrawl of red and orange flames at its base and the spark of flashing emergency lights nearby.

Melinda heard agitated voices coming from the radio clipped to the officer's vest but couldn't make out the words.

"We've got a situation over there that's got this highway shut down." The deputy was nearly shouting now, pressing his cap down over his face as he tried to block the wind.

"Tornado came right through, the house was nearly wiped away but some of it collapsed into the basement. They're trying to get those people out. The barn caught fire when the power lines snapped."

He paused to wave through another county vehicle, sirens blaring, that had come up behind Melinda.

"Emergency vehicles only, sorry." The officer shook his head. "You could head back to the last intersection, try the long way around. Was anyone at your place when the storm hit? Is everyone accounted for?"

Melinda's chest tightened as she recalled Doc's eerie visit to the Emmersons' that morning. Hadn't Mabel once said their place was on the county highway? She closed her eyes, tried to steady herself.

"No people were at home, no. But I've got animals and ..."

A blare of sirens and flashing lights approached from the west and the deputy stepped aside as an ambulance flew past, racing for the junction with the state highway.

"Godspeed to them," the deputy called to Melinda. "And good luck to you."

* 19 *

Melinda turned into the eastbound lane of the county highway and drove back to the last intersection, the hum of her tires on the wet pavement accompanied by the "splat, splat" of enormous raindrops hitting her windshield. As she headed south from the blacktop, she tried to gather her emotions and her courage.

In one moment, she told herself the storm may have missed Horace's farm. The house would be unharmed, the barn and sheds intact. The sheep were inside, safe from the stinging downpour, and Hobo and the cats were napping in the grain room. Melinda tried for a smile as she imagined Pansy sulking by one of the chicken coop's windows, her afternoon of pecking for grubs ruined by the rain.

In the next, she feared finding the farmhouse smashed, rafters and siding tossed into the road, and the barn reduced to a jumble of debris. The garden might be nothing but a tangle of shredded stalks, the mangled remains of the front maple tree pinning the broken lilac bushes into the ditch. And the animals ...

"Oh God, no," she prayed. "They all have to be OK. They have to!" A wave of guilt came over her, but didn't pass.

She hit the steering wheel with her hand. "Why couldn't this have happened when I was home? I might have been able to do something."

She drove slowly, cautiously, as she wasn't familiar with this gravel road and random bits of tree limbs littered the ditches and shoulders. The first crossroads finally appeared and she turned west, through a mile where the two farms had only minor damage. The crops looked tired and hail-beaten but were still upright. At the next intersection she'd continue west, cross a bridge and pass Angie and Nathan's farm, which was up on a hill.

Melinda braked hard at the crossroads and stopped, not sure what to do.

The creek crossing was still more than a quarter of a mile away, but a heavy tree that once hugged the waterway's bank had been ripped free and thrown across her approach to the bridge. The willows lining the creek bed were ripped from their roots, tossed about like ábandoned toys, and the wooden post for the yellow "one lane bridge" sign was sheared off a few feet up from the ditch.

Beyond and up the hill, the decades-old windbreak on Angie and Nathan's farm was now just a jagged line on the horizon. She took a steadying breath and went left, her only option to drive around the mile section and reach Horace's farm from the south.

There seemed to be fewer twigs down from the shrubs and trees along these fence lines, but her hands became icy as she turned at the final crossroads. It had seemed like she would never get home, but now she was almost too afraid to drive that last half mile.

"I have to face it," she said to herself, gripping the steering wheel tighter. "Whatever it is, I need to know, I need to see it. Please, God ..."

The tears returned as she recalled her first cautious drive on this gravel road nearly two months ago. She'd not only come from the other direction, but from a completely different point of view. Her motive had been simple curiosity, to pass the time on a lazy, sunny afternoon.

And now, she was overwhelmed by how much this farm, these animals, meant to her. Hobo's face flashed through her mind, and Horace's too. This place had helped her start her life over, and she couldn't bear to see it destroyed.

Just one more small rise in the road, and the farm came into view. The barn was still standing, as was the house and the windbreak beyond it.

"Maybe it missed us." She felt the smallest stirring of relief as she turned in the drive. "Maybe it's not so bad."

The lilacs were haggard but still rooted in the front yard. There was a torn tree limb across the driveway, and she got out to drag it to the side. While the rain had slowed to a trickle, the temperature had dropped and a stiff, cold wind caused her to shiver as she got back behind the wheel.

As she pulled up to the garage, it became apparent the farm's buildings hadn't been totally spared. There were a few toothy gaps in the barn roof where shingles had peeled away, exposing the wood underneath. The upstairs bathroom's storm window had been shattered by hail. More ragged balls of ice, some as large as golf balls, littered the yard. Twigs and sticks were everywhere, but she didn't care. Picking them up would take hours of backbreaking work, but it could have been so much worse.

But oh, the garden. Melinda's elation drained away as she sidestepped the hailstones and downed branches to reach the back porch door. What that morning had been healthy and strong was now wind-whipped and bedraggled, the beans' fence bent over and nearly touching the ground, the tomato cages crumpled and teetering under the weight of their plants. It was just as well the rhubarb season was long past, as the top-heavy leaves were shredded and limp.

An indignant squawk made Melinda jump. Two of the black-and-white hens, their feathers fluffed in irritation, were huddled in the drooping lilies next to the back steps. She peered around the garage toward the coop. Three of the run's wood posts were askew, a torn gap visible between two of the wire panels.

"So you escaped, huh? And you don't like it much out here, do you?"

The chickens just clucked and squirmed closer to the house's foundation. Melinda didn't see any other hens in the yard, and wasn't sure if that was a good or a bad sign. Hobo, the cats and the sheep would all be in the barn, safe. But she couldn't shake the feeling that something wasn't right.

She dropped her things on the back porch bench and anxiously flipped the ceiling light's switch. If the power had ever been out, it was back on. She pawed through the overstuffed closet and pulled out a flame-orange sweatshirt, then folded its cuffs up to meet her wrists. With her phone stuffed in a front pocket she reached for a flashlight, encouraged that the first one she picked up made at least a faint beam on the wall. She couldn't imagine she would need it, but its weight in her hand made her feel ready, prepared.

She wanted to try Angie again, and call Ed and Mabel. But first, she had to assess the damage. She pulled the sweatshirt's hood up against the wind and closed her eyes in despair as she trudged past the garden, hail stones crunching under her sneakers.

"Hobo!" she called in the direction of the barn. "Come on out, Hobo! Help me look around."

There were only a few shingles missing from the chicken coop's roof and the main door was still bolted. A round of agitated clucks answered the creak of the door's hinges as she entered, and four pairs of eyes caught in the gray light from outside. One of the skittish hens hopped down from her roost and ran for the far wall, her neck working in nervousness.

"That means two more of you are still missing." Melinda studied the gloomy corners to make sure she hadn't miscounted. She slid the cover over the chickens' access to the run, then latched the main door securely behind her.

The shabby little building between the coop and the machine shed was now a heap of splintered wood, its broken roof held up only by whatever junk Horace had stashed inside. Melinda wandered into the windbreak, stepping carefully in the shaggy, wind-flattened grass. A brown-tipped evergreen that was probably dead before the storm appeared to be the only tree down. She was circling back past the machine shed, which seemed unscathed except for a few torn shingles, when her phone rang in her pocket.

"Melinda! Are you all right?" She could hear the fear in Kevin's voice. "I heard about the tornado."

Her shoulders relaxed. She didn't feel so alone anymore.

"I'm fine, I'm OK. It missed Prosper, and Swanton, too, thankfully. I was at the store when the storm came through. I just got home and, well, I guess it could be worse. I'll start with the house ..."

Kevin wasn't worried about the small shed. The Schermann family was already organizing to come out to the farm that weekend and clean up, and he would track down someone to repair the bathroom's storm window and replace the outbuildings' missing shingles. "I'm glad it's not too bad. The two hens might be in the windbreak. They'll come out when they calm down and get hungry. Other than a few runaway chickens, sounds like the animals are fine."

Melinda stopped short, stared toward the barn. Hobo hadn't come out. She'd been so busy examining the chicken coop, then Kevin called, and ...

"Well, I think so. I mean, I'm sure they're OK." She tried to keep her voice light. "It's just that I haven't seen anyone else yet. But I haven't made it to the barn."

Kevin didn't seem concerned. "The sheep and cats and Hobo are all smart enough to head for shelter. And there should be some wire in the grain room to close that gap in the chicken run. I'll call Horace and let him know you're holding your own out there. If he's been anywhere near a TV this afternoon, he must be worried."

Melinda passed the concrete pad where the windmill used to stand and craned her neck to see the peak of the barn's roof. How many storms had this structure stood tall against over the past century? It would take time to clean up, but Horace had been lucky.

"No, we've all been lucky," she said softly, patting the main barn door's flecked red paint as she slid the metal latch to the side. The barn's familiar, comforting smell was still there, just as it had been that morning.

"Hobo! Where are you? Storm's over, buddy, you can come out now."

There was no answering bark, no echo of padded feet coming her way. And no sheep, either, she realized as her eyes adjusted to gloom. Only an uneasy silence.

"They have to be in here." She flipped the light switch and hurrying down the aisle. "Here, sheep! Here, Hobo!" She rapped her fist on the metal lid of the grain barrel, checked the lambing pens in the back of the barn. Nothing.

The haymow offered no sign of Hobo or the cats. She called again, her now-shaky voice reverberating through the cavernous space.

Downstairs once more, she could see that Hobo's flap-covered door in the north barn wall was clear of debris.

"Don't panic, it's been a long day," she whispered to herself, but her mind was already racing. "The ewes have probably gone back outside since I got home, I just didn't see them. Maybe Hobo got over a fence and in with the sheep, and he's outside, too."

Melinda passed through the gate into the sheep's feeding area, pausing only long enough to make sure the metal latch was soundly locked. She hurried out the east pasture door and circled through the lot, nearly stumbling over the gopher holes hidden in the unevenly chewed grass. The rough wind racing in from the west carried off her frantic shouts to Hobo and the sheep.

Only a few bushes lined the fence rows, but several gnarled evergreen trees had long ago banded together in the far southwest corner of the pasture. Several light-colored shapes were moving among the low-hanging branches.

"At last!" She ran back into the barn for a bucket of oats. "Hobo must have herded the sheep into that little grove." There were two rope halters hanging on a nail next to the inside gate and she pulled one down, hoping she wouldn't have to figure out how to use it.

She ran across the pasture, her heart pounding in her ears, then eased her pace as she neared the patch of trees. She needed to approach the sheep slowly, casually, to have any hope of keeping them together. And if Hobo got too excited, he could cause the whole flock to bolt. If she could get one of the ewes to follow her, the others should fall in behind.

Another line of inky black clouds was dropping in from the west, heavy with rain and possibly hail. She had to hurry.

"Here, sheep! Here, sheep!"

Finally, one of them sent back a distressed "baaaa" in return. Melinda counted twelve fuzzy charcoal heads turning her way, but there was no sign of Hobo. She scanned the wild grasses growing tall around the pasture's perimeter, looked carefully under all the trees in the grove, called him again.

"He's not here. He's not out here!"

In this far corner of the pasture, away from the shelter of the farm yard, Melinda felt small and alone, frightened by the vast stretches of hail-beaten fields and ominous skies. There was a threatening strength in the cold wind as it stung her face and uncovered hands.

She couldn't call anyone for help, not now, when all her neighbors were dealing with the same problems, or worse. She set down the oats bucket and the halter, tightened the hood on her sweatshirt and briefly warmed her hands in its pockets. "I'll have to find Hobo later. Right now, I need to get these sheep inside."

The ewes were pacing back and forth, nudging each other, their eyes wild. By the terror etched on their faces, Melinda realized the sheep may have never made it to the barn, had possibly rode out the storm in the thin shelter of these scraggly trees.

"Ladies, I need you to come with me," she announced in a careful, low voice, gently shaking the grain bucket. "Let's all go back to the barn. I'll set out a good supper and you girls can rest. I'm home now."

But I wasn't home in time to protect you, she thought with a pang in her chest.

Or Hobo. Or the chickens or the cats. She told herself that Sunny and Stormy were surely tucked away in the haymow, their tails puffed with fear but otherwise safe, and pushed all those other thoughts aside.

"It's OK, it's OK," she cooed to the sheep, shaking the grain bucket again, not knowing what else to try.

Annie, always the bossy one, began to bellow, her nose leading her toward the bucket but her wary eyes catching sight of the halter in Melinda's other hand. Melinda hid the halter behind her back and Annie relaxed.

"So you don't want to see the rope, is that it? Annie girl, I know you're smart. How about you help me out here?" She shook the grain again and took a few steps back, but Annie wouldn't follow. The ewes resumed their anxious chorus and, with a grunt of impatience, Annie joined them.

Melinda would need the halter. She turned her back to the flock and worked the twisted rope in her hands, getting a feel for its rough strength and loosening the loop. Even if she couldn't get the halter properly fastened on Annie's head, she might be able to at least get it around her neck.

The sheep began to calm down a bit. They were all watching Melinda, waiting for her next move, looking to her for guidance. She slowly set the bucket down, hiding it in the long grass, careful to not look Annie in the eye and keep the halter behind her back. Annie decided Melinda no longer had anything to offer, and started to turn away.

This was her chance. Just before Annie flanked to the left, she quickly tossed the halter over the ewe's head. Annie let out a surprised grunt and tried to leap forward, but Melinda held tight even as she felt the burn of the scratchy rope in her palms. Her heart racing and her hands trembling, she managed to tighten the slip rope just enough to keep it around Annie's neck.

"Annie, shhh. Annie, stand still," she whispered.

Once Annie realized she couldn't get away, her breathing slowed and so did Melinda's. Thunder rumbled away to the west and a large raindrop splashed on Melinda's forehead.

"OK, let's get that grain." Gripping the halter lead in her left hand, she reached over and snatched up the grain bucket, shook it back and forth. "You're the leader of the pack, Annie. Let's take everyone home, huh?"

Annie jumped but Melinda pulled on the rope, bringing the ewe up to the bucket. The ewe tentatively set one hoof forward, then plunged her nose into the oats. Melinda let Annie enjoy a good mouthful before taking two steps back. Not only did Annie follow, this time with confidence, but three of the other sheep began to move their way.

"Let's go, girls, let's get back to the barn," Melinda called over the rising wind. "We need to hurry."

She rattled the grain bucket and more of the sheep came forward. Then she took three steps back and tugged on the rope. Annie walked toward her, the others clustering behind. Four more steps. Five. Then she turned her back on the sheep and pulled, felt the rope go slack as Annie followed.

Shaking the grain bucket again, Melinda called, "here, sheep! here, sheep!" as more rain drops splattered the hood of her sweatshirt. Then the skies opened. She tried to walk as fast as she could without tripping, blinking the rain out of her eyes, comforted by Annie's weight on the end of the rope.

The rain slashed at her face until she at last rounded the southeast corner of the barn. With the towering walls offering shelter from the roaring wind and the open barn door beckoning, the sheep began to "baaaa" with excitement.

Melinda hurried Annie inside and tied her halter rope to a fence brace, then scattered the rest of the grain into the feed bunk. It wasn't much, but enough to encourage the last of the sheep to enter the barn. She counted twelve wooly backs before she reached out into the downpour for the handles of the divided barn door. There was a satisfying slap as the bolt on the top half slid closed, locking the sheep inside. Melinda loosened Annie's halter so she could slip free and, with an indignant bellow, the ewe joined the rest of the flock.

Melinda was shaking all over, cold rain soaking through her sweatshirt to run down her scalp and through her clothes.

But she'd brought the sheep in, and they were safe. She and Annie had done it together.

She leaned against a post, the tears coming in a torrent as the heavy rain drummed on the barn roof. Hobo was out there somewhere, night coming on in a few hours. What if he ran away before the storm hit, and not after? She knew animals could sense the weather and Hobo was a smart, sensitive dog. He could have taken off, trying to stay ahead of the approaching storm, and been caught out in a field somewhere, terrified and alone, with no shelter in sight.

"I have to find him!" She wiped her nose on her sweatshirt sleeve. "I can't let Horace down. Oh, Hobo, where are you?"

The ewes were silent, watching. Even Annie was still.

∗ 20 ∗

The adrenaline rush that helped her get the sheep to safety drained away in the few minutes it took to scoop out their evening ration of grain.

She was suddenly so tired. And hungry, too. She'd rest for a few minutes at the kitchen table with a sandwich, then fix the chickens' run and start looking for Hobo.

But first, one more check of the haymow. No one answered her calls. But just as she doubled back to the stairs, something along the east wall caught her attention. A golden glimmer, just behind a pile of straw bales.

"Kitties? Are you there?"

A second reflective orb became visible as her eyes adjusted to the shadows between the stack of bales and the wall. Then, Sunny's fuzzy ears. And finally, another set of frightened eyes: Stormy huddled behind his friend.

"It's OK, it's OK now." Melinda crouched down to the level of the cats, who made no move to leave the safety of their crawlspace. "I'll bring supper up here, just for tonight."

She fetched a scoop of kibble from the back porch and filled one of the bowls in the grain room, then rinsed and refilled the cats' water dish. "I'm back now," she said softly, setting the bowls down near the straw bales. His nose working at the smell of the kibble, Sunny put his paws up on a bale, debating whether he should make the leap.

"I know better than to press my luck with you two," Melinda cooed. "I'll leave so you feel safe coming out to eat. I'll see you kitties in the morning."

She shivered as she stepped out into the damp yet again and checked twice that the barn door was secure. The rain had slowed but the wind was still strong. Her cell phone started to ring as she kicked away her sodden sneakers inside the back porch. It was Angie.

"Oh, thank God." Melinda tucked the phone under her chin as she opened the kitchen door and peeled off the soaked sweatshirt. "Is everyone OK over there? When I tried to get home, I couldn't get over the bridge by your house."

"We're going to lose the barn, but Nathan and I and the girls are all right and that's what matters." Angie sounded strangely calm. "It came up so fast. We crawled under the workbench in the basement and rode it out. But what a mess! We've got people over here rounding up the sheep and goats and cows. We're trying to get them settled in one of the sheds, moving stuff around and putting down straw and setting up fence panels."

Angie took a deep breath, then her voice started to rise in pitch. "The animals are so terrified, and we're afraid they'll crash through what's left of the pasture fences overnight if we don't get them locked inside somewhere. The barn is just smashed, Melinda, the whole top half is gone."

"Oh Angie, I'm so sorry. But I'm relieved you are all OK. I tried to call earlier, I was so worried. I couldn't get Ed and Mabel, either."

"I talked to them a bit ago, and they are fine." Angie sniffled, and tried to get her emotions in check. "Just some tree damage. Ed said it sounds like the tornado was west of here, then bended more to the east once it got closer to the blacktop. If it had turned sooner, we all would have been right in the worst of it. How bad is it there?"

"There's some shingles off the barn and outbuildings, tree branches down all over. Some of the hailstones were as big as golf balls but I think there's only a few storm windows broken on the house. The garden looks terrible; I'm glad Horace isn't here to see it. The sheep were hiding in that little grove at the far corner of the pasture, but I got them inside."

"Wow, look at you, Little Bo Peep." Angie's voice brightened. "I bet Hobo was excited. He likes to think he can herd sheep."

Melinda said nothing, and concern flooded Angie's voice.

"What is it? Something's wrong, isn't it?"

"Oh, Angie, Hobo is gone." Melinda slumped in a chair and tried to keep her voice steady. "I can't find him anywhere. He's not in the barn. He wasn't with the sheep. I have to find him. Kevin called, and ..."

"Does Kevin know about Hobo?"

"No, I still thought Hobo was in the barn when he called. I don't know how I'm going to tell him, and Horace will ..." She glanced at the clock above the sink. It was already past seven. "I need to get back out there and keep looking."

"Listen, don't call Kevin back tonight," Angie said gently. "Hobo could have headed for the creek, or he's hiding in a ditch somewhere, scared but OK."

Melinda thought of Stormy and Sunny, how they were safe but too afraid to leave their hiding place. "You're right." She took a deep breath. "I don't want to worry Kevin unless I have to. I'll check the windbreak again, walk the road."

"I'll talk to you tomorrow. And don't worry, I'm sure Hobo will turn up. If nothing else, he'll get hungry and come home. Just promise me you'll take a well-charged flashlight and wear study boots. No city-girl shoes, OK?"

Melinda managed a small laugh. "Yes, ma'am. And you let me know if there's anything I can do to help over there."

Talking to Angie made Melinda feel better. That, and a hastily arranged sandwich eaten in the comforting light of the kitchen. Her friends were safe, but not everyone had been so fortunate. She thought of that ambulance, lights flashing and sirens blaring, as it sped away down the blacktop.

She changed into an old pair of jeans, thick socks and a long-sleeve thermal top. She didn't have any boots, but there were rubber waders on the porch she could pull on over dry sneakers. The orange sweatshirt, drying on a peg next to Horace's chore coat, was replaced with a yellow slicker found in the porch closet.

She was anxious to keep looking for Hobo, but she had to get the runaway chickens inside before night came on.

"Girls, I've got a confession to make," she whispered to the two hens now roosting under the back porch steps. "I'm scared of the dark. At least, out here anyway. There. Doesn't that make you feel better? Aren't you glad Horace picked me to look after you? Yep, I'm sure you are."

The chickens would be safe inside their coop for the night, but Melinda didn't like leaving the run open to predators. Besides, she may not have time to fix it in the morning. She found the wire in one of the dusty corners of the barn's grain room, just as Kevin said she would, and wire cutters in the toolbox on the shelf.

The chicken run was a haphazard mess, but there was no time for elaborate repairs.

Melinda gave one corner a shove with her shoulder, trying to square the frame as much as she could. It took several lengths of wire, crisscrossed this way and that, to pull together the large gap where all four chickens escaped. She made a hurried inspection of the rest of the run, threading smaller pieces of wire through a few other spots where the panels threatened to pull loose from the frame.

"There." She stepped back to observe her work. "Is that tight enough to keep out a fox, or a raccoon? Can't they squeeze through really small spaces? I don't know. But this will have to do."

She heard a faint "cluck, cluck" coming from just inside the windbreak, and hurried out to find the other two hens huddled in a feathery pile under one of the cedar trees. She stared at them for a moment, then had an idea. "Wait right there," she called over her shoulder as she ran for the house.

"Good thing I brought all these totes with me," she said as she bumped across the yard with two of the larger plastic tubs. She slowly approached the hens in the windbreak, then gently set down the containers, their lids already loose. Before she had time to get nervous, she snatched up one chicken, plopped her in the tote and snapped on the top.

The other bird tried to scoot away but Melinda was quick, catching the hen just before she got out of reach. With those captives safely inside the coop, she repeated the process by the back porch steps, drawing those frightened ladies out with a bit of cracked corn.

Melinda allowed herself a moment of elation over her luck with the chickens, then gathered up her totes and started back for the house, the yard already falling into twilight. The reassuring glow of the yard light guided her to the back porch and kept the worst of the shadows away. But the gathering darkness hovered just outside the light's beam, waiting for her down the driveway and on the gravel road, in the empty, silent places she would have to visit tonight if she had any hope of finding Hobo.

She discovered a cheerful little red lantern on the porch shelf, then rummaged in the kitchen junk drawer for fresh batteries for both the lantern and her flashlight. With all the farmhouse's downstairs lights aglow, she pocketed her phone and keys in the yellow slicker and paused on the back steps.

"If I were a scared dog, where would I go?" she asked the stars, which were beginning to peek out from the thinning clouds. The moon was barely a sliver, unable to offer any additional light for her search.

She decided to walk the yard first, just in case Hobo had returned while she was inside. Then she would trudge back through the windbreak, where the trees' leaves trembled in the unexpected chill, and shine her light into the shadows. She passed through the front pasture gate and followed the barn's foundation with her flashlight's beam, pausing only to aim it into the foreboding darkness of the windswept grass. She kept close to the barn, too afraid to step away from its comforting walls.

"Hobo! Hobo, where are you?"

The only answer was a startled sheep's "baaa" from inside. She let herself out the pasture gate on the west side of the barn, then traced the concrete footings of the machine shed with the flashlight and skimmed the pile of lumber that used to be the little building. The circle of light next caught the windows of the chicken house and the far edge of the wrecked garden.

She stepped carefully into the windbreak, the downed limbs and twigs crackling under her galoshes. The flashlight's beam bounced off the debris, throwing a maze of shadows on the ground. Melinda half expected to flush out a rabbit or even a raccoon, but saw no signs of life. The usual summer-night noises also seemed to be missing, like the incessant chirp of crickets, or the occasional croak of a toad that had wandered away from the creek.

The creek. Her mind churned, trying to visualize where Hobo might be. If he had seen the storm advancing from the southwest, he might have run toward the waterway. It was lined with shrubs and trees that would signal shelter to a frightened dog, as would the crawlspaces under the bridge.

As much as it frightened her, she had to go down there. If Hobo was simply hiding in the tall grass of the fencerows, or crouching in a ditch, wouldn't he have turned up by now?

"If he's alive, he would have." She pushed the rest of that thought from her mind.

Her sneakers were clumsy inside the heavy-soled rubber boots, the galoshes crunching the gravel as she started down the lane and farther away from the safe glow of the house. Even with fresh batteries, the flashlight's beam was only a pinprick in the dense darkness.

She stopped at the end of the driveway to switch to the plastic lantern, which threw off a wider circle of light. The edge of the metal drainage culvert under the driveway caught her attention. She hesitated, then stepped off the shoulder of the gravel road into the weeds.

Melinda was glad the rubber boots came up almost to her knees. Who knew what she might stir up in this long grass in the dark? Snakes could be the least of her worries. Anything might be out here, lurking around.

"Hobo! Hobo, where are you?" Yelling, she decided, might do more than bring Hobo to her. It might scare away anything else crouching in the ditch.

She nearly slipped on the slick grass, and grasped the rusted top of the drainage tube for support. Closing her eyes for a second to gather her courage, she crouched down and shined the lantern into the murky blackness of the culvert. It was desolate and empty, a sludge of muck and water clinging to the bottom and clumps of dead leaves plastered to the rusting metal. The wind made an eerie whistling sound through the culvert, and she felt a chill snake down her spine.

It was good to stand up again, scramble back to the openness of the road. She adjusted her gear and made sure nothing had fallen out of her pockets. The lantern's pool of light ebbed and flowed as she turned left and then right, checking the ditches for any sign of her friend. She called Hobo again and again, with no answer, as she followed the gravel's packed-down tire tracks north to the bridge.

This crossings' metal guardrails were still square, the "one lane bridge" sign no more dented than it had been that morning, but several smaller branches littered the road. It was maybe ten feet down a steep slope to the water's edge. The grass here was taller, nearly three feet high in some places, making it impossible for Melinda to see her feet. She nearly lost her balance and decided to slide the rest of the way on her bottom rather than risk a fall.

She snapped the lantern off for a second, listened for any stealth movements along the creek bank. There was only the rustle of the wind in the bushes and the "swoosh, swoosh" of the creek as it rushed off toward the damaged bridge east of Angie and Nathan's farm.

The bank was muddy, so soft that Melinda's galoshes threatened to keep her rooted in one spot. She began to call for Hobo again, shouting until she became hoarse, as she shined the lantern along the creek bed.

There were animal tracks in the mud. Some were smaller than others, but they all followed the water's edge. Melinda wished she had paid better attention in sixth-grade science class, could decipher what creatures might be watching from the shadows. But the younger Melinda could never have dreamed she would be roaming a lonely ravine on a strange night like this, risking a broken leg to find someone else's dog.

Tears began to well up in her eyes. Hobo was Horace's dog, but he was her dog, too.

He helped her feel at home here, had been her constant companion. He'd eased her loneliness and made her laugh, gave her someone to care for when she needed that most.

"We've helped each other heal," she said, then raised her voice. "Oh, Hobo, where are you? I need to bring you home. We need to go home. Let me know if you're out here." Losing hope, she barely paused for a response before following the tracks to the underside of the wooden-plank bridge.

The vastness of the black sky and the void of the empty gravel road had been unsettling enough, but the dark tunnel under the old bridge was worse.

Melinda shivered as she shined the lantern toward the shadowy recesses where the creek's banks met the bridge's support beams, half hoping she'd see a set of eyes glowing back at her, half hoping she wouldn't. But the crawlspaces were empty. Hobo wasn't there.

Or was he? Melinda turned, surveying a pyre of downed tree limbs and waterlogged weeds on the south bank. The creek would have been higher and swifter during and right after the storm, beaching debris as it slowed to make its sharp turn just past the bridge.

"It must have gone down nearly as fast as it came up." Her voice echoed back out of the shadows. The ragged stack was over two feet tall, high enough that ...

Her stomach dropped. She didn't have gloves on, but it didn't matter. Hands shaking, she set the lantern at her feet and tugged at the closest broken tree limb. The rough bark scratched her palms and the chunk of wood was heavier than she expected. With a grunt of effort, she dragged it aside and reached for another, then another.

"Please, don't be in here," she whispered, her voice shaking. She was moving faster now, tossing branches aside with both hands.

"I want to find you, but not here. Not here."

Her heart filled with despair. Why hadn't she been home when this happened? And the forecast had called for severe weather. Why hadn't she thought to lock Hobo in the barn that morning?

He wouldn't have liked the change in routine, but he would be safe now.

And she wouldn't be here, in the dark cavern under this bridge, praying not to find her friend buried in the rubble.

She worked feverishly, stopping now and then to shine her lantern into what was left of the tangled limbs and branches. There weren't any pockets left where a dog could be trapped, but she couldn't stop until she reached the bottom, until she was sure.

Only when her raw hands touched the slimy muck of the creek bed was Melinda able to stand up and step back, tears of relief streaming down her face.

"Oh, thank God," she sobbed, and lowered herself to a large limb, putting her head in her hands. "He's not here. He's not trapped under here. But where is he?"

Hobo could be anywhere. Any stand of grasses along a fence line. Under any random tree in a field. There were drainage culverts under every farm drive in the county. How would she ever find him? Her shoulders slumped, and now the tears were from exhaustion as well as defeat. "I might as well go home. He might be gone for good."

Her arms ached and her back complained as she braced herself to stand up. Stiff and sore, the lantern handle heavy in her scoured hand, she picked her way back along the creek to where she'd slid down the bank.

She crawled up through the wet weeds, keeping low so as to not slip on the steep slope. By the time she reached the edge of the field, her old jeans were as soaked and muddy on the front as on the rear.

Melinda's heart was so heavy, and her galoshes so cemented with mud, that she wondered how she would manage the half mile walk home. She'd failed. The one thing Kevin had asked of her, the one thing Horace had wanted her to do, was to look after the farm, especially Hobo.

She dreaded the call she would make in the morning. How could she tell Kevin that Hobo was missing?

She was exhausted by the time she reached Horace's property line but trudged through the ditch again to follow the outline of the acreage, her lantern beam searching through the tall weeds along the fence line. At last she came full circle, passing the front of the pasture and reaching the driveway.

Melinda remembered her first evening here, when she'd walked down the lane to find Hobo stretched out, head on paws, watching the road for Horace's return. How she'd rubbed his ears, told him it was going to be OK. They'd sat together in a comforting silence for over half an hour.

Hobo hadn't followed her back up the lane that night as she'd hoped. But the next day it seemed as if something had changed, and for the better.

In a second, Melinda knew what she needed to do. She carefully placed the little red lantern right where the lane widened to meet the road, right where she and Hobo had sat that evening.

The lantern's glow radiated only a few feet, but Melinda was out of ideas. She imagined Hobo, hiding somewhere in the darkness but somewhere close, seeing the lantern's small beam and heading toward it.

"Please come back," she pleaded. "Please be safe and come home."

There was nothing more to do tonight. She slowly clomped up the driveway to the back porch, the heavy mud still clinging to her boot, the farmhouse's soothing glow urging her to take just one more step, then another.

She kicked her boots off on the porch floor, then trudged through the house and upstairs to change out of her muddy, sodden clothes.

She went into Wilbur's old room, where she could just spot the end of the driveway out the lone window. The battery-powered lantern still glowed down there in the dark, a steady but small and fragile beam. Melinda said another prayer for Hobo and shuffled to her room, collapsed on the bed and fell into a deep sleep.

✳ 21 ✳

"Looks like you could use something stronger than this coffee." Auggie pressed a warm mug into Melinda's hands. "Back in the day, your grandpa had a special bottle under the counter, over there on the right side. Just for emergencies, you know."

"Don't worry, Auggie, your coffee is hearty enough to wake the dead." Doc took an appreciative sip and sighed, the creases around his eyes more visible this morning.

"Even so, it's going to take a few pots of this stuff to keep me going today."

Melinda held the hot coffee as close to her face as she dared, hoping the steam would rejuvenate her senses. Her feet ached, her hands were still raw and her shoulders sore. It felt like she had been up all night, even though she'd fallen into a deep, exhausted sleep once her head hit the pillow. And the moment her eyes opened, there was that heavy sadness in her heart as she remembered that Hobo was gone.

She called for him again and again, and checked around the outbuildings, but all she found was the silence that had been there the night before. She retrieved the lantern from the end of the driveway and fed the sheep, the ewes all but racing to get out to pasture once Melinda unlatched their door. Sunny and Stormy were still wild-eyed but waiting in the grain room for their breakfast.

The early-morning light took a critical view of Melinda's hurried attempts to repair the chickens' run, but all that mattered was she counted eight hens inside the coop, strutting around as if nothing had happened. The garden got only a sigh and a promise. At least it wouldn't need to be watered for several days. She called Kevin but he didn't answer, much to her relief, and she left him a message with the bad news.

Even with Hobo missing, she had been one of the lucky ones. And while she was tired, her friends had even more reason to nod over their coffee this morning.

Doc and Bill had been on duty most of the night with the volunteer emergency department, going farm to farm to evaluate the damage and make sure no one was missing. The fire Melinda saw was indeed at the Emmersons' place. Both Will and his wife, Helen, were still in the hospital, Doc reported, but there had been no fatalities from the storm and only a few minor injuries.

Bundles of branches and sections of cut-down trees were already being stacked along Prosper's streets when Melinda drove into town just before seven, the roar of chainsaws assaulting her ears when she crawled out of her car. Jerry had returned late last night and was now over at City Hall, organizing an official cleanup effort.

George's chair was also empty. Despite his age and against the wishes of his wife, he had been up until midnight helping neighbors clear downed tree limbs. He'd left a message on Prosper Hardware's answering machine, telling the others not to worry when he didn't show up for coffee. "I'm too old for this," George had said, his voice muffled by exhaustion. "Off to bed." Auggie had kept the co-op open until eleven and came back in at four that morning, the phone ringing constantly with farmers needing feed after their silos and barns were damaged in the storm.

Through her tears, Melinda told Doc and Auggie about Hobo. The two friends exchanged looks of concern but offered much-needed words of encouragement.

Auggie said a neighbor's dog once disappeared for two months and then suddenly returned one morning; she was found lounging on the patio as if nothing had happened.

Melinda had set up a Facebook page for Doc's clinic just before the Fourth of July parade, and he urged her to post Hobo's photo right away.

"I'm sure he'll turn up," Doc said. "Animals sometimes run away after a storm, I doubt he went very far. Sounds like the damage at your place wasn't too severe. He likely wasn't hurt, just scared. Kevin will understand."

"And you're not a failure." Auggie patted Melinda's arm. "I didn't know what to think at first when you said you were taking on Horace's farm. A city girl, out there with all those animals to look after? But you've done more than you know, and given Horace peace of mind to boot. Frank and Miriam would never have gotten by this long without you, either."

"What about me?"

Doc and Auggie looked shocked as Aunt Miriam hustled up the main aisle from the back of the store.

"Oh, come on, now. You boys aren't the only ones with keys to this place." Miriam elbowed Bill, who was yawning and pouring himself a cup of coffee. Melinda wasn't sure where her aunt had found her energy and high spirits.

"Everybody, I've got an idea, been working on it since last night." Miriam slapped a palm on the oak counter, unable to contain her excitement. Doc gave her a questioning look over his coffee mug. Auggie jumped in his chair, and Melinda realized he'd nearly fallen asleep.

"We've come through with not much more than a broken pane of glass in the front door. But sadly, many people around Prosper can't say the same. I hear the Emmersons are still in the hospital. So, Frank and I were up late, talking about how we might help. It was all I could do to keep him in the house. He wanted to go pick up tree branches, can you imagine? But here's what we're going to do."

Miriam pulled up one of the vacant chairs gathered around the sideboard.

"For the next two weeks, we'll sell all building materials at cost. That's the plywood, lumber, screws and nails, you name it. If someone asks for it and you're not sure if it qualifies, don't worry about it. Just give it to them at wholesale."

"Miriam, that's a wonderful idea." Doc reached over to put an arm around his longtime friend. "People will sure appreciate it."

"Well, this community has done so much for us these past months. This is one way we can give back, say thanks." Melinda could see a few tears of gratitude in her aunt's eyes.

"The construction stuff doesn't make up much of our sales these days, not like it did decades ago. It won't break us to do it at cost for a little while. Besides, this way people won't have to drive so far to get what they need, they can come here rather than drive to Mason City or anywhere else. I've got the cost sheets up in the office. Bill, I'll get those to you and put a copy up here under the counter."

"Sounds like we may need to increase our supply order for next week." Bill was exhausted, but he was smiling.

"Melinda," Miriam turned in chair, "can you get something together to put on the city's website? Nancy can post it for us, and I don't think Jerry would mind. And out to the media?"

Melinda felt her despair start to ease. She needed something to pull her focus away from the fact that Hobo was missing. And Aunt Miriam's good mood was infectious. "Of course. And you might gain some new customers out of all this, too."

"That's true. You are always thinking ahead like that, I love it. Now, let's see how many people we can help out. Speaking of help, I made Frank promise he'll stay inside today and let our dear neighbors clean up the yard so I can be down here at the store. I think we'll be busy. It is a Saturday, after all."

Aunt Miriam was right. Three people were waiting outside when Melinda unlocked the front door at eight. Two customers from the hardest hit areas northwest of Prosper had pulled up in the back even before then, their pickup beds cleared out to haul plywood and lumber.

Miriam guided people to the correct screws and nails and other supplies they needed, and was quick to give comfort as residents shared their harrowing stories of survival. Esther showed up before noon, insisting she couldn't sit at home when she knew Prosper Hardware was having one of its busiest days in years. Her first task was to make more coffee and set out cups for the customers.

Melinda, running the register, could barely catch her breath as people continued to pour into the store. Many of them lingered, anxious to talk to other shoppers and ask after old friends or distant relatives.

It was an emotional day. Everyone was tired, disheveled and reeling from the storm, but the goodwill circulating in the store gave Melinda just enough of a lift to power through. Friends hugged each other, tears of sympathy and relief on their cheeks, and promised to lend a hand with repairs. Strangers were connecting over their shared troubles, parting with warm handshakes and pats on the back.

One man paid for his purchases and then slipped Melinda two twenty-dollar bills, asking her to put them toward the tab of "anyone you think needs it most." He left the store before Melinda could flag Aunt Miriam down and try and find out who he was.

"This is small-town Iowa at its best." Esther beamed as she sacked purchases. "Everyone pulls together when things get tough. We always find a way to make do, don't we?"

"We certainly do." Melinda felt a lump in her throat as she reached for the next customer's items on the oak counter. Seven customers were waiting in line for the register, but no one was complaining or cross. All these people were willing to help each other, whether it was to swing a hammer or just offer a kind ear to someone who was worried or scared.

She was proud to be from here. Actually, she was proud to *be here*, right now, be a part of the healing that was taking place right there in the store. But she was so tired ...

"You need to take a break." Esther put a hand on her arm. "You had a long night, and today's going to be the same. Why don't you go upstairs for a few minutes, take a nap if you like? I'll give you twenty and I'll come up and wake you."

"Thanks, Esther, I will." Melinda took her purse from under the counter and saw her phone blinking with a message from Kevin.

She settled in on the faded couch in the upstairs office and, with trembling fingers, dialed into her voicemail.

Kevin urged her not to worry, and said several Schermann family members would arrive at the farm by nine tomorrow morning. "There's still hope Hobo will show up." His tone was reassuring, but she could hear the sadness running through it. "I won't tell Horace about Hobo just yet. He can't do anything to help and it'll just upset him."

Melinda barely remembered closing her eyes and was startled when Esther gave her shoulder a shake. The rest of the day passed in a whirlwind, the store's entire display of screws and nails reduced by half and every tarp on the shelf and in storage sold before the store closed.

"Good work today, everyone." Aunt Miriam sighed as she locked the front door, then looked at Bill and Esther. "I don't want to see either of you here Monday morning until at least noon. And Melinda, Monday is still one of your days off, so you stay home."

Bill started to protest but Miriam kindly cut him off. "You've all done more than enough. I can manage by myself Monday morning, I'll line up someone to stay with Frank. I think most people needing large amounts of lumber have already come in, and I'll help any stragglers as best as I can."

As they walked out, Melinda told Miriam the Schermanns were coming in the morning to clean up the acreage.

"I can understand Kevin taking that on, and maybe a few close relatives, but it sounds like there's going to be a whole team," Melinda said.

"I felt so alone and afraid last night, and tomorrow I'll have more than enough help. It's almost overwhelming."

Miriam gave her niece a hug. "What goes around, comes around, my dear. I don't know what I'd do if you weren't here. I know your parents love having you back, if only for a summer, but Frank and I are running a close second. And," she turned more serious, "I'll be praying that Hobo finds his way home. You've done all you can, it's not your fault."

"I know it's not my fault," Melinda said to herself as she drove home. "But I still feel sick about it. I wasn't home when the storm hit. Even if I'd left the store the minute the skies darkened, I couldn't have made it there in time to do anything. Why am I still beating myself up about this?"

The answer came swiftly and, for the second day in a row, she found herself blinking away tears as she turned off the county highway.

"Because I love that dog." She shook her head, wiped at her face with the back of her hand. "Because I love that house, and that farm feels like home. Hobo's my best friend here in Prosper, despite all the wonderful people I've met. I can't give up on him, on any of it."

Melinda slowed as she approached the jag in the gravel road, then bumped across the creek bridge and pulled over to the narrow shoulder. She couldn't go home until she checked the ravine again.

The birds had resumed their songs in the willows, and the squirrels chattered at Melinda as she side-stepped partway down the creek bank. She looked up and down the waterway for any sign of movement, called for Hobo to come. The terror she felt last night under the bridge didn't return, but there was no sign of her friend.

No one ran to greet her when she came up the driveway. Melinda usually changed her clothes before chores, but not tonight. She hurried to the barn, calling for Hobo as she crossed the yard and opened the door. She had cautioned herself to not get her hopes up, but she was still discouraged when Hobo didn't appear.

The ewes came tumbling in from the pasture, crowding at the feed bunk. Their fear long forgotten, they were only interested in how quickly Melinda could scoop out their supper and reach over the partition to give them a few quick pats on their heads.

Stormy and Sunny watched from behind the grain room door, and mewed and circled their dishes while Melinda added to their kibble and refreshed their water. She held out her hand, and Stormy tentatively leaned forward and touched her fingers with his nose, then quickly stepped back.

"I need to look after the ones still here, no matter what else happens. Isn't that right?" she asked Sunny, who hesitated for a moment then bravely brushed against the leg of her jeans.

Maybe the cats will learn to trust me after all, she thought. *There's always hope that they'll change.* She had wanted to make friends with the cats from the first time she saw them, but now, with Hobo gone, it seemed more important than ever to win them over.

The hens clustered at the front corner of their run when they saw Melinda coming. They, too, wanted their supper. She scattered their feed, relieved to see that her rough repairs to the run were holding. She dumped out the waterers, then lifted the red plastic bucket off its hook inside the coop door.

Hobo enjoyed filling the bucket at the hydrant, drawn by the squeak of the iron handle and the whoosh of fresh water splashing on the ground. He'd always tried to sneak in a drink before Melinda got the bucket in place, although she gave him plenty of time to enjoy the rushing water when she was done. She smiled at the memory of Hobo dancing at her feet, his enthusiasm for even the simplest joys on the farm. Every chore, every routine reminded her of him. How was she ever going to fill these lonely moments?

Melinda tried to turn her focus to what it would take to restore the acreage. She was picking up branches as she made her rounds and had started a decent pile of limbs and sticks next to the garden, but wished she'd gotten more done. At the very least, she wanted to straighten up the house tonight and bake something to share with the volunteers tomorrow.

She was just renting the place, only staying for a few months, and the repairs were ultimately Kevin's responsibility. But this was her home, even temporarily, and she planned to be out here with everyone else, pitching in.

Hobo's disappearance wasn't her fault, she knew, and few people besides Auggie had expected the storm to be as severe as it was. But the damaged acreage shook her confidence.

She had learned so much about living in the country in just a handful of weeks, was so proud of how the garden and the animals were thriving under her care. But now, she saw just how uneducated she really was, how wrong she had been to assume she could spend the summer just reading in the front porch swing and enjoying the fresh bounty from Horace's garden.

She had a huge mess on her hands, and one of her dear friends was missing. And she hated to think about it, but what else might happen?

"Apparently, lots of things," she muttered as she lugged the bucket of water back to the chicken coop. "And we can pick up every twig in this yard, and fix the shed roofs and try to save the garden, but none of that will bring Hobo back."

Living in the country might be peaceful, but it could turn dangerous or frightening in a matter of minutes. Unpredictable weather was only one of the challenges. An animal could suddenly become hurt or sick. Would she have even the faintest idea what to do? What if Doc couldn't come right away? It was just short of a miracle that none of the sheep had been injured during the storm, or worse.

She thought back to last night's trek through the windbreak, her slide into the creek ravine. She was living alone out here, and she needed to be careful. If she got hurt and her phone wasn't within reach, it could be hours, or days, before someone might realize she needed help.

Melinda hadn't known that before, hadn't thought of it until now. Trouble had come, and she wasn't prepared. And that made her uneasy.

* 22 *

Melinda was just finishing her cereal the next morning when Kevin's truck slid past the kitchen window. Less than a minute later, she spotted a car coming up the lane. And then another. Following that was an SUV, adding to the kick-up of gravel dust that danced in the humid sunshine.

She glanced sideways out the kitchen window to where the Schermann relatives were gathering under the light pole by the garage, hugging, shaking hands and unloading rakes and toolboxes out of their vehicles. A chainsaw appeared, and then a wheelbarrow was lifted out of the back of the SUV.

"These people mean business." She went out to the back porch for a better look. Kevin, in grungy jeans and a faded T-shirt, slid the garage door open and start to hand around more tools, then roll out Horace's wheelbarrow and the grill.

Melinda was as ready for her guests as she could ever be. She'd scrubbed the kitchen and the downstairs bathroom last night, then dusted and decluttered the main rooms. The banana muffins she baked this morning, cooling on the counter, were packed with walnuts and oats for energy and chocolate chips for a sweet finish.

Some of Kevin's relatives were looking toward the house. Melinda imagined a few were evaluating the structure, checking for signs of storm damage, but many were probably more curious about the tenant that hadn't yet appeared.

"I'm the one who's really the guest here." She subconsciously brushed at her jeans and tee shirt. "I need to get out there and say hello."

She smoothed the wavy hairs already escaping her ponytail and reached for one of Horace's faded caps hanging next to the door.

Kevin was at the back steps, ready with an unexpected hug. "I see what you mean about the mess. But we'll get on it." He introduced two friends Melinda had assumed were family, then went around the group calling out names and how everyone was related.

"And without further delay," Kevin waved forward an older woman who was already beaming at Melinda, "this is Ada, my mom."

Melinda instantly recognized Ada's blue eyes, as they were shared by both her brother and her son. She was notably younger than Horace, probably in her early seventies, with cropped silver hair and a broad smile.

"Oh, Melinda!" Ada offered a welcoming hug. "I'm so glad to finally meet you. Kevin can't stop going on about all you've done out here, caring for the animals, the painting and on and on. I can't wait to see what you've done inside."

"Well, I'm trying to keep things going." She was touched by Ada's warmth. "The house may have come through the storm pretty well, but I'm afraid I can't say the same for Horace's garden."

"You'll be surprised at how quickly those plants might bounce back." Ada dropped the tailgate on Kevin's truck and nimbly climbed in the back. "How about we get this cooler into the house? I brought hot dogs, chicken and burgers with all the trimmings."

The two women nearly had the cooler to the back porch steps when again there came the hum of tires on the gravel. Diane and Roger parked alongside the other vehicles in the yard, and Roger popped the trunk lid.

"More food?" Melinda gasped. "I was just glad you could help out for a while, I didn't expect ..."

"What's a potluck without potato salad?" Diane reached for a cooler. "I threw in some fruit, and your dad insisted on bringing his special calico beans." Ada approached Roger for a "hello" and held the back door open as he carried the slow cooker into the house.

"Ada's got a whole bunch of stuff to grill," Melinda said. "And I made muffins last night. We definitely won't starve."

Then Ed and Mabel arrived. "Ada Schermann Arndt!" Mabel called out as soon as she had the car door open. "It's been far too long!" Ada hurried across the yard to her old friend.

"Can you tell they grew up only a half a mile apart? You'd think they were kids again." Ed shook his head, grinning. "They only talk on the phone at least once a week." Mabel reached in the back seat for a cake safe and Melinda's mouth watered. She knew what was in it.

"You got it worse than we did," Ed said as he studied the yard, "but things can be cleaned up. We got a lot of our work out of the way yesterday, two of our kids and their families came over. Angie and Nathan have a full crew helping them, so when Ada called us last night, we figured we'd stop by. I almost hate to ask, but ..." he gave Melinda a hopeful look.

"No, sorry," she sighed. "I wish Hobo was back. He's the one thing that can't be replaced. I'm trying to not give up."

"Dogs are smart." Ed clapped her on the back. "It's amazing what they are capable of. Give it a few more days, see what happens."

"Mabel, I'm so glad you're here," Melinda said as they started for the house. "I promise to not ask you to can anything today, at least. The garden's a wreck. I should've tried to set things right out there last night, but by the time I got home ..."

Mabel patted Melinda's shoulder with the hand that wasn't toting the coconut cake.

"That garden's not done yet. A few weeks and it'll be out of control again, you'll see. We brought some extra cages and stakes, just in case you need them."

Melinda finally had a chance to help Ada lift her oversized cooler into the back porch. "I can't wait for you to see the results of our painting, Ada. I hope you like it. I tried to pick colors to blend with the bird wallpaper in the dining room."

"That's no easy task. Well, let's give it a look." Ada breezed through the kitchen door, instantly at home again, then gasped and threw up her hands.

"It's a decorating miracle! Melinda, this looks wonderful." She hurried through the dining room and into the living room. "I don't know which I love more, the cream walls in the kitchen or this beautiful light gray in here. You've managed to make those crazy bluebirds almost stylish."

Ada gestured at the wallpaper and sighed. "I don't know what possessed our mother to put that up, what, forty-some years ago? Wilbur and Horace didn't have the patience to rip it down, and neither did anyone else. My brothers aren't much for decorating, but even they would be impressed with what you've done in here."

"How are they doing, Ada?" Melinda was genuinely interested but didn't want to pry. On one hand, she was living in their house. On the other, she'd only seen Horace once and never met Wilbur.

"Wilbur's doing better now that Horace is there." Ada's sparkling eyes turned tender. "He seems a bit less forgetful, with Horace there to prompt him. Horace is the one person Wilbur consistently knows. Horace says he plans to come home in a few months, but I think he secretly likes the nursing home. All those people to talk to, the good meals. He was sort of isolated out here, alone."

Ada put an arm around Melinda's shoulders. "You came along at just the right time. You are just what Horace needed. He's always so pleased when Kevin tells him how you are doing out here, how you've bonded with Hobo." Her face fell and she turned silent.

Melinda wiped away a stray tear. "I miss him so much. It's like I'm missing an arm or something. He was just always here, and now ..."

"Let's not lose hope yet," Ada said quietly. "I truly believe everything happens for a reason, we just don't always understand it, that's all."

Melinda told her about the notes Horace left behind, the scrap of paper taped to the pouch of dog treats in the kitchen cabinet and the letter about the cats she found in the barn.

"Oh, that's Horace," Ada said with a laugh, shaking her head. "He's a man of few words sometimes, especially in a large group of people, but he's a sharp one. Speaking of those cats, I hope I get to see them today."

Fourteen people gathered around the picnic table for a round of muffins and coffee while Kevin organized the work crews. Their laughter and enthusiasm were contagious, and Melinda felt energized as she looked around the yard.

There was so much to do, but just one day's work could sweep away most of the damage and restore the acreage's character and charm.

Kevin backed his pickup over to the fallen-down shed, and his friends and cousins donned heavy work gloves and pitched the worst of the busted boards into the back. The crippled roof was cut into sections and added to the truck's bed. Any pieces usefull for another project were stacked in the unused feeding area in the northwest corner of the barn.

"We'll sort through that iron and stuff after lunch," Kevin told Melinda. "Maybe Mom will know what some of it is. Anything we don't need or can't save will go to the landfill."

Mabel herded the chickens into the coop by offering them fresh water and a treat of cracked corn, then slid their hatch closed. Under Roger's guidance, a group of volunteers ripped away the run's honeycomb fencing and squared its posts. Additional boards were nailed along the top and near the bottom to further stabilize the frame, and new fence panels were installed.

The barn's randomly ripped-away shingles would have to wait until another day, but Kevin's cousin Dave hoped to fill in the bare spots on the chicken coop's peak and the machine shed's roof yet that afternoon.

Melinda had discovered that morning there was a small crack in the storm window in the farmhouse's stairwell. That pane and the one for the bathroom would be replaced later, as they had to be measured and ordered.

Several people fanned out across the property, gathering the largest branches and limbs and adding them to the pile Melinda had started next to the garden. Others followed with rakes, lifting away the smallest twigs and the still-green leaves that had been ripped from their tree limbs by the high winds.

Melinda, Diane and Ada tackled the garden, raising the tossed-over tomato cages and straightening the fence panel that was home to the bean vines. The pepper plants' stakes were twisted and broken, but were soon replaced with the ones shared by Ed and Mabel. The below-ground crops, including the carrots and radishes, were windblown but otherwise unharmed.

Every plant was checked, fussed over and watered, and shorn-off vegetation and blown-down sticks were cleaned from among the rows.

"The garden is really starting to take shape," Diane said as she met Melinda across a row of carrots. "I'll be sore tonight, but it'll be worth it." Melinda didn't respond and pulled Horace's cap lower over her face.

"What's wrong? Do you need to take a break? You've been pushing hard for days, both here and at the store."

"Hobo would have loved all this." Melinda wiped her face, leaving a dirty smudge across her cheek. "He'd have loved all the excitement, all the hustle and bustle. If he could get home, wouldn't he be back by now? It's been almost two days."

"Well, look at it this way." Diane's expression turned grim. "You haven't found his body yet. He wasn't in the ditch, or the culvert, or down by the creek, or out behind the barn. You don't know for sure that he's gone for good."

"True. But I may never know what happened to him. And that's what I cannot bear."

Kevin started up the little round grill just before noon. Soon the volunteers were filing through the kitchen to load their plates, then finding a seat at the picnic table or in their own lawn chairs. After the meal there was time for a quick rest in the shade.

Sunny and Stormy, much to Melinda's surprise and delight, made a brief appearance by the garage before ambling off to lounge under the evergreens north of the house. She was sure the grilled chicken and beef brought them to the party, rather than an eagerness to mingle.

Both cats refused Ada's offers of affection but graciously accepted an array of meat scraps. They wouldn't eat, however, until Ada and everyone else gave them a wide berth.

"I wonder where they came from? They're such nice kitties," she said wistfully.

"They aren't talking, at least not yet." Kevin elbowed Melinda. "But Melinda's working on that."

The cleanup continued through the afternoon, the humidity soaring along with the temperature. Sweat ran down Melinda's neck as she cleared twigs out of the pumpkin patch, determined to have the garden fully restored. She was just about to call for a shade break of coconut cake and ice cream when her phone vibrated in her pocket. It was Doc.

"Wait a second," she called to Diane and Ada, who were debating the merits of tomato fertilizers as they filled a wheelbarrow with garden debris.

"Hey Doc, what's going on? I'm surprised to hear from you. Everything OK?"

"I had to call right away!" Doc was so excited he sounded nearly out of breath. "It's about Hobo."

Melinda's knees buckled and she felt dizzy as she eased herself into the soft garden dirt. She couldn't speak, only grip the phone tighter.

"He might be alive! Someone called the clinic, it rolled over to my phone. A farmer east of you found a stray dog yesterday. Their daughter was on Facebook a bit ago and saw your photo of Hobo." Doc was talking so fast now that Melinda's mind raced to keep up. "They called the dog 'Hobo' to see what it would do, and it wagged its tail!"

"Where? I have to get over there!" She motioned to Diane, who jumped over a row of lettuce with hope and excitement on her face. "Go get Kevin. It's Hobo." Diane ran across the yard, waving to the crew working by the downed shed.

Melinda was elated, nearly gasping with joy. But there was still a chance it wasn't Hobo. She had to be sure.

"Doc, where do they live? How ... wait ... didn't he have his collar on? Is he, I mean, is the dog hurt?"

"I don't know. They didn't say. But I can tell you where they live."

Melinda didn't recognize the name, but the farm was only two miles east of Horace's. Hobo could have run that far in the past two days, it was certainly possible ...

Kevin and Dave sprinted toward the house, Diane right behind. Melinda met them at the back steps.

"Let's take Dave's SUV." Kevin could barely contain his excitement. "If it really is Hobo, we'll need room to bring him home."

Melinda rode in the back seat and called out Doc's directions as they reached each gravel crossroads. Soon they turned up a long lane leading to a large brick farmhouse surrounded by white outbuildings. As Dave parked on the side of the drive, Melinda looked down to see her knuckles were white from gripping the seat cushion. Kevin was nervous, rubbing his palms together. He took a deep breath before they started toward the house. "OK, let's just see what we can find out. We can't get our hopes up just yet."

A middle-aged man came around from the back of the house, a worn ball cap shading his face from the sun. He extended his hand to Kevin. "I'm John Olson. You must be here about the dog. I hope he's the one you're looking for."

Melinda struggled to speak, her emotions getting the better of her, and could only nod as she scanned the still, drowsy yard for any sign of Hobo.

John smiled kindly at her. "Ma'am, we've got him resting back here." He gestured for them to follow him to an old garage behind the house.

"I must tell you, he's got a few scratches, but we cleaned them up as best we could. Doesn't look too serious. If he had a collar, he lost it somewhere along the way."

John reached for the garage's side door and lowered his voice. "He was so scared yesterday when he turned up here, we set him up in this shed so he couldn't run before we tried to find his family."

Before Melinda could adjust her eyes to the cool shade inside, there was a rustle and a high-pitched whimpering. Hobo bounded up from a thick stack of blankets in the corner and ran toward her, wriggling and shaking his head as he picked up her scent. She dropped to the floor and wrapped her arms around him.

"Oh, Hobo, you're safe!" She began to sob as those desperate, terrifying moments under the bridge rushed back in her mind. "Oh, I missed you, I was so worried! Oh, thank God." She glanced up and noticed all three men casually rubbing their faces, but she could see their happy tears.

Then Kevin was also on the floor, and Hobo was happily trying to sniff him and kiss Melinda at the same time.

"Where ya been, buddy?" Kevin's voice cracked. "Melinda looked everywhere for you. I couldn't sleep, not knowing where you were. Did you decide to outrun the big tornado? Had to get away?"

Melinda let go of Hobo long enough to allow Kevin to put his arms around the dog and rub his dusty fur.

"It's a mystery," John said, smiling and shaking his head. "Doc said you live right west of here, about two miles? Hobo made it that far in less than twenty-four hours. Wonder if he came all that way Friday night? Or went partway, slept somewhere and got up yesterday, disoriented, and started out in the wrong direction?"

"When exactly did he show up here?" Dave asked.

"Early afternoon yesterday. Maybe he got hungry and saw our farm, decided to take his chances. I was gone at an auction. Couldn't believe it when I got home and my wife said there was a stray dog here. Our dog, Boots, had started barking and my wife found Hobo stretched out by the barn, exhausted. She got him some water and food and he seemed grateful, but shaken. Like I said, he's got some scrapes on his coat but nothing serious. He was muddy, too, even had dry mud caked on his belly, like he'd maybe been in the creek."

Melinda and Kevin looked at each other.

"The creek," Melinda nodded as Hobo tried to climb into her lap, still wriggling with excitement. "That's one of the first places I looked. I thought he might have been down there, but ..." she swallowed hard. "I can't thank you enough for what you've done. Please let us pay you something for your trouble, for the food at least."

"Oh, I can't take anything." John waved away her offer. "I'm just glad he had the courage to come into our yard. You can thank Facebook, I guess. My daughter gets the vet clinic's updates and saw Hobo's photo."

"He means so much to us," Kevin said. "He's my Uncle Horace's dog. He is at the nursing home and Melinda's looking after the acreage. I hadn't even had the nerve to tell him Hobo was missing."

Hobo had calmed down and was burying his nose in Melinda's shoulder. "Are you sure we can't offer you more than our gratitude?" Dave asked.

John smiled. "Oh, no, forget about all that. I'd want someone to do the same for Boots, if she ever ran away. It wasn't anything, really. I'm just glad we could help."

"I'm sorry I haven't met you before now." Melinda got to her feet and extended her hand. "I've been out here almost two months but haven't ventured too far around the neighborhood."

"Well, it's good to meet you, regardless of the circumstances." John gripped her hand firmly. "Don't be a stranger, now."

"I sure won't. And thanks again, you've done so much."

"Well, there's one thing we didn't do." John began to laugh. "My daughter wanted to give Hobo a bath, but I told her he'd been through enough already."

"I'll be glad to do it," Kevin said. "We're over there today cleaning up. I guess we can add 'dog bath' to the list."

Hobo was a bit uncertain about Dave's unfamiliar vehicle, but once Melinda got in the backseat, he jumped in and settled his head in her lap with a contented sigh. She worried about Hobo's dirty paws, but Dave just shook his head.

"Never mind all that. I'm honored to be Hobo's driver. I'll need to clean out the truck, anyway."

She held Hobo close, burying her face in his fur. The dust in his coat nearly made her cough, but she didn't care. Dave and Kevin were talking, but she couldn't focus on what they were saying.

She didn't know what tomorrow would bring, or next week. Her future might be uncertain, but it was also a clean slate. She had her family. And friends, both old and new. She had a job, an interesting one, no matter how unexpected it had been or how temporary it might be.

Life was never going to be easy, but her fears had vanished in the few seconds it took Hobo to dash across John Olson's garage and into her arms.

"I have you," she whispered to Hobo. "And Stormy and Sunny, and the chickens and the sheep. Even Annie might be glad to see you. I can handle whatever else might happen this summer as long as you are here. What do you think?" Hobo touched his nose to her cheek.

As they turned at the last crossroads and approached the farm, Hobo pushed past Melinda to look out the side window. He began to make excited yips and wriggle, and clods of dirt flew out of his thick tail.

"He knows where he is!" Kevin beamed, watching from the front seat. "You're right, buddy, we're almost there."

"There's the welcoming committee," Dave announced as they drove up the lane. Everyone had gathered under the yard light, shielding their faces with their hands.

Many of them were trying to peer into the vehicle, to see if Hobo was inside. Melinda noticed both her dad's and Mabel's hands clasped in prayer.

"I'll get out first and tell them the good news," Kevin said. "I'll ask them to stay quiet and stand back, give Hobo some room. He's really had a hard time."

Through the windshield, Melinda saw the elation on everyone's faces as Kevin made his announcement. After the clapping and hugging and high-fives dwindled away, Kevin motioned for Melinda and Dave to bring Hobo out. Dave held the door and, before Melinda could even rise from the seat, Hobo pushed past her and jumped out into the grass, sniffing the air and wagging his tail with pure joy.

Ada disappeared inside and quickly returned with a small dish. Hobo met her halfway, Melinda right behind.

"Somehow I knew you'd want this," Ada told Hobo, trying to hold back happy tears as he scarfed down a chopped grilled chicken breast. "I was putting away leftovers when Mabel came running into the kitchen, waving her arms like the barn was on fire, saying you might have been found."

Ada eased down into the grass next to Melinda and put her arm around Hobo, who had finished his meal and was now trying to lick Ada's face.

"My dear boy. You've always been here to look after my brothers. Do you know how special you are? And now, we are all going to look after you." She gave Melinda a wink.

"That's right," Melinda said as Hobo scooted over and laid his head on her shoulder. "I'm here," she whispered. "We're all here. You're safe, and you're home."

WHAT'S NEXT

"Harvest Season" sneak peek: Melinda's journey is just getting started! Read on for a special excerpt from the second book in the series..

About the books: Details on all the novels follow the excerpt from "Harvest Season." Then discover "A Tin Train Christmas," a short story set on the Schermann farm during the Great Depression. And look for Book 5, "Songbird Season," to arrive on April 30, 2019!

Recipes and more: Part of the fun is discovering what Melinda is cooking up in her farmhouse kitchen. Head over to fremontcreekpress.com and click on the "extras" to find recipes inspired by the series!

Stay in touch: Visit the "connect" page on the website to sign up for the email newsletter. You won't hear from me too often, but when you do, it'll be something worthwhile ... like release dates for future titles.

So, what did you think? Did you love "Growing Season?" Or do you wish you could get those hours of your life back? If you're reading this, you probably made it all the way through, so I'd like to ask a big favor. Please hop on to Amazon and/or Goodreads and leave a review. While I'd love for everyone to love this book, that's not likely to happen. So if you were annoyed by a character or hated the ending or whatever, go ahead and say so. But if you did enjoy it, please tell your friends, or recommend it for your book club.

Thanks for reading!
Melanie

Sneak peek: Harvest Season

August: Prosper Hardware

Prosper's Main Street was quieter than usual as Melinda drove into town just before seven. Auggie, Doc and Jerry were already sipping their first cups of coffee, and she had to smile at the two vacant chairs pulled up to the vintage sideboard. One was waiting for George. The other was for her.

She waved and set her purse behind the oak counter. "Jerry, how do Miriam's flowers look? Do they need another shot of fertilizer?"

Jerry was a certified master gardener, along with his official title of mayor. More than once this summer, he had given Melinda advice that kept Horace's garden thriving.

"I think you're good for another week. They're holding up, considering how hot it's been. I'm glad you and Bill had time to take them down before that bad storm a few weeks ago. Miriam worked so hard to get those baskets planted."

Melinda had just returned from watering the flowers when the front door's bell jingled again and George shuffled into the store. "Good morning all, had to drive over today because Mary sent us a special treat."

Melinda knew it was going to be a hot day, as he had chosen a short-sleeved shirt to pair with his pressed overalls.

"What is it?" Auggie leaned forward, expectant.

"Some kind of applesauce bread." George set the container on the sideboard and started to place slices on napkins and pass them around.

Doc seemed especially buoyant. He had his slice gone in a few large bites, then looked around the group with a big smile on his face. "Everybody, it's fitting that we have treats this morning, because I've got a special announcement to make."

Melinda wasn't sure how old Doc was, maybe in his late fifties. Surely he wasn't retiring?

"Well, out with it, Doc," Auggie said. "Because I can see you're about to burst. Must be a pretty big deal. Are you adding on to the clinic or something?"

Doc's practice was based out of a dark-green building with sharp white trim at the far end of Main, by the water tower. While he made farm calls for large animals and cared for cats and dogs inside the clinic, it wasn't unusual to drive by and see a calf or sheep staked out front.

"Well, not really, but that might have to come in a year or two. You see, I've hired another vet, an assistant. I'm not ready to retire, but I will someday. And I can hardly keep up with the calls. Anne says I need to slow down a bit, and I guess she's right. The new vet's got her degree from ISU, has been working in a small-animal clinic in Cedar Rapids for about ten years. But she grew up on a farm over by Storm Lake and wants to get back to small-town life."

When Melinda heard "her degree," she paused with the coffeepot in her hand. The guys didn't seem to catch on at first, as they were so shocked by this news. Doc had been the only veterinarian in Prosper for more than twenty years.

"Hey, that's great!" Jerry stood and clapped Doc on the back. "Glad you'll be able to slow down a little."

Then Jerry did a double take. "Wait ... did you say *she*?"

Auggie's head snapped around and George's blue eyes widened in surprise.

Melinda dropped her chin and tried to keep from laughing. The modern era of veterinary medicine was coming to Prosper. She just wasn't sure if these guys were ready. Or many of the area's farmers, for that matter.

Harvest Season is available in Kindle, hardcover and paperback editions

ABOUT THE BOOKS

*Don't miss any of the titles
in this heartwarming rural fiction series*

Growing Season (Book 1)

Melinda Foster is already at a crossroads when the "for rent" sign beckons her down a dusty gravel lane. With her job gone and her prospects dim, it's not long before she finds herself living in a faded farmhouse, caring for a barn full of animals, and working at her family's hardware store. And just like the vast garden she tends under the summer sun, Melinda soon begins to thrive.

Harvest Season (Book 2)

Melinda's efforts at her rented farmhouse are starting to pay off. But even in Prosper, nothing stays the same. One member of the hardware store's coffee group shares a startling announcement, and a trip back to the city makes her realize how deep her roots now run in rural Iowa. As the seasons change, Melinda must choose between the security of her old life or an uncertain future.

The Peaceful Season (Book 3)

As a reflective hush falls over the fields, Melinda turns her thoughts toward the coming holidays. She has a list of what will make the season perfect: Prepare her acreage for the coming winter, host her family's Christmas dinner, and use her marketing smarts to upgrade Prosper's holiday festival. But when a mysterious visitor arrives, she is reminded there is so much more to the Christmas season.

Waiting Season (Book 4)

Melinda finds herself struggling to keep the worst of winter's threats from her door. She pushes on because Horace's offer still stands: He'll sell her the farm in the spring. But as winter tightens its grip on rural Iowa, Melinda's biggest challenges are still to come. A series of events threatens to break her heart and shatter her hopes, and it will take all of her faith to see the season through.

Songbird Season (Book 5)

The first blush of spring finds Melinda filled with great expectations. But as the songbirds return and the garden's soil is turned, not everything's coming up roses. When Uncle Frank makes a shocking discovery in the town's archives, the fallout threatens to dim Prosper Hardware's bright future. As friendships are tested and family ties begin to fray, can Melinda restore the harmony in her life?

Coming April 2019

———————— ✳✳✳ ————————

A TIN TRAIN CHRISTMAS

Travel back in time to Horace's childhood for this special holiday short story inspired by the "Growing Season" series

"A Tin Train Christmas" is available in Kindle format as well as a paperback version that's perfect for holiday gift giving!

From the author of the heartwarming "Growing Season" novels comes this old-fashioned story of family and faith to brighten your holidays!

The toy train in the catalog was everything two young boys could ask for: colorful, shiny, and the perfect vehicle for their wild imaginations. But was it meant to be theirs? As the Great Depression's shadows deepen over the Midwest, Horace and Wilbur start to worry Santa may not stop at their farm. But with a little faith and their parents' love, the boys just might discover the true spirit of Christmas.

And there's more: At the end of the story, you'll discover three holiday recipes handed down in the author's family!